S [illegible] DEATH

An AJ Conti Novel

SYNDICATE OF DEATH

James A. Bacca

Luminare Press
www.luminarepress.com

Syndicate of Death

Printed in the United States of America

Cover Design: Melissa K. Thomas

Luminare Press
442 Charnelton St.
Eugene, OR 97401
www.luminarepress.com

LCCN: 2020902744
ISBN: 978-1-64388-306-9

To my Mom, Nan, and to Sam and Anne,
for the strength only parents can give.

Acknowledgements

Many thanks to Pat for sharing and for his guidance, and not only in this endeavor.

Many thanks to Rick and Lynn for always being there.

CHAPTER ONE

Viktor Laine sat in the lobby of his civil rights attorney, Aaron Vasquez, wondering what he would want to talk with him about given he had already received settlement payments several days ago.

"Mr. Laine, first congratulations on winning your lawsuit, thanks to some alert citizens using their phones to film the beating you received…but it is my duty to inform you, another client of mine went missing under suspicious circumstances not long ago." Aaron shook his head. "His case was settled almost two years ago and we won a settlement for him under identical circumstances. Police using excessive force during his arrest."

Aaron walked around his desk, sitting in the chair next to Viktor.

"You see…he moved to Arizona and six months later died in a suspicious trailer explosion. I'm telling you to be careful. Watch your back."

"Hell, after expenses and your cut, I'm only walking away with a couple hundred grand," Viktor scoffed. "Not enough for them to get excited about."

"Mr. Laine, I cannot go into details, but trust me, it is a much bigger issue. Sources tell me they are targeting anyone who costs them money…to send a warning message."

"Wow, sounds like it'd make a good movie," Viktor

laughed until he saw Aaron stare back at him. "Okay. I promise. I'll let you know if I see anything weird or strange. Happy?"

"Yes, thank you. Now, go celebrate."

North Valley, Albuquerque, New Mexico

Their orders were clear—find Viktor Laine. Nothing else need be said; nor would it. Suits always tried protecting themselves with plausible deniability. Officer Trevor Johnson and Sergeant Rob Pace were in a black Chevy Tahoe with dark tinted windows, while Officers Brody Sachs and Jerry Bodner were in the other. Trevor felt everyone needed a moniker, so he unofficially came up with one for each of them. Being the youngest of the group, he settled on the name they called him…Rook.

Sergeant Pace, a former Marine naturally became Gyrene.

Sachs became OM, short for Old Man of the group.

Bodner became Sly, primarily based on Trevor's reservations about him. Trevor had thought about all of them getting the same tattoo to make them legit, though he had not said anything about it—yet. It only took a few weeks of him using the monikers before everyone started buying into them.

"We got him," Sly said. "Viktor is walking right toward you guys."

Walking north on Fourth Street, Viktor began to get excited and picked up his pace. In one more block, he would get the meth from his supplier. He had already started to count his profits. It would be a large sum after cutting it several times before he delivered it to his buyer.

Cross San Andreas Avenue and the laundromat's right there, Viktor thought, thankful the meeting with his attorney didn't take long.

"Almost there...oh yeah, I see him," Rook called out.

Viktor had taken three steps into the intersection when he saw the black Tahoes pull into the left turn lane on Fourth Street directly across from him.

"Fuck," Viktor said before he froze, oblivious to the cars on his right honking. He spun around and took off running.

"He's crossing...shit, he's running your way," Rook yelled into the cell.

Sly thrust the phone in front of him, a grimace on his face as he stared at it. OM laughed, knowing Sly hated the inability of rookies to remain calm.

Viktor had run before to keep from going to jail. This time, he had a different purpose—to stay alive. His mind strained trying to think of where to go. Hearing squealing tires behind him, Viktor sprinted left around the corner heading toward Mountain Mahogany Community School. He knew there were several buildings on the campus and various directions he could go.

I can lose 'em there.

"We're coming up the other driveway," Sly said into the phone. "There he is." Sly pointed to his left, seeing Viktor through the bushes. "Punch it!" he yelled. "Don't let him get to the school." True to his moniker of OM, the old man stayed steady, accelerating only slightly.

Passing the Son Broadcasting building, Viktor believed he'd make it and looked over his shoulder one last time. Turning his head back around, the second Tahoe came to a screeching halt right in front of him causing his feet to slip as he tried to avoid running into its front end. When his knee hit the bumper, he flew several feet before hitting the pavement.

Excruciating pain surged through Viktor's leg as if his knee had exploded when four men, dressed in black fatigues and black sunglasses, converged on him. Viktor's fear took his breath away, causing the knee pain to become a vague memory.

"You forgot about the school's driveway being U shaped, didn't you?" OM growled, squeezing Viktor's swelling knee as Rook zip tied his wrists behind his back. Viktor screamed until an elbow caught him in the gut. "You're gonna like where we're taking you."

His wrenching fear eclipsed the physical pain when they grabbed ahold of him and threw him in the back seat of one of the Tahoes. One cop pushed him into the middle seat as two others sat on either side. One had him around the neck while the other put a hood over his face. Viktor could not help but remember the warning his attorney had passed on to him.

"Yeah. We're gonna give you five hundred thousand reasons to wish you had never filed a lawsuit, and then we're gonna kill you!" Sly smiled.

"I didn't get five hundred thousand," Viktor said, gasping for air, tears rolling down his cheeks. "I only got two hundred thousand. My attorney and expenses took up the rest."

The cops looked at each other and laughed. "All right, we promise only to give you *two* hundred thousand reasons then. Is that better?" OM smiled. "Starting with this." He drove an ice pick into Viktor's right femur and smirked when Viktor passed out and his body slumped.

CHAPTER TWO

Gyrene drove north on Fourth Street to Osuna Road and turned east. Rook followed wondering what they were saying to Viktor.

Turning north on Jefferson, Gyrene drove to their warehouse tucked behind commercial buildings past Paseo Del Norte Boulevard. The first button on his visor opened the electric gate to the warehouse and the other two opened the bay doors. Gyrene shut the doors behind them.

Dragging Viktor out of the Tahoe they threw him on the solid metal workbench covered with clear plastic, which extended fifteen feet on all sides down to the cement floor. Four-point restraints had been attached to the bench and fed through slits in the plastic. With the restraints in place, Viktor could not move. After they removed his hood, OM pulled the ice pick out of his leg wiping the blood on the Russian's jeans.

Viktor gasped for air and tried to talk, his lip quivering like a toddler trying to explain himself.

"Relax," Sly said. "We're only trying to get your attention. We aren't going to kill you, unless you don't cooperate."

Several seconds later the words registered to Viktor... *cooperate and live!* He took a few deep breaths, trying to regain control.

"I'll do...I'll do whatever you want," Viktor cried. "Please, don't kill me."

Sly nodded to OM, who punched Viktor in the jaw before grabbing a one-inch thick metal pipe. Rook stuffed a rag into Viktor's mouth seconds before OM struck Victor's arms and legs with the pipe.

"Grab the saw," Sly said to Rook.

Viktor's eyes shot open as he turned his head to see the young one heading for the saw. Whirling back, his head gyrated from side-to-side staring at the restraints while he tried to break free. All the possibilities of what might happen next flashed through his brain.

Rook hated the *hands-on* stuff. He had no problem being a gopher and handing the compact circular saw off to one of the other three, but he knew Sly would not go for it. He could appeal to Gyrene as the group leader since he was a sergeant and had been in the Marines, but his appeal would be redirected back to Sly. Rook shuffled his feet heading back to the table with saw in hand.

Maybe we're just going to scare him. Rook hoped.

Sly nodded once and pointed with his eyes to tell Rook what he wanted.

Rook started putting on coveralls and heard Viktor's muffled screams. Trying to ignore it, he put on goggles and surgical gloves before picking up the saw. In seconds, Viktor's finger lay on the table, detached from his hand.

Rook turned away—retching.

When Viktor began to regain composure, Sly walked over to the table and put a hand on the man's shoulder while the other grabbed the rag.

"I hope you now know we're serious. You make any kind of a screaming sound when I pull out this rag and you'll watch us cut off more than your finger."

Viktor nodded, his choices were limited, but he held out hope he still had a chance to live. When the rag came out Viktor took a deep breath.

"Where's the settlement money…what'd you say, two hundred thousand?" Sly asked.

"They wired it directly into my bank account," Viktor replied.

"Is it all still there?"

"Yes." Viktor blurted out before thinking. "No. Well, most of it."

"*Most* of it," Sly growled. "What the fuck's that supposed to mean?"

"I had them wire sixty-eight thousand into my mom's account so she could pay off her house. She's all alone, and…."

"Forget about it," Gyrene said from his chair back in the corner, steam now rolling off the coffee cup in his hand.

Sly shot Gyrene a look as if to say he was crazy, but he dared not ever say it aloud. He believed Gyrene's Afghanistan missions left him unstable.

"Is the rest of the money still in your account?" Sly asked.

"Not exactly," Viktor said. "Wait, wait, wait, I can explain." He knew it had to be quick or they might do him in.

"I took out five grand to do a meth deal. It's, you know, where I was headed, when you guys saw me. I planned on getting the meth and cutting it. I had this chick…she's throwing a party, and I planned on making a profit."

"Ah, a businessman at heart," Sly said.

OM rolled his eyes; he hated the slow pace instead of letting him get straight to completing the job. Sly grabbed his iPad and made a wire transfer from Viktor's account into the group's account taking the remaining one hundred and twenty-seven thousand, along with removing the five thousand in cash from Viktor's pants pocket.

Sly held Viktor's phone to his ear, the evil look in his eyes staring back at Viktor conveyed a loud message...*don't screw it up, or else.*

"Simeon, it's Viktor."

"Where are you...you're late!"

"I know, I know. I can still make the deal if you still have the product?"

Several seconds of silence followed. Sly instinctively knew why, Simeon no longer trusted Viktor. Sly whispered in Viktor's ear and Viktor repeated it. "Look man, I'll throw in another five hundred for being late. I need it."

Silence again, this time for only a few seconds.

"I lost faith in you, dude." Simeon hesitated, and said, "A thousand."

When Sly nodded, Victor said, "Done!"

"Forty-five minutes, same place. *With* the extra cash." Simeon hung up.

"Great job, Viktor," Sly patted him on the shoulder.

Viktor would have to worry about Simeon later, right then and there he had to stay alive. His hope was he increased his chances since they were going to get the meth.

Sly confirmed Viktor's meeting place with Simeon and turned away. Viktor didn't see Sly nod at OM.

OM yanked Viktor's head back and jabbed the ice pick between his chin and Adam's apple. Viktor never felt the repeated stabbing in different areas of his brain stem without OM removing the pick.

"All right, you guys know what to do," Sly said, as he and Gyrene were heading for their Tahoe. "We have some drugs to steal and a drug dealer to kill if he tries to stop us."

Sly rolled down the window and called out to Rook. "Bury the body parts in the West Mesa dump site the serial killer used a few years ago. No one will expect another body dumped there."

Rook nodded, knowing he got the shit jobs because he had not been a cop long enough to lose rookie status. Rook looked over at OM who still had a grin on his face staring down at the dead body.

A bunch of sick bastards...Rook shook his head.

CHAPTER THREE

"Where did AJ Conti go?" I heard Kenny Love asking from his living room and knew it would only be a short time before he found me. Though I wasn't hiding from anyone, I happened to be spending a little alone time reflecting, as much as one could be alone at a going-away party.

The time would come for all of us someday to give up the *rush* of police work, whatever our particular *rush* happened to be. Kenny Love decided to leave for the big computer geek bucks, which made the party bittersweet since we had gone to the academy together a decade and a half earlier. Kenny had made a name for himself in the computer forensics world, so leaving for a large six-figure salary seemed wise.

Most of the new guys around me were good. Still, it wasn't the same. The only one who remained was a weasel named Willie. My long-time evidence tech, Knox, had a heart attack and decided to hang it up in order to enjoy time with his family. Seth, the man I admired and thought would replace me took a job with the union as a rep and contract negotiator. And now…Kenny.

"So, how much longer before you wise up and get out while we're still young?" Kenny asked, sliding next to me staring out over his swimming pool.

"I've been standing here thinking…the team's gone. Hard to get motivated with a bunch of new faces. Guys like you, Seth and JT made it fun. Now what?"

"It's been close to a year since you returned from Italy and you've been able to deal with Bethany's death and go forward," Kenny said. "Maybe it's time for you to move on from here…and from Bethany."

"He's right you know," Seth added, moving next to me on the other side.

I stood silent falling back into memory.

When one of my homicide suspects murdered Bethany I struggled to make it back. The trip to Italy helped me regain some semblance of sanity and now standing here listening to my good friends giving me advice gave me a good feeling. They were right. And meeting Donatella in Italy had been the closest I got to dating someone. Returning, I buried myself in my work, like the old me before Bethany.

Seth's question brought me back. "Is there any reason you can't hang it up, I mean…financially?"

I chuckled. "No reason, I did better on Kenny's investment advice than he and Macy did." *I never told anyone the amount of money Bethany left me after she took care of her sisters and nieces.* "No. Money is not an issue."

"We're all good friends here, right?" Kenny asked.

"Yeah, the best. Why?" I stared at him.

"You ever going to tell us how the life insurance lawsuit thing ended?"

I hesitated, my eyes shifting between them. They already knew Bethany had changed life insurance policies once she began receiving the notes from Stalker, the man who ultimately took her life. Each threatening note she received prompted her to increase her policy.

"I think Bethany's sisters were happy with the settlement in the end," I said. "Bethany made sure she took care of us all."

Both men stared at me, silently waiting. We all knew I skirted the answer, which would work with most people, but not the two closest to me.

"My part of the settlement turned out to be around...one point one...million. Plus, after Kenny got me going with the investing, I ended up with a broker who took me under his wing and really helped me to understand the stock market. I never had to worry about a family or any of those things. So, I gained a little over another million from taking a few risks, which worked out to my benefit. Like I said, money is not an issue."

Silence.

I had to smile. The looks on their faces, eyes wide, and their mouths hanging open enough to catch flies. The shock of it all, how could I not smile?

"What the...your Mustang's the most you've ever splurged on," Seth stumbled over his curiosity being so surprised.

Kenny said, "Hell, you live in a modest house...if *we* never guessed you had that kind of cash, I guarantee nobody else will."

"I figured if modest were good enough for Warren Buffet, it would work for me. What can I say?"

They shook their heads as the reality set in. I could only grin.

"All right then, you made this easy...my advice now, step away," Kenny patted my shoulder. "You'll find something to do. Hell, go mold young minds at a university and put the law degree, you never did anything with, to good use. Hell, you can afford to be an underpaid professor."

"You might want to try dating again, too," Seth smiled.

Now, they were smiling like kids in a candy store as my mom used to say. Looking me straight in the eyes, they raised their glasses and Kenny made the toast. "To good times, AJ!"

THE UNLAWFUL GROUP NEVER GAVE ROOK A CHOICE about using his own vehicle to dump Viktor Laine's body parts. He loaded the eight orange buckets in the back of his Chevy Equinox and headed for the west mesa.

When Rook got to 118th Street he turned right and noticed new housing subdivisions lining the east side of the road. After pulling over to the dirt shoulder across from the subdivisions, he saw two mattresses propped against the barbed-wire fence where he noticed an opening. When he checked for bystanders or other vehicles, there were none. From his vantage point, he could see what looked like dirt roads out in the mesa and guessed they'd been made by four-wheelers.

Housing construction prevented Rook from going to the serial killer's dumpsite near Amole Mesa Avenue, so he decided where he was now seemed close enough. He guided his Chevy into the mesa over several berms with his lights off until he could no longer see the subdivision and made a U-turn so he could drive away quickly if needed.

After digging seven shallow holes and dumping a bucket of body parts in each one, Rook covered them up. He finally reached for the bucket in which they collected Viktor's blood as they dismembered his body. He walked the bucket to the back edge of his Equinox when a flash of light to his right grabbed his attention. He could not hold the weight of the bucket as it started to tip over the ledge of the bumper, sliding off it headed for the dirt as the light flashed back toward him.

Striking the ground, the bucket's lid flew off and blood splattered the dirt below. Still, Rook kept his focus on the spotlight coming his way...*a patrol car of some kind.* The vehicle turned and drove through the opening in the fence with the headlights shining into the mesa.

Rook scrambled to grab the other buckets and shovel, throwing them in the back of the Equinox. He grabbed the blood bucket last before he did a quick look around the back corner of his vehicle. Seeing the patrol car turn around toward the road, Rook sat on the bumper and caught his breath with a deep sigh of relief. Fifteen seconds later, he heard a distant siren and decided he had to get outta there.

He realized his good fortune, no blood splashed on him or his vehicle. He had been told to dump blood around each of the body burial sites to attract coyotes. Looking at the bloody dirt, which was nowhere near the body-parts sites, he shrugged. *What the hell...none of the guys will ever find out.*

CHAPTER FOUR

It took District Court Judge Murtagh *Mac* McDunn almost a year to ask out Lisa Stevens. Her work had surpassed other news reporters and on a couple of occasions, she showed up at his office under the guise of needing to ask follow-up questions for an article. She had also been spotted several times sitting in his courtroom during cases she had not been assigned to cover.

Mac had one woman he loved dearly, who died of cancer ten years before. She had been married and Mac's love for her was from a distance, never interfering in any way. Only after she divorced did he let his true feelings for her be known, only to have her leave his world less than two months later.

Burying himself in his work, Mac regularly spent eighteen hours a day in his chambers. The dividends to his career were dramatic, and Judge Murtagh McDunn became well known and respected by most in the legal and law enforcement community. The debt to his health loomed equally large, forcing him to back away a bit and take care of himself.

Lisa's smile and her ease of communicating with all types of people were what he noticed first. Mac found himself reading her articles in the Albuquerque Journal newspaper, enjoying her willingness to ask the tough questions and loved her dogged determination to get to the truth. His taking so long to ask her out had nothing to do with her, it had to do with his vulnerability of getting hurt again. Fortunately for Mac, his sister convinced him to go for it. The last fourteen months with Lisa in his life finally made Mac feel whole.

Mac sat in the booth patiently appreciating how Lisa's work hours were nowhere near as regular as his. He figured she wouldn't be long since he chose her favorite Mexican restaurant on Fourth Street.

As Lisa slid in next to him, Mac asked, "So, how are things at the Journal?" Her endearing kiss and the happiness in her eyes told him it must have been a good day.

"It's great," Lisa exclaimed. "My article on police corruption is getting close to being featured. The editor wants me to clear up a few more things and then I think we run it on a Sunday edition. At least I hope so."

Mac congratulated her, unable to hide his concern for her safety. Lisa could read him like an open book.

"What's bothering you? Bad day at work, or is it the corruption story?"

"No. Not at all," Mac replied, but waited to elongate until the waitress took their drink orders and left.

"Look, we know the police department's ROP team went rogue, way beyond trying to stop the repeat offenders for which the program was designed. But, they were shut down years ago and reassigned."

"Yeah, okay," Lisa said.

Mac could tell she was really saying *where the hell you going with this.*

"I told you about the note I got in my mail several weeks ago at the beginning of the civil trial against the Albuquerque Police Department with Aaron as the plaintiff's attorney," Mac said. Leaning closer and lowering his voice he continued. "I got two more I never told you about, and the last one's rather disturbing."

"Why didn't you say something," Lisa snapped, anger sparking in her eyes, her cheeks flushed pink.

He raised his brows to stare at her, his way of telling her to calm down.

"At the time I didn't want to hear you hounding me about them probably being from someone at APD. I didn't want to believe it. Now…I'm starting to wonder."

He described how the original note was in a plain white envelope with the misspelling of his name, *Mc DONE,* stuffed in the middle of his personal mail the first week of the trial. It suggested Mac back off and recommended the case be thrown out on some technicality. It hinted at some danger to Mac, although having received threats before, he ignored it.

A week later Mac received another white envelope, same misspelling, along with a definite death threat if there was a payout to the plaintiff. Mac contacted the Albuquerque Police Department. Their lack of investigation surprised him considering he had an excellent working relationship with the rank and file. Detective Sergeant Montez told him the threat seemed too random and lacked credibility. Mac felt both letters were credible on several levels. Still, he sensed Montez lacked an understanding of the matter as he responded how danger appeared to be unlikely—Montez did not care.

"And today, the third envelope arrived in my office, buried in my mail exactly like the others."

When their waitress delivered the food, Lisa ignored it. Sitting sideways in the booth she only stared at Mac.

Mac described opening the envelope with his letter opener, trying to hold it by the edges. He had no idea who to get to fingerprint the envelope. Still, he held out hope to find someone he could trust and not go through Montez.

Reaching under the table, Mac pulled his briefcase to his lap and retrieved a plastic bag with an envelope inside. Using his napkin Mac drew the white stationary paper from the envelope.

"It's exactly like the others in black ink, and a distinct flow to the writing, possibly from a woman's hand," he said, showing it to Lisa.

Too late. The payout is complete. Too bad Viktor won't be able to spend it in his scattered state. Your choices have consequences, and certain ones have deadly consequences. Figure it out, YOUR HONOR!

Mac described reaching for his phone after opening the letter to have Alex, his Trial Court Administrative Assistant, locate Aaron Vasquez, Viktor's attorney. When his instincts told him otherwise, he hung up and pulled out his cell and texted him.

"My good friend AJ Conti, the homicide detective in California I've told you about…AJ has told me for years to quit trying to rationalize everything and trust my gut once in a while."

"Maybe, he's right."

"Maybe. I'll admit, I have an eerie feeling about all of this. Not like I'm being watched, more like…I'm being targeted. I kept my text to Aaron generic, asking him to meet for lunch."

"You didn't tell him *why*? I mean…."

"No. I specifically avoided anything about the case."

"I don't understand."

"I don't know. Cautious I guess."

"Probably wise. The more I dig into my story, the more I realize the depths some of those unethical cops will go to. So, when are you two meeting?"

"Not sure, Aaron never responded."

CHAPTER FIVE

I reached my goals of getting back to work and making it past the anniversary of Bethany's death. Now, all the important people on my team had left for personal reasons, albeit good ones, and I no longer had the desire to stay. I really hoped Kenny and Seth were right about something being out there waiting for me.

After putting a call into the Public Employees Retirement System I had several appointments with a representative who walked me through the entire process of freezing my retirement until I was old enough to draw it. Sitting in a chair across from the rep in a conference room, I felt it. Stress was leaving with every word she said.

I sent a text to a small group of important people in my life letting them know of my impending departure. I appreciated the comments and support, helping me accept the idea I made the right decision. Thirty minutes after the teasing died down, I got a second text from Mac.

Mac and his siblings were like family. I could count on him to listen when I needed it and he never blatantly suggested what I should do. Getting another text from him did not surprise me; but his proposing I come to Albuquerque did. Something had to be amiss.

It was after five there, so I gave it a shot by calling him. Mac answered on the fourth ring.

"Retirement? What are you going to live off? You're younger than me," Mac said.

"I'm better looking too," I replied.

"*Ha*. Debatable," he shot back with a hint of laughter.

"Most things are to you *attorney types*."

"I have to agree," Mac said.

"So, what's up?"

"What do you mean?"

"Something's wrong. I'm not a dentist, Mac. Don't make me pull it out of you. Just tell me."

The phone went quiet, except for the rustling of papers in the background. In my mind I could see him weighing out how much to tell me, if anything.

I waited, knowing many people feel a need to fill the silence.

"Nothing really," Mac said, his voice trailing off. "Just a bit overloaded. Thought it might be good for you to come visit and I could take some time off."

"Got it," I tried to sound like I bought it. "When you can indemnify the route, drop me a line. Gotta go. We'll talk again." I hung up, hoping he grasped my play on words.

I thought about Kenny who had his own secure web site for law enforcement types interested in computer and cell phone technology, but he had also let in some Army Rangers and Navy Seals who worked together. One of them he called Ric, although I knew it wasn't his real name, had convinced Kenny Al-Qaeda's use of cell phones helped them prepare for many missions in Afghanistan because they were so insecure and easily tracked. Something told me Mac's work phone and cell phone might already be compromised.

Mac set the cell on his desk. Instinctively his elbows rested on the oak surface, his hands together in front of his face, secured in place by his thumbs under his chin.

He and AJ had an affinity to communicate in various modes, often leaving others bewildered. They developed it when they were younger, but time and distance had put it on hold.

Mac knew AJ would call when he sent the second text. He presumed he would have time to figure out the right opportunity to mask his purpose. He had not expected AJ's directness so early in the call.

Indemnify the route....

AJ's actions and word choices meant he understood, although his return message had Mac puzzled.

Indemnify the route?

Mac's eyes narrowed, his lips pursed, and one nod followed.

"Alex," Mac yelled.

I smiled when my desk phone rang. I knew I had a secure line, figuring Mac did, too. Now!

"Detective Conti," I said in case.

"It took me a few to figure out you were referring to a secure line," Mac said. "And, I wanted to get to a more neutral area."

"Perfect. What phone?"

"It's Alex's, my administrative assistant. You remember him, right?"

"Yes. Perfect. So, something's up for you to be worried enough to contact me, I know you have a great relationship with a lot of cops there. Plus all the concern for security, what's going on?"

"Long story short, I recently finished a civil trial where the plaintiff sued the city and the police department. Aaron, the plaintiff's attorney, has sued APD and won several times and he won this one too, for half a million."

"Not sure I like where this might be headed."

"Yeah, well, me either. During the trial I received two threatening letters about making the case go away. Then a couple days ago I get a third one, also a threat, this time bearing out knowledge of the settlement, *and* it speaks of the plaintiff as if he is dead because of me."

I felt the hairs on my neck bristle as I thought…*there's a similarity to the letters Bethany received before her murder.*

"Enough said. You can fill me in when I get there. I've already taken care of everything here. I gotta clear out my desk, say goodbye to a few people, and then I can work on the flight."

"Are you sure? I mean…."

"Positive. I'll text Alex when I land. And Mac, be careful."

CHAPTER SIX

"Alex, I'm headed to my meeting with the Chief and Sheriff about cameras," Mac said.

"Ought to be fun," Alex snickered.

"Yeah, loads," Mac responded without looking over at him. Mac knew Alex always wanted to jump up and get the door for him when he had a briefcase over his crutch handle. By not looking over, Alex could be uncomfortable in private. Mac never wanted polio to be how people defined him, although most everyone did.

Mac made sure he arrived fifteen minutes early and sat at the conference table on the opposite side of the doors so he could see them walk inside. Chief Dick Baylor walked in on time and they were finishing their greetings when Undersheriff Morris LeBlanc opened the door.

"Where's Tom?" Chief Baylor asked, his scrunched brows giving away his disappointment in seeing Morris.

"Good morning, Your Honor," Morris said looking at Mac. "Hi Dick, it's good to see you too. *The Sheriff*...had another meeting." Morris stared until Dick grabbed a chair and pulled it out. Morris looked at Mac and rolled his eyes, causing both to grin.

"Morning Morris, good to see you again," Mac said, rubbing it in.

Over the course of the next hour Baylor pushed Mac on why they needed to put video cameras in every courtroom and at the county jail. The Chief felt it prevented having to transport inmates for every motion or preliminary hearing, thereby saving money and time.

Mac was aware the Sheriff and the county had money for things they really wanted. He designed a specific program for probation violation offenders to be seen in a separate location the county paid to refurbish, as well as paying for new judges to oversee the program, based on their feeling it took the judges too long to adjudicate cases. Mac did not know the exact reason Chief Baylor argued so adamantly for the cameras, but he knew it had to be political. Had it been a priority for the county, the Sheriff would be here doing the arguing.

"It's important for judges to see defendants face-to-face," Mac said. "Over ninety percent of the judges agree with me. You all sat here and assured me this would not be an issue when you proposed a new jail site instead of the one across the street. Therefore, we will continue doing business as usual. No cameras."

Chief Baylor slapped his binder closed as the screeching from the metal chair legs filled the room when he pushed back and stood. Without a word Dick Baylor yanked open the door and left.

Mac looked at Morris, raising his shoulders and pursing his lips. Morris nodded and grinned.

"Dick and the Mayor are really pushing this, but the Sheriff is not," Morris said. "He knows those two are aspiring for higher positions and he doesn't want to cut off his nose to spite his face. As difficult as it is, he's trying to stay neutral."

"Not a problem," Mac said. "Tell Tom not to worry, I'll

be the bad guy on this one."

"Thanks, Your Honor. I'll tell him."

"AARON VASQUEZ IS IN YOUR OFFICE" ALEX MOUTHED while lifting the mic end of his desk phone above his head when Mac entered.

Good. Hopefully he can let me know where his client is, Mac thought.

"Aaron, how you doing?" Mac asked, "Did you get my message?"

"Yeah, sorry Mac. Way too much going on." If they did not respond to one another's message before 9:00 a.m., any lunch or dinner suggestion was automatically off.

Aaron and Mac had been friends from their early days at the office of the Public Defender. Each had experienced discrimination and prejudice, Aaron from being gay and Mac being handicapped. Mac appreciated Aaron always calling him by his name when they were alone, in its own way validating their friendship.

"What can you tell me about Viktor Laine?" Mac asked while working to release his leg brace locks.

Aaron looked perplexed. "What do you mean?"

"Sorry. Not very clear, was I? Let's start over. What's the status of his case? Have you received your checks?"

"Oh, yeah. A day or two ago. Normally the city appeals, but Viktor's settlement was so low they realized paying was cheaper than appealing, especially given their track record. He had his wired to two accounts." Aaron paused, the strangeness of it all now registering. "Why are you asking? You've never asked me anything like this before."

Mac slowly pulled his chair closer to his desk and opened

the top center drawer. He handed Aaron the third note.

Bewildered by the clear plastic bag, Aaron took the corners cautiously between his thumbs and index fingers. Reading the note, Mac watched his confusion drift away… replaced by concern.

“I told him to be careful and to let me know if he saw anything suspicious,” Aaron said. “He hasn’t contacted me so I am presuming he is okay.”

“Do me a favor and try to locate him as soon as you can. We know I’ve received a bunch of threats, most of which don’t amount to anything. This one wasn’t directed at me, and the writer already knew of the payout. Plus ....”

“It speaks of Viktor in the past tense,” Aaron said, finishing his sentence.

He set the bag on the desk in front of Mac when he stood. “I’ll get my investigator on it right away. I’ll let you know when I hear something.” Aaron turned and headed for the door, his cell phone already in his hand.

“Aaron,” Mac called out. He stopped and turned. “You already told Viktor to let you know of anything suspicious. What is it you know?”

“Let me find Viktor and make sure we get him to safety first,” Aaron said. “I’ll explain everything then. But it has to be at your house. Not here, not my house, and definitely not in public.” Without waiting for a response Aaron pushed the button and was already speaking with his investigator when he walked through the doorway.

Mac had never seen a hint of fear in Aaron—until now. He looked across the room to the small table with the family picture of Alex, his wife Monique, and their two daughters, Maya and Sophia.

“Alex,” Mac called out.

CHAPTER SEVEN

Sitting in the Sacramento airport I pulled out my laptop and started to research the Albuquerque PD. They had their share of being in hot water with DOJ and the FBI, all of which appeared to be almost a decade ago. The Chief of Police and the Mayor had retired shortly after the investigation and from what I could tell there had been at least two Chiefs and Mayors since. I found several articles detailing how a rogue unit had been shut down and some of the other reforms required by DOJ. Reading about bad cops working in the city where I was raised took me back in time.

My father died when I was very young. My mother, a wonderful person, married a man who by all societal standards was a good person, too. Though, in the privacy of our home he was very different, preferring to punch and kick instead of talk. Many an Albuquerque cop had been in our home, only to assure us nothing else would happen–until the next night.

Mac's parents watched over me, presumably due to being the youngest of my siblings. Watching how the McDunn's dealt with adversity, always displaying dignity and class, stuck with me. I saw firsthand how they were never violent or harsh to those expending mental, physical or psychological abuses on them as to how Mac having contracted polio and needed to wear leg braces and walk with crutches.

Many years went by before I recognized the juxtaposition of my early childhood becoming the framework for my being a detective. I had been taught how to treat everyone with respect…up to the point when they escalated to violence. Fortunately, I also learned to fight through pain and to win the battle so I could go home every night. Somewhere in there I formed my belief; right is right, and wrong is wrong, with little gray area. Quite the foundation.

I BECAME LOST IN MY OWN WORLD UNTIL A FEMALE voice brought me back to reality.

"Evil, the place is evil," the woman hissed.

It took me a second to realize her comment was meant for me.

"Excuse me?"

"That place," she declared, her index finger bouncing in the direction of my computer screen. "It's evil." Reaching into her purse, she took out more gum even though her jaws were working overtime on her existing lump.

She wore her blonde, shoulder length hair, pulled into a bun. Her blue skirt and jacket, along with her carry-on bag made it easy to define her career.

"Are you one of the attendants on the flight to Albuquerque…?"

"Shannon. Yes. Thank God we head out to Dallas shortly after we land."

"Don't want to stay in Albuquerque, huh?"

"Hell no," she snapped as she attacked the new piece of gum.

"Sorry, Shannon, if I've caused you any undue stress. I'm doing some research on the police department, although I can close it out if it bothers you."

"It's okay...."

I could tell she was waiting to hear my name.

"I'm sorry, pretty rude of me," I said. "AJ. My name is AJ."

"Nice to meet you, AJ." Shannon turned and went behind the counter looking for a trashcan to dispose of her gum wrapper.

"So AJ, why is it you're doing research on the police department? You applying for a position there?" Her eyes broadened as she realized she may have already stuck her foot in her mouth.

"No. You can relax." I half chuckled, which encouraged her to take a deep sigh of relief. "I'm only going there to help a friend."

"Your friend in trouble with the police?" Shannon straightened up, as if she might be afraid of the possible answer.

I did not want to answer her question so I decided instead to ask her one.

"What can you tell me about APD? I mean it's obvious there's something about them you don't care for."

"You don't look like an attorney."

"Thank God," I exaggerated, bringing a slight grin to her face.

"You must be some-kind-of private eye...or a lunatic. I'm telling you most people wouldn't go there to help a friend in trouble with the police."

I kept looking at her, waiting for an explanation.

Shannon's eyes darted side-to-side before she drifted over to the large window overlooking the tarmac, her back toward me. I closed my computer and set it on my seat and inched up next to her making sure not to invade her personal space. I looked out on the tarmac at the workers rushing to get the baggage on the plane and waited.

Staring out the window, her arms crossed on her chest, Shannon whispered her utter distaste for APD. Turning around, she looked at me out of the corner of her eye.

"They killed Celia's husband and added insult to injury when they denied her requests for compensation. She's about to lose her home to foreclosure." Shannon shook her head and sighed. "We've been friends since high school. Her husband, Peter had worked his way up to sergeant."

My brows raised as I looked at Shannon. She read the shock on my face hearing how a police department would kill one of their own.

"I know. Right," she mumbled.

"From my research it seemed like the Department of Justice took care of that several years ago."

"Yeah, well…it only got better for a couple of years. Now they're back to the same old stuff."

Law enforcement is no different from any business where CEO's surround themselves with like-minded people. I knew that an administrator who had been promoted in an environment where the chief allowed rogue activity would likely be the same kind of chief given the opportunity, especially if they became the chief in the same agency. Add greed and money to the equation and city leadership can become straight out corrupt.

My head tilted, but I kept my eyes on hers.

"Celia told me Peter was one of a group of officers who did not agree with the police tactics of violence and abuse. Peter was the most outspoken of them so they killed him."

I watched a tear form in her eye before she turned back to the window and lowered her head.

Kyle Lansing had worked for the El Paso Police Department for ten years. His hatred of Mexicans became apparent to his coworkers the day after his probation period ended and he received union protection.

Kyle's father had taught him well. As a young man his father's desire to become a labor attorney had been thwarted by alimony and child support payments from several marriages. He settled for the next best option, becoming a union labor rep for the large industrial plant in Texas where he worked. He often shared closed-door session information with his son so Kyle would know how to stay out of trouble.

Directly out of high school Kyle joined the Army and served two years of a four-year stint before the bigotry complaints against him began to mount. Putting to use what his father had taught him, Kyle leveraged his colonel's affair with a fellow soldier's wife against the bigotry complaints, managing an honorable discharge with his early release.

Kyle's intelligence helped him finish third in his police academy class. The consummate rookie, he did everything by the book, paid attention to his training officers and treated everyone as if they were equal...while on probation. Despite policy against bigotry, Kyle knew it would be difficult to prove in a city where the Mexican population was so high. It took nine years for the El Paso Police Department to build a case capable of standing up in court, and for the union to finally quit paying for Kyle's attorneys.

It didn't take long before Kyle became a police officer again. Albuquerque PD hired seven lateral transfers, five of whom had been fired by previous agencies. The public had been assured by Deputy Chief Freddy Chamberlain the five previously fired transfers would never carry a gun, while at the same time stating it would be foolish not to utilize the group's experience to help the Police Department in other ways.

Four of the five officers originally part of Deputy Chief Chamberlain's promise, including Kyle Lansing, were working as police officers in less than six months…and carrying guns. Within two years Lansing became part of the ROP unit, unofficially known as *ROPE* for the hangman noose tattoo inked on most of the officers. The specialized unit had been designed to target repeat offenders and parole violators.

Lansing had not been with ROP long when the Federal Department of Justice required massive reforms, one of which was shutting down the ROP unit citing its obviously rogue tactics along with escalating situations in the level of violence rather than working toward peaceful endings. Although the violent unit had been shut down many officers continued to overstep their authority, including Kyle. He and another officer shot and killed an undocumented Mexican man. Lansing had been caught in a compromising position due to audio and video evidence of him telling other officers he was going to shoot the man, a known illegal alien, the department had dealt with many times.

Both officers had been on administrative leave with pay for over a year as Kiley Hildebrand, the District Attorney, struggled with whether or not to file charges. Despite Hildebrand having an excellent relationship with Albuquerque police officers, the risk of filing charges against the two made her worry about jeopardizing her own career. After seeking advice from several people she trusted, Hildebrand ultimately filed murder charges against them. Trying a common defense tactic, she hired two different sets of jurors and put on mock trials. Only after both juries deadlocked did Hildebrand decide to drop the charges.

Two months after returning to work as a patrol officer, Lansing got approached by Deputy Chief Freddy Chamberlain for a private meeting at a coffee shop. The following Monday afternoon both men arrived in casual attire.

After purchasing two iced Frappuccinos, Chamberlain surveyed the possibilities before he chose a small two-chair table tucked in the back of the shop. Lansing followed, letting the Deputy Chief call the shots. He felt ambivalent about their meeting. Still, he was intrigued by the fact the DC wanted to meet with him. He remained cautious after everything that happened and the negative press he drew.

Chamberlain looked past Lansing to ensure there was no one within earshot. Even so, he leaned forward resting his elbows on the table and spoke in a low tone.

"The DOJ investigation has created some changes," Chamberlain said. "They wanted us to shut down ROP… so we did. Still, sometimes you've got to be willing to take risks to get ahead." He took a sip of his drink while staring at Lansing. "You agree?"

Trying to appear *bought-in,* Lansing nodded as his right hand flared open.

"Good. Let's put it this way, certain officials and one guy from DOJ are prepared to take a few risks. Could we count on your support?"

Lansing settled into his chair holding his Frappuccino wearing a smirk on his face. “I’m listening.”

Chamberlain nodded, relaxed into the back of his chair and sensed he had brought another one into the fold.

“Excellent!”

CHAPTER EIGHT

My flight landed close to 1:00 p.m. and I thought about contacting Alex. Instead, I decided to wait until I had a rental car. In no hurry, I stayed back to let passengers not going to Dallas exit the plane.

"Thank you for your insight," I said to Shannon when she came out from the attendant area.

"You're welcome," she said with a smile.

"Is there any way you could do me a favor?"

Shannon tilted her head and squinted as she contemplated. "It depends," she said, still a little unsure.

"I'm going to give you this business card with my cell number on the back. Can you pass the number on to Peter's wife, Celia, I believe you said, and if she's up to a few questions she can call me?"

Shannon looked at the card, then me, then back at the card. She slowly reached out to take it.

"I'll do it, but I don't think you should sit around expecting her call. She isn't likely to reach out to you."

"I understand. I would even be willing to meet her anywhere she would want if she had concerns about me coming to her house. If not, please let her know I understand, and I'm sorry for her loss."

The corners of Shannon's lips turned up into an appreciative smile.

“You know, you’re fixin to put yourself in danger, poking around like you’re about to.”

Gently, I placed my hand on her shoulder. “Thank you for caring. Enjoy Dallas.” I smiled and turned, walking towards the front of the plane.

“AJ,” she said after I passed the wings.

I half-turned.

“Please, be careful?” she said, a pleading look on her face.

I winked, and continued on.

While heading to baggage claim I passed three pairs of Albuquerque police officers. One pair looked caught up in their own conversation and never saw me. It felt to me as if the other officers focused on me while I approached. I could not tell if my short hair and cop appearance had something to do with it, or the fact I assessed them as much as they did me. It would be nearly impossible to tell the good cops from the dirty ones in passing, but I had no intention of blindly trusting them solely based on their wearing a badge.

When I grabbed my suitcase off the conveyor I headed for the restroom. I wanted to get my Glock out of the lockbox in my suitcase and I knew there were no cameras in there, especially in one of the stalls. After I got my holster in place I waited. When I heard a couple of hand dryers start, I seated the magazine and racked a round into the chamber. I put one extra magazine in each front pants pocket, and put the lockbox back in the suitcase.

The fairly short line for a car rental surprised me and in under ten minutes I stood at the counter talking with the young clerk.

“Got any Ford Mustangs?”

“Boys and their toys,” she said, her eyes never leaving the computer screen.

"Mustangs are for men, not boys."

She chuckled. "Well then, you would probably appreciate the 500 GT we got back this morning."

"Music to my ears, young lady. A V-8 engine with four-hundred-sixty horsepower, music to my ears!"

She laughed. "Let me see what I can do."

In less than thirty minutes I had a contract in my hand and a set of keys to a beautiful, black Mustang. Sitting in the car listening to the engine purr I sent Seth the picture I had taken of the car hoping he might be a little jealous. Then I texted Alex.

Ralph had worked as an undercover cop in Dallas for ten years. A nasty fight with one of his informants, crazy after taking PCP, led to Ralph's left leg being broken in several places after being pushed over a metal railing and falling eighteen feet to a cement floor. The informant went at Ralph with a metal pipe. Ralph's first three hits with his Glock 23 to the informant's chest did not stop the advance, despite two hits later determined to be kill shots. The last two rounds Ralph fired were headshots. Ralph medically retired after several surgeries to repair the leg, but the injury left him with a noticeable limp.

A chance encounter with civil rights attorney, Aaron Vasquez, years later at a gym in Albuquerque prompted Ralph to get his private investigator license and work for him. His diamond earrings, brownish grey ponytail, thick mustache and goatee helped most of Aaron's clients to immediately relax with Ralph. His undercover experience helped him put even the most hardened at ease.

After receiving Aaron's call about Viktor, Ralph confirmed with Viktor's mother he had not been home for several days. Though worried, she had not called anyone since Viktor had done so several times in the past.

Two hours later Ralph located information about a meth dealer named Simeon , who supposedly had been looking for Viktor, too. When Ralph found Simeon he understood why.

"The mother fucker's dead when I see him," Simeon fumed.

"What happened?"

"He narced on me, man. He's supposed to show up with five grand. He don't show. A couple hours later he calls, wants to still deal. Offers to give me incentive for not showing the first time. I agree. Then the frickin cops dressed in all black showed up where I'm waiting to meet Viktor. They beat the shit outta me and took my meth, then drove me halfway to Santa Fe before they kicked me outta the car."

"Really?" Ralph's one raised brow bore out his disbelief.

"No, man, I'm lying. *Hell yeah*, it's the truth. Viktor's gonna pay too, one way or another."

"What'd they say to you, I mean, when they kicked you outta the car?"

"Said if I didn't want to end up like Viktor…I better keep quiet. Said I had time to think about it while walking back to Albuquerque."

Ralph looked at Simeon like he was an idiot for telling him.

"What? What's the look for?"

Ralph opened his palms and leaned back. "Why do you think?"

"Ah, yeah. They meant not to repeat it to any cops, right? You ain't no cop, you help out the defense attorney Viktor used. Besides, I figure when you see Viktor you can tell his ass I'm getting my six G's back. One way or the other."

CHAPTER NINE

Gary and Barbara O'Brien owned a large, upscale house in the foothills of the Sandia Mountains. They had been trying to sell their home, although according to their daughter, Julia, there had been some tension between them and their realtor, Nick Sandoval. When Sandoval discovered their dead bodies a few days later, he instantly became the focus of the investigation.

After hours of sitting through grilling by detectives, despite being told it was simply an interview, Sandoval said he wanted an attorney. Within hours he hired one of the city's well-known defense attorneys, Gordon Rogers.

Albuquerque police detectives conducted a search of Sandoval's residence and subsequently arrested him, charging him with two counts of first-degree murder. The district attorney's office changed the charges initially to second-degree murder to lessen the burden of proving specific intent. They were prepared to re-charge Sandoval with first-degree once they had all the police reports and evidence… if the charges were justified.

The warrant the detectives utilized to search Sandoval's home had been signed by the district attorney's office only minutes prior to 9 p.m., followed by one of the district court judges thirty minutes later, although the judge warned they needed to serve it *before* 10 p.m. because he did not authorize nighttime service. Detectives assured the judge how other detectives were ready to serve the warrant immediately so they did not need nighttime authorization. The actual service of the search warrant began minutes *after* 10 p.m.

The case of The State of New Mexico versus Nick Sandoval ended up in Judge Mac McDunn's courtroom. Gordon Rogers immediately filed a motion to suppress the search of Sandoval's house based on the warrant not being authorized for nighttime service, and the search began after 10 p.m. Judge McDunn granted the motion, suppressing the search and all evidence from it deemed "fruit of the poisonous tree."

McDunn had been surprised at the display of anger by the detectives having previously been warned by one of McDunn's colleagues about nighttime service. Their anger was trumped by the public comments of Dick Baylor, Albuquerque Chief of Police, and Mayor Raymond Sampson. Over the course of the next several weeks they openly commented about how it had been wrong for Sandoval to be released on bail. They also spoke of the deaths of two prominent citizens needing to be solved, blaming the justice system for preventing it from happening.

Deputy District Attorney Misha Hanson and defense attorney Gordon Rogers took their seats across the desk from Judge McDunn.

When the direct line to Alex on the desk phone buzzed, Mac picked it up instead of using the speaker.

"He's at the airport," Alex said. "You want me to have him come here?"

"Yeah. This meeting isn't going to last long," Mac said for the attorney's benefit. He hung up, put his elbows on the desk and rubbed his hands together.

"Let's get started. Ms. Hanson, what do you have?"

"Well, Your Honor, we have learned the cameras used at the crime scene had a different time zone stamp, Central time zone, and not Mountain Standard Time. Therefore, the warrant on Mr. Sandoval's home had been served prior to 10 p.m., thus making it a *lawful search*."

"And we know this how?" Mac asked, in a slow, almost non-believing manner.

"When Detective Tanaya called the company, she ascertained the cameras used at Mr. Sandoval's had originally been set up with Central Standard Time."

"This is preposterous, Your Honor," Gordon Rogers said with a raised tone. "She's beating around the damn bush, sorry Your Honor, darn bush. If she would have been able to validate it with a report, everyone knows she would have been flashing it around and handing it to us before a word ever came out of her mouth."

Mac looked at Misha, brows raised, his expression all but asking the question.

"I do have a report from Detective Tanaya regarding her calling the camera company."

Rogers opened his mouth to blurt something out when Mac put up his hand.

"Let me guess, Ms. Hanson, there's nothing in the report about specifically who the detective spoke with, or how the time zone issue can be directly validated to those cameras," Mac said.

"I don't believe so, Your Honor."

"She knows so," Gordon growled.

"Relax, Mr. Rogers. Now, Ms. Hanson, if this case were to be going to trial anytime soon, do you believe you would be the lead attorney?"

Misha's eyes got big. "No way."

"And yet, they have had you file five motions up to now to add evidence in order for me to essentially reverse my earlier decision to uphold the suppression. None of those motions were worthy of such a ruling, and frankly, some were pretty weak. Especially the last one, trying to say the bullet casing in the bag had been overlooked, despite the earlier photos already shared with defense not showing any casing in the bag."

Misha started to blush and looked at the ground.

"I think we all realize, thanks to the police chief and the mayor reminding us in the news every day, this is potentially a major case. Not to mention political. I would even guess they are putting pressure on your boss, who undoubtedly is putting pressure on you."

Gordon turned to look in time to see Misha nod her head. He smiled.

"Ms. Hanson, I understand you are only doing your job by trying to do anything possible to keep all of the evidence from the search from being excluded, not to mention keeping Ms. Hildebrand off your back. Still, the fact remains, nothing you have presented before today, and nothing today quite candidly, makes me believe I can trust the police investigation on this case. I would not ask you to tell me your thoughts, although I would venture to say even you know this whole investigation appears shoddy at best, a travesty in some people's eyes, based on how it has the appearance they are trying to do anything they can to go after Mr. Sandoval. Including possibly falsifying evidence, or so it appears."

Misha looked up without raising her head, embarrassed by what she was being asked to do.

"I feel like a pawn in a game I don't even want to be involved in anymore."

"I understand, Ms. Hanson. I will give the prosecution one last chance. Bring me validation from the company regarding the specific cameras used at the search of Mr. Sandoval's residence were, and always have been, set to Central Standard Time, otherwise I will uphold the motion to suppress."

Misha thanked Judge McDunn as she stood, taking rapid short steps towards the door. Gordon began laughing the instant the door closed behind her.

"You nailed it when you said political," Gordon said. "I'm used to pointing out mistakes made by cops and detectives. There's something about this one though. I don't have a good feeling about it."

"Yeah, well, I wish I could tell you more," Mac said. "Suffice it to say, I'm not going to be well liked if and when I uphold your motion to suppress."

Heading for the door Gordon said, "You know it's when, not if."

Mac nodded, thankful Gordon could not see him.

CHAPTER TEN

While driving to the courthouse I flipped through radio stations when I came across Syd and Shelly, radio DJs discussing the killing of a homeless man by two Albuquerque police officers.

"It doesn't make any sense. Drop the charges?" Shelly said questioningly.

"It seemed like a slam dunk case," Syd said. "I mean, officer…what was his name?"

"Kyle Lansing."

"Officer Lansing says he hates illegal Mexicans and he's going to shoot the guy and it's all caught on tape. Then he guns down the unarmed man shortly after making those statements to fellow officers. I mean, come on."

"I would like to hear from our listeners what they think," Shelly said. "Is the District Attorney, Kiley Hildebrand, afraid to prosecute police officers, or is it a political move on her part? Give us a call…."

I lowered the volume so I could concentrate on finding a parking spot close to the courthouse. Before one opened up my phone rang. The area code confirmed a New Mexico number…the rest of the numbers gave me no clue.

"Hello, AJ?"

"Yes. Who's this?"

"My name is Celia Howard. Shannon gave me your number."

That was quick, I thought. Before I could answer she continued.

"Shannon said she thought I could trust you, especially since you're not from around here. We can meet at my house. Can you be here within the next thirty minutes?"

I sensed her about to chicken out if I didn't jump on the opportunity. "Sure," I said, hoping she didn't live too far away.

Celia gave me her address on Parsifal, and suggested I take the Wyoming exit off of Interstate Highway 40 after I told her I was downtown.

The instant she hung up I dialed Alex's cell.

"AJ, how you doing? Are you lost already?"

I laughed. "Man, wasting no time getting some jabs in."

"Well, it's been like ten years since we saw you last, so I figured you couldn't remember how to get to the office."

"No. Not lost, not yet at least. I just got a call from Sergeant Peter Howard's widow. She's willing to talk with me, if I go over there right now."

"Wow, I'm surprised."

"Why? What's up?"

"From what I understand she has been pretty tight lipped. She even told Mac she didn't know who to trust and would not talk with him. Peter and Mac were decent friends."

"Quickly, tell me what happened to Peter? I don't want to put my foot in my mouth."

"He was driving home around midnight after getting off his shift, maybe six months ago now. Shortly after he turned onto Constitution from Wyoming a car pulled up next to him and opened fire. Peter drifted right and crashed into a light pole, dead from the gunfire."

"Any witnesses?"

"No. Although it happened on a Sunday night, early Monday morning thing. Not much traffic, and the strange thing about it…none of the people in the houses just south of where he crashed heard any gunfire…but several heard the crash."

A silencer? I wondered.

I asked Alex to let Mac know what I was doing and I'd catch up with him later.

"I HAD A MEETING WITH DEPUTY CHIEF CHAMBERLAIN this morning," Gyrene said. "He gave me some directions on what we are supposed to be focusing on for the next few weeks…possibly longer."

Rook raised his chin as if pointing across the lounge area toward Gyrene's office. "Who's the dude?"

Gyrene remained straight faced, but the others shook their heads. When Rook talked like he was a surfer, they cringed, wishing they had a more mature, seasoned officer.

"DC Chamberlain wants to bring another guy on the team," Gyrene said. "He wants the guy to work with us for several days to see if we approve." Gyrene went to his office, and returned with the officer.

Sly jumped up with a huge smile on his face. "Kyle Lansing, long time no see." They gave each other the standard bro hug, like athletes on television. "This guy is legit people. We worked together in ROP, and I'm telling you, he's perfect for this group."

The others stood and shook hands with Lansing. Rook went last, as if shuffling to do what was expected. All he could think about was the new guy had more experience than him meaning he'd still be the rookie of the group.

Gyrene could tell it wouldn't be long before Lansing officially became part of *The Syndicate of Death*, as Rook had dubbed their group.

"It's good to see you back in uniform after all the crap that bitch of a DA put you guys through," OM said.

"Thanks, man. It's nice to be back. She took so long deciding what to do, I actually thought she might try to prosecute us."

"Thank God she's smart enough to know where her political bread is buttered," Sly added.

"Wait a second. You're the one who shot the Mexican dude?" Rook inquired.

"Da! Surfer dude is finally starting to catch on, dudes," OM teased.

Rook was not fazed by the laughter directed at him.

"Shooter."

"What," Gyrene asked. "What'd you say?"

"Shooter," Rook said, nodding his head in approval of himself. "His moniker is going to be Shooter."

Sly looked at OM and shrugged. "Appropriate. Finally, the rookie gets something right."

Everyone laughed, including Rook.

CHAPTER ELEVEN

Celia Howard sent me a text requesting me to park away from her house. When I turned onto Parsifal Street I saw her house on my left. I passed by, turned left on Meylert Road, and parked along the curb.

Walking up her driveway a petite woman, about thirty-five, wearing a red sweatshirt and jeans, pushed open the screen door.

"AJ, I presume? I'm Celia."

"Thank you for seeing me," I said, reaching the door. "I know how difficult a time this is for you."

"How can you *possibly* know?" she growled, still holding open the screen and standing in the doorway as if I were no longer welcome.

"My fiancé was murdered almost two years ago. I'm the one who found her."

Celia's eyes widened, her hands covered her open mouth as tears formed in her eyes. She turned and ran to the bathroom, the screen door slamming behind her.

I walked into the house and closed the door. I figured if she wanted me to park around the corner, the last thing she'd want would be me standing on the porch waiting for her to return.

Similar to when I had been left alone in an attorney's or judge's office, I started to look around. There were several pictures of Celia and Peter, many with a young girl who looked to be around ten. A number of photos were of the little girl doing gymnastics, competitively by what I could tell.

I felt bad for making Celia cry and had hoped my opening up to her would help her trust me. Right before I heard the bathroom door open, I picked up one of the pictures of Peter hugging his daughter.

"This is a wonderful picture of the two of them," I said, as I turned towards her. *I learned the hard way about trying to replace something quickly and making a mess being worse than a person asking you not to touch their things.*

"Thank you. It's one of my favorites," she said, followed by a sniffle. "I'm so...."

I put up my hand to stop her.

"Your heart's been broken. The last thing you need to be concerned about is me. I really do understand."

She mouthed, "Thank you," before grabbing a tissue and sitting on the couch with her legs underneath her.

After I replaced the picture I took a seat in a chair.

"Shannon said you were here to help a friend who might be in trouble with the police."

"Yes. I have a good friend who feels as if the police might be targeting him."

"Besides saying you were cute, Shannon said she didn't know why...she just felt I could trust you."

It was nice to see the faint smile come across Celia's face, probably from my blushing at the *cute* comment.

"You've mentioned the word *trust* several times between the phone call and now."

Celia stared at me for several seconds, the assessment time she needed without being rushed.

"I've been afraid to trust anyone since Peter's death…his *murder.* I believe with all my heart it was corrupt people from the police department who killed him. He'd been looking into corrupt practices and dealings and had been warned to back off."

When the front door creaked Celia's eyes shot wide open, jetting back and forth between me and the person now entering. I stood, sensing it might be her daughter and Celia might not want to talk in front of her.

A four-foot little girl who looked all of fifty pounds walked into the room and ran to hug her mother. Then she looked over at me with an infectious smile. "Hi, I'm Brooke," she said with a little wave of her hand.

"Hi, Brooke!" I smiled.

Celia's face displayed worry with her eyebrows rising and creating a furrow along her forehead as her cheeks drew in.

"My name is AJ…I'm here to see if you and your mom are doing okay. She told me all about how great a gymnast you are."

For the next ten minutes Brooke proudly showed me some of her medals and awards. At one point, when Celia went to make coffee, Brooke leaned in close and whispered, "I know I'm done with gymnastics after the next meet in Denver. My mom says we can't afford it anymore…since my dad…."

The tears forming in her eyes swept me away and I gave her a hug. With her head buried in the crook of my neck I whispered, "Try to have faith." When she sat up to look me in the eyes I asked, "Can you promise me you'll try?"

She nodded. "I promise."

"Let's go see what your mom's doing."

"Okay."

When she backed away I wiped the tears from her face.

"Why don't you go in the bathroom and put some cool water on your face, so your mom won't know you were crying. It's good for her to see your beautiful smiling face."

She gave me a quick hug and ran off to the bathroom.

"She's wonderful," I told Celia as I sipped on coffee.

"At first I worried about what you would say. Thank you... for making her smile. I've been missing it. I don't want to talk about any of this with Brooke around. Please, don't hesitate to text me if you would like to talk another time."

Standing on the front porch saying goodbye to Celia, Brooke ran up and gave me a hug.

"What's the name of your gymnastics team, in case I want to watch you practice some time?"

Brooke's face lit up. "Star Gymnastics. It's close to here. It's on Tramway, near Indian School. We're getting ready for the meet I told you about, so we're practicing every night at six."

"You've got to promise me if I show up you won't do something crazy like fall off the beam and break your noggin."

Brooke giggled and ran off.

"I haven't seen her laugh for a while now," Celia said. "Thank you."

I felt good having helped them both to relax, even if only for a little bit.

Walking away from the house my thoughts shifted. Right before Brooke ran up and hugged me, I had noticed a patrol car creep by. The male cop stared at us the entire time he rolled by. I wondered if he'd still be in the area.

Approaching the corner I saw him parked along the

curb to the right of the intersection. With my car to the left, I knew I had a fifty-fifty chance he did not see me drive in. If not, then he'd want to see what I left in. I took the chance and turned right, walking in his direction and saw a gray Chrysler 300 parked near him along the curb three houses down.

I made my way into the street and when I got close to the car I slowly pulled out my keys when I got by the trunk. When I looked over the cop stared right at me, so I decided to play his game by staring back. Within seconds he started the squad car, turned on the emergency lights and drove off. I smiled and nodded when he looked over at me as he passed by. I took note of the identifying number on the front quarter panel of his patrol car before acting as if I was about to get inside the Chrysler as he drove out of view.

Jogging to my car, I left before he could make a return pass, knowing I could only pull off the charade once.

CHAPTER TWELVE

"Alex, how the heck are you?" I asked walking into the office. Alex had been Mac's Trial Court Administrative Assistant for over ten years and we had met several times.

"AJ, I'm doing great." He stood and we shook hands.

"How is Monique, and the girls, Maya and Sophia?"

Alex's wide smile showed he was impressed I remembered their names.

"They're great. Monique recently got a promotion, so now she oversees three of the ten stores in the city. The girls are doing well in school. Both are playing soccer and they love it. It eats up our weekends, but it's fun to watch them. And, how about you? Mac says you left the police department."

I knew by the way Alex referred to the judge as Mac, he was part of the inner circle. Alex seldom called him Mac to anyone unless they were family or close friends.

"Yes, a few days ago, in fact."

Alex said Mac was busy with a phone call and offered me a bottle of water.

After he sat at his desk, he looked around as if someone else had snuck in the office. He pulled his chair close, laid his forearms against the edge and leaned towards me.

"I'm glad you're here," he said in a low voice.

I tilted my head and squinted, curious about what he had to say.

"I haven't seen him this...*concerned*, outside of trials, of course, since his good friend lost her battle with cancer several years ago."

Alex was intelligent, so I felt sure when Mac asked to use his phone and left the office the other day, Alex went on guard.

"What do you mean?" I prompted.

"He actually asked me if there were someplace where I could take my family away from Albuquerque if he told me to do it."

I still did not know much, but it seemed like a good suggestion, in case things escalated.

"Well, do you?"

Alex jerked back, sitting up straight, confusion in his eyes.

"I can tell by the way you're looking at me you went from thinking Mac might be stressed or something, to realizing, 'Oh crap.'"

He nodded as he leaned into the back of his chair.

"Look, I don't know a lot yet, but I do know if Mac is concerned enough to call me and to warn you, we probably ought to have faith in him." I knew Mac trusted Alex implicitly, so I figured I could, too. "Plus, Celia Howard said some interesting things. Pretty enlightening."

"AJ, come on back," Mac yelled.

I went in, walked around his desk and bent over to give him a hug. "It's good to see you. Too bad it's under these circumstances."

"I agree," Mac said, with the closest thing to a downcast look on his face as I had ever seen.

"Alex," he yelled, "if anyone comes in the office please shut my door."

"Yep," came echoing back.

"What's the deal with asking Alex if he had someplace to go?"

"I don't know. I wish I could tell you. All I know is I feel… cautious, I guess. The last note I received suggested the plaintiff is dead because of my not listening to whoever is sending the notes. If it's true, and by the way, the attorney's investigator has not located him yet, it makes sense to put those close to me on notice. Right?"

I paused, taking it all in. I never pretended, not even remotely, to think I was a profiler. Still, after years of investigating a number of serious crimes, I developed a reasonable feel for how many of the criminals think. Wearing a uniform did not stop nefarious thinking.

"You're right. My take, so far, is they, whoever they are, are not quite ready to go so far as to kill a judge. But those around him…maybe. As for your plaintiff, he's dead. I'm certain of it."

"Really? What makes you so certain?"

"It is exactly like a gang, or the mafia. You don't send a message by saying you did something when you didn't. They probably had no issue with taking him out. It's like snuffing out a prostitute, killers think no one is going to miss them."

"Makes sense when you put it that way." Mac thought for a few seconds before shifting gears. "So, Alex told me you got a call from Peter Howard's widow."

I explained the research, Shannon's telling me Albuquerque police were not to be trusted, and how I left a card with her for Celia.

"She surprised me calling so quickly, solely based on what Shannon told her. Long story short, I think she's scared, she doesn't know who to trust. I got the feeling she wants to trust someone…but, she doesn't know what to do."

"You're aware Peter and I were pretty good friends. As much as a judge and a police officer could be. We often got together to go shooting at the range."

"Yeah, Alex commented briefly about it. The funny thing is, Celia never asked about my background, or anything. So she still doesn't know I came here to help you. She simply trusted Shannon's belief I was someone who could help her."

"What do you think is going to happen when you tell her you were a cop, and about knowing me?"

"I'm inclined to say it will be fine, but who knows. I never asked a single question about anything important, I only listened…I wanted to build rapport. When their daughter, Brooke, got home from school, I spent time chatting with her, getting her to laugh and open up about her gymnastics. She was giving me hugs by the time I left."

"Pretty crafty."

"Maybe. I prefer to think of it as being sensitive to their problem."

We heard a slight snicker on the other side of the doorway and knew Alex had listened in. I smiled and did a short jab with my head towards the door.

Mac leaned forward and whispered, "I don't blame him. He's probably concerned about the safety of his family and wants to know as much as possible. It's kind of why I had you leave the door open."

I nodded. This wasn't one of my homicide investigations. If Mac had no problem with Alex listening in, neither did I.

I'm only here to help my friend.

CHAPTER THIRTEEN

"So, you said the DC gave us some directions," Sly said. "What's up?"

"It appears McDunn is struggling to get the message," Gyrene said. "Just in the last couple days he refused the chief's request for cameras so not every prisoner needs to be transported from the county jail on bullshit stuff like a ten-minute continuance hearing."

"Apparently killing Viktor wasn't enough to convince him," OM said.

"Apparently not. He also sent the Deputy DA packing again on the O'Brien murders. His time as a public defender has clearly clouded his judgment. The Chief has that realtor, Sandoval, squarely in his sights, and he wants Sandoval to go down for it. The DC wants us to make sure McDunn doesn't get in the way. Let's make it clear Sandoval killed the couple."

"I'd be happy to pull the trigger," OM blurted, bringing his hands together in front of him as if he was shooting someone across the room.

"Not so quick," Gyrene said. "We may have to at some point, but the last thing they want is DOJ back here doing another investigation. There are other people we can go after to get the message across."

Gyrene's cell rang and he checked the caller ID. "Yes, sir.

Having it right now, sir." He turned and walked to his desk in case he had to scribble notes.

"Yeah, well, when the time comes, I'm doing it," OM said, looking at each member to make sure they understood.

"Something must have happened for you to want to take care of it so bad," Rook said.

"When he was a public defender, he made a fool out of me on the stand once. I ain't never forgot it."

Sly was the first one to start laughing, followed rapidly by the others.

"What's so funny?" Gyrene asked after he hung up.

"OM thinks McDunn is the only reason he looked like a fool on the stand," Sly teased. "He obviously hasn't looked in a mirror lately."

Everybody started laughing harder, including OM who finally cracked a smile once he realized why.

Gyrene cleared his throat to get everyone's attention.

"The Chief and the Mayor told Chamberlain they didn't want any more lawsuits and we need to send a clear message. Everyone should know who the focus is squarely on now."

Rook nodded along with everyone else, despite not having connected the dots from their last murder.

"Also, they told him the Hispanic chick on the city council, the married one not the divorced one, is getting too ballsy; she's starting to gather some listeners. Remember, our primary goal is to protect them for two reasons. One is our financial future, and two is so when they get what they want, we all will have the fast-track on moving into cushy positions to pad our retirements."

Everyone agreed, each seeing a bright future in what they were doing.

"Oh, Chamberlain's the one who called," Gyrene said.

"No shit," OM declared. "Like we couldn't figure it out from your, 'sir, yes sir, anything for you sir, I'm here to please you sir.'"

Everyone laughed, except Gyrene. Looking above their heads as though he were contemplating, he said, "Hmm, let's see. Someone gets to decide who pulls the trigger on whom. I wonder who gets to decide."

"He got ya, big guy," Sly said as he patted OM on the back.

Gyrene let the chiding of OM go on for a couple of minutes. "Back to the DC. Apparently Celia Howard had a visitor, and according to our guy the visitor looked like a cop. White guy, looked to be mid-thirties to early-forties, easily six foot, maybe a couple inches taller, short dark hair and a big scar on his cheek. Our guy said he got into a gray Chevy 300, New Mexico plates, but he didn't get any numbers."

"Ain't it a Chrysler 300?" OM said more than asked. "How the hell did that guy make it past training?"

Tension and fidgeting filled the room. None of them had a problem dealing with taking care of business and killing Peter. Doing something to his wife and daughter went beyond their comfort zone. Gyrene could see it and instantly knew why—he had the same feeling. Internally he marveled at the irony, every one of them could kill a woman, but messing with a cop's wife seemed somehow taboo. Even if she could bring the house of cards down on them.

"Don't worry. We're only interested in the guy. Rank and file have been quiet ever since Peter got eliminated. We need to figure out which area and what shift this guy works so we can make sure he isn't going to try to pick up where Peter left off."

Gyrene spent the remainder of the time making sure everyone knew the petty stuff was over for a while...they needed to focus on recon before turning up the heat. He passed out assignments and told Shooter, as the new guy, he would be buying the beer, right after they located Emilio, one of Gyrene's old informants. Gyrene had long-ago figured out a little relaxing first helped focusing when he needed it.

LISA STEVENS HAD BEEN EMPLOYED AT THE ALBUQUERQUE Journal for seventeen years. She had worked her way up through strong writing skills, her ability to make the reader feel as if they could see what she saw, and her in-depth research. Some peers referred to her as Clancy, in reference to the famous writer well known for his thorough research.

The door to Mike Sanders' office had a six-inch wood frame with a long strip of glass in the middle. Mike liked seeing people approaching before they got there, and he often stood in his office looking out at the employees. In his mind he didn't consider it spying, he needed to see who deserved the *tough but sought-after* stories.

Mike saw Lisa coming the instant she stepped on the carpet from the stairwell. He had seen the look on her face many times and knew it would be important. He grabbed his cup and walked over to the coffee pot all the while praising himself for having made a fresh pot.

I'm probably going to need it, he thought.

The tap on the glass came when Mike started walking to his chair. With a head tilt, he gave Lisa the okay.

"Mike, I need your advice," Lisa blurted out before she even took a seat.

Mike took a sip of coffee, lauding himself once more. When Lisa talked fast, things were serious.

"And, I need you to promise me what I tell you stays between us."

Mike sipped and stared.

"Plus, you need to promise me you won't give this information to someone else to write the story if I decide not to."

Mike took another sip. The five seconds of silence was Lisa's way of telling him she would wait for a response.

"Lisa, we've been through this before. If information is credible and the story needs to be told, we are going to tell it. Period."

Lisa looked at the files she held as if trying to decide what to do.

"Mike, this is different. I'm technically not supposed to know it."

Mike could read between the lines, part of the reason he was one of the most successful editors the Journal ever had.

"Let's start with a hypothetical," he suggested.

Lisa's eyes sprang open. "Hypothetically, a judge in a civil trial received several threats about making the trial go away, or else."

Mike's lips pursed in reflection and he nodded.

"Okay. Go on."

"So, hypothetically, what if the plaintiff is said to be dead because the judge did not listen. Then, let's say the plaintiff cannot be located."

"We need to stop there before I reach a point where I cannot listen to hypothetical anymore."

"What should I do? My story on corruption is due to come out soon, but hypothetically, information like this could blow the lid off."

"I'm inclined to say your story proceeds on schedule. Any potential new information deemed credible could lead to a nice follow-up story."

Lisa took a deep breath, ready to let loose. Mike raised his hand, his palm facing her.

"Before you get all flustered and say something you can't take back, I promise I won't say anything to anybody."

Lisa sighed in relief when she heard the promise and smiled, knowing she would have been perturbed.

CHAPTER FOURTEEN

I followed Mac to his house so I could drop off my car. He had called his girlfriend, Lisa, to meet us for dinner, but she said she was working on her story and would catch up with us later.

"Before we go eat can we go someplace?"

"Sure," Mac replied, indicating I had piqued his curiosity.

"Just something I want to take care of right away, so I don't forget."

"No need to explain," he said sensing the importance and got into his car.

We arrived shortly after five-thirty and the parking lot was fairly large. I had no idea what kind of car they'd be in so I could only hope we were early.

Holding the door open, we went into Star Gymnastics. I did a quick scan inside the thirty by fifteen multipurpose area and Celia and Brooke were nowhere in sight. Along the outer wall to my right was a narrow hallway and looking through the glass to the gym floor I saw little activity.

"Can I help you?" The woman behind the counter asked, looking over the top of her reading glasses.

"Yes, I was wondering if you could tell me about Brooke Howard's account?" I asked timidly, not really having planned what to say.

"We don't share people's personal information," she answered, now paying full attention to me through squinted eyes.

"Sorry, sorry."

"Smooth," Mac said slightly above a whisper.

My quick glance told him to *shut up*, but his, *who me* grin showed I was too late. Turning back to the woman, I cleared my throat. "I understand Mrs. Howard will not be able to afford for Brooke to continue doing gymnastics."

I paused, expecting her to say something, but she did not say anything while she continued to stare.

Mac scoffed, having a good time with my rising discomfort level.

"Well, uh, I would like to pay for her to continue here for the remainder of this year and all of next year." I kept my eyes down while I pulled out my credit card.

Her stare turned to a huge smile when she took my card.

"Why…how very generous of you," she stole a glance at the card, "Mr. Conti."

When I looked over at Mac he stayed leaning on his crutch, his head tilted and face grinning.

"What? You know her chances of success are much greater if she can have something she loves to focus on."

"I'm not saying anything," he said, rolling his shoulders.

I signed the bill, put my credit card and receipt in my wallet, and put it away as several girls came through the door.

Brooke lit up when she saw me as she ran over and gave me a hug. I introduced her to Mac about the same time her mother walked in. When Celia saw me she stopped, right in the middle of her conversation with one of the other moms.

"Hi, Celia. Thought I would stop by to watch for a little while." Although she did not say a word to me, she politely excused herself from the other mom before looking back at me, the gentle curve of her lips and her soft eyes telling me she was touched.

I explained to Brooke we could only stay for a short time, but promised to come again. She thanked us, gave me another quick hug, and raced through the door out onto the mats.

Celia moved forward, her face seemed caught between emotions. I pointed with an open palm and she went to the seats directly in front of the window. I followed and sat on her far side, while Mac sat in the first chair.

"Celia, this is my good friend Mac."

"Judge McDunn," she extended her hand. "My husband spoke fondly of you."

Mac shook her hand. "I enjoyed being around Peter. We had some great conversations. I'm so sorry for your loss."

"Peter really enjoyed them, too." She turned to me. "Is Mac the friend you're here to help?"

I nodded. Celia looked over at Mac, then back to me. The tenseness in her shoulders diminished as she settled into her seat and looked out at Brooke.

Parents began taking seats, although no one came to the open chairs near us in the first row. We could feel the buzz in the room about two men sitting with Celia. We spoke in low voices, which only added to the intrigue. Fortunately, there were two moms who could have easily been heard from another room, and they enjoyed verbally competing for the *best mom* award by trying to one-up each other.

"So, if AJ is here to help you, then you must not trust certain people in uniforms either?"

"Sad, but true." Mac tried to stealthily steal a glance around the room, being a little uncomfortable with sharing too much, especially with it being crowded. Ironically, the opposite could almost be said about Celia's comfort level. The safety she felt with others around spoke volumes.

In the forty-five minutes we were there, Brooke looked over several times, each time with a cute smile. We even got a quick hand raise once. Celia informed us the instructors always wanted the girls' full-attention, so Brooke might get in trouble despite trying to hide it. Before the practice started, I had seen the woman I paid walk out and say something to one of the instructors, before both looked over at me. Apparently my kindness may have helped Brooke receive a little slack for her couple of smiles and one wave.

Once Mac and Celia established they both had similar trust issues, the remaining thirty minutes centered on Brooke's well-being and how she was coping with her loss.

"Was this intentional?" Mac asked as soon as both car doors were closed. "Having me meet Celia?"

"There was no malice aforethought, if that's what you're thinking. It didn't hit me until we were walking up to the door. Look, I know you. Sometimes you can hide behind your own fears of what others might think. I knew neither one of you would agree to a formal meeting, plus, I had to let Celia know the truth soon. This evening took care of the whole thing."

Silence filled the car while Mac drove to a Greek restaurant not far from his house. He parked and looked over at me. His pursed lips and slight head nod his way of acknowledging my answer, in the very least held merit, even though I could see he still did not like it.

Once inside the restaurant Mac filled me in on everything about the notes he'd received, including his concerns. Then he told me Lisa was about to get a major article published on police corruption. Although I felt ready to jump in with both feet, I explained to Mac how I needed to spend a day visiting my sister and her husband. They lived in Los Ranchos De Albuquerque, a suburb along the Rio Grande River. I had not seen them for quite a while and looked forward to the visit. More importantly, I wanted to make sure they were aware of what I had agreed to do. Based on what I already knew, they needed to be keenly aware of possibly being targeted by the police.

CHAPTER FIFTEEN

City Councilwoman, Anita Trujillo, had been holding forum meetings once a week for the last month. Although the issues people brought up were important, what pleased her most was the growing attendance each week. Anita genuinely believed she could have a real shot at being the next mayor if she could tackle some of the issues surrounding the police department.

She had hoped to get home at a reasonable hour, although such an opportunity had long passed. She had met with three local pastors at the Denny's restaurant on Coors Boulevard and prepared to leave. Anita texted her husband and was not surprised when he did not answer—as owner of a construction company he endured long days of early mornings and late hours. She texted Amy, her thirteen-year-old daughter, who answered immediately. Anita told her she wanted to say goodnight since it would be at least an hour before she got home, and asked Amy to put her phone away and go to sleep. Anita appreciated how Amy seldom questioned their house rules, unlike a number of her teen peers who constantly battled their parents.

Whenever she felt stressed, Anita stopped at the Sandia Casino off Interstate Highway 25. With the casino only a few miles from her house, she felt there was little risk of anything happening if she had a drink or two…a welcomed bit of relaxation after long nights of listening to people's troubles. The casino was less than two miles from her home and no businesses or residences occupied either side of the road for the majority of the drive. After eleven p.m. traffic dropped down to a car or two every hour. Only twice had she seen a police car in all of the time she had been going to the casino.

Anita walked into the Casino around ten thirty and went straight to the dollar slots…her credit card in hand.

"Busy night?" Cherise the waitress asked.

"Oh, hi, Cherise," Anita said. "It's been a stressful week."

"Want your usual drink?"

"No, tonight I think I'll do a Jim Beam."

"You weren't joking, girl. You are stressed. I'll be right back."

"Thanks, Cherise."

Anita settled in and relaxed on the end seat, thankful she only had one female on the last machine to her left and nobody on the machines around her.

ROOK AND SHOOTER FOLLOWED ANITA FROM DENNY'S. Shooter parked the black Tahoe two rows over and fifteen spots from where Anita parked. She never looked his way when heading to the main entrance.

Rook went inside and milled around until he found an open seat at a Blackjack machine where he could keep an eye on Anita. After their meeting the other day when Gyrene told them to start focusing on the Hispanic city councilwoman they began to follow her. One night she stopped at the casino for an hour so he hoped for the same this evening. The waitress taking Anita a shot of Jim Beam instead of a Bud Light surprised him because she only had two beers the previous night.

Will she stop after two drinks tonight? He wondered.

After a couple of shots, Anita had two Bud Lights before leaving close to midnight. Rook had cashed out and did not hesitate to leave the five-dollar credit on his machine. He kept his distance and she had no idea he was following her.

"What the hell took so long?" Shooter blurted out as Rook got in the car.

"She had a couple of hard drinks before her usual two beers. She must have won a few bucks. She was all smiles talking with the waitress about it when she got her last beer."

"Ah, hell. It'll all work out," Shooter commented, trying to calm himself.

THEIR RELUCTANT PARTICIPANT, EMILIO, HAD SWEAT running down his face as he sat in the rear of the Tahoe. They had been parked for over an hour and the longer he sat, the more he felt he made a mistake. Dirty cops offering him two grand along with stolen meth had been hard to pass up…his addiction made the decision seem easy the night before. He'd been told he'd get a grand when they were done, and another grand in a few days.

Emilio heard the loud voice on the radio saying, "she's leaving." Emilio kept rubbing his hands together and bouncing his leg…the option to back out no longer existed.

JUST AFTER THEY PASSED THE PARKED TAHOE, SHOOTER turned on the emergency lights. The blue Ford Edge pulled over to the gravel shoulder and Shooter approached the Ford.

"Ma'am, do you have any idea why I pulled you over?"

"No, I'm sorry, I don't," Anita slurred.

"You were weaving, and you crossed the center line twice." Shooter looked over the car to make sure the others had everything in place.

Anita never saw the second SUV pull up with all the lights off...her awareness thwarted by her nervously trying to figure out how she could get out of the situation.

"Officer, I'm Councilwoman Trujillo...I'm less than a mile from my home."

"Yes, ma'am. I need you to step out of the vehicle so I can conduct some field sobriety tests."

Anita tried twice more to finagle her way out, only to give in when the officer said he would happily drag her from the car if he had to. Getting out, she got a better look of the officer's face, recognizing he had been the one all over the news for killing an unarmed man...her heart sank.

A split second before she started to scream she felt a punch hit her stomach, taking her breath away.

A second officer came up and slapped a piece of duct tape across her mouth. With one hand he wrenched her arm behind her back causing severe pain, and with the other he grabbed a handful of hair and yanked her head back. The two officers dragged her off the side of the road into a small gulley hidden by a six-foot bush where a blanket laid on the ground.

When Anita saw two other men, thoughts of being gang raped, or worse, flooded her mind. Each time she tried to fight they subdued her with a sharp pinch to a nerve on her shoulder blade or a punch to her gut. In less than a minute she lay naked on a blanket, her embarrassment of exposure and trying to close her legs only served to help the men hold her down.

A man in all black fatigues knelt above Anita's head saying, "You quit fighting, and you go home. You will not be raped, unless you do not cooperate. If we rape you, we kill you. Do you understand?"

Anita nodded while tears rolled down her face.

Emilio emerged from the darkness, naked, and every bit as scared as Anita. He was instructed to lay beside Anita, and place his leg on top of hers and his hand on her breast.

"Don't scream, or they'll kill us both," he whispered.

Anita saw the fear in Emilio's eyes, the truth of his statement settling in. Someone ripped the duct tape off her mouth while another began taking photographs. What seemed like several minutes, took less than thirty seconds, and the photographer stopped. One of the men told Emilio to go get dressed, while another threw Anita her clothes. She silently said a prayer as she dressed, feeling a small ray of hope they were going to let her go.

CHAPTER SIXTEEN

Anita drove home in a daze, not knowing how she ended up in her driveway. Thoughts and images flooded her mind, all of which kept her fear inside intensified. She sat in her car for several minutes, crying and shaking.

Every few minutes she would tell herself she should be thankful not to have been raped, and more importantly, grateful to be alive. Those thoughts were replaced by new waves of nausea and shaking as Anita recalled the pictures they showed her of her daughter Amy in front of their house and Desert Ridge Middle School, dressed in the clothes she wore to school earlier in the day. The threats of what they would do to Amy resonated above all else.

After thirty minutes she wiped away the tears and slowly exited her car, trying to gather herself in case her husband or daughter were awake. When shutting the door she looked around, hoping none of the neighbors had seen her sitting so long in the car.

She scanned west, then her eyes swung past the intersection to the house across the street when it registered… her eyes darted back to the black Tahoe on the shoulder of the road and her hands began to shake.

The doors to the SUV opened with two men emerging, both in dark clothing. She could feel their stares as they walked to the front of their vehicle and leaned against the hood. Anita could not move.

The tall one lit a cigarette and took a long drag before extending his right hand in Anita's direction. The way he leaned his head with his arm fully extended and hand in front of his eyes, Anita knew he was simulating shooting her. Her knees nearly buckled.

She recognized him as the one who wanted to kill her rather than take pictures, settling for kicking and hitting her several times instead. One of the voices in the darkness yelled not to leave any obvious marks – none that she couldn't cover up. Subsequently, all of his blows were to her buttocks, lower back and the back of her head.

Anita knew she needed to get in the house, but the thought she would already be dead if their goal had been to kill her gave her the strength to close the car door. Telling herself not to look back, her steps were paced and deliberate, though she wanted to run. At the front door her key touched the lock several times, bouncing around the hole before she reached up with her left hand to steady her right… the key finally hit its mark.

In the back of her mind she knew the locks on the door were not enough to keep them out if they wanted to get in for her, or her family. Yet, the turning of the deadbolt on the inside of the door provided a semblance of relief. Setting her purse on the foyer table, she nearly knocked over a small vase…her mission to be quiet had been trumped by needing to get to Amy's room.

Seeing Amy sleeping tranquilly, her clothes for the next day laid out, gave Anita peace of mind for a brief second. She closed the door and raced down the hall to the bathroom, dropping to her knees in time to direct the vomit into the toilet. She stood, took a cloth and wet it with cold water before sitting on the toilet lid. When she began to wipe her face, her emotions erupted. She let the cloth cover her face while she sobbed…slowly rocking back and forth.

SLEEP FOR A HOMICIDE DETECTIVE CAN BE SOMEWHAT elusive, something you long for but never really expect. After Bethany's murder I struggled with flashbacks and nightmares for months, only averaging a couple of hours of sleep at a time. Once I got past those times, I became accustomed to four hours each night.

After Mac went to bed, I headed to my room and tried to stay quiet. My body still functioned on California time, so I tried to figure out the rogue cops next moves. An uncomfortable feeling settled in while I thought about it all, the fact they were dirty cops the most likely reason. Every agency has their fair share of bad cops, most are intelligent and capable of putting on a front, starting with learning how to pass a polygraph and the interviews one goes through to get hired. By the time they get off probation some have constructed a plan of evildoing, which only expands their experiences of what they can get away with. Most agencies are fortunate not to have their delinquents hook up with other cop offenders. Albuquerque PD had become the exception…a culture most likely started three to four Chiefs ago.

To my knowledge, they had killed two people, one a fellow officer, and threatened a district court judge. I had no way of knowing positively if their driving by Celia's home with regularity had to do with their concern about another officer going there to collect what Peter might have gathered versus watching out for a fellow cop's widow. My gut told me they couldn't care less for his widow, along with telling me it would soon get worse. Killing has a way of becoming easier the more one kills, and for dirtbags…they start to enjoy it.

CHAPTER SEVENTEEN

Celia parked in the driveway knowing she would be going to pick up Brooke in a couple hours. The screen door rested against her back as she started to put the keys in the lock. When she touched the door it creaked, moving no more than an inch. Instinctively she looked over her shoulder to scan the area, but not seeing anything suspicious did nothing to quell her feeling *they* were there and *they* were watching.

Closing the door, she went to the kitchen, setting her purse and keys quietly on the counter before grabbing the largest knife out of the wooden block. Methodically she made her way throughout the house taking inventory. She started to doubt her fear about someone having been inside since nothing appeared to be disturbed. Turning, she started down the hallway seeing Brooke's room exactly like she left it before going to school. But, her fears were confirmed when she made it to the last two rooms…her room and the spare bedroom.

She saw the money she left on her dresser, along with her diamond earrings and necklace still where they belonged. Her laptop left on the bed seemed to be the only item taken. She walked to the spare room used as their unofficial office. It seemed clear their search centered on the office. She had a sickening feeling in the pit of her stomach when she stepped inside.

The remaining dust on the desktop outlined where the keyboard, computer stand, and mouse pad had been. Several of the smaller items from the desktop were on the carpet and all of the desk drawers were pulled open. Looking closer, she noticed the zip drives missing from the top of the middle drawer. Her eyes shot open and she felt the blood rushing from her face as the reality set. The intruders were people Peter worked with.

"Oh my God," she gasped, dropping the knife, her hands moving up to her temples. "They're looking for his information." She closed her eyes, afraid of what it might mean. Her thoughts went to Brooke, now afraid for their safety.

Somehow she made it to the dining table, pulled her phone out of her back pocket and sat. She sent the text and waited. When it buzzed, she looked at the response, stood up, grabbed her purse and keys, from the kitchen and left out the front door. When she got to the car she paused and went back inside, heading straight to the nightstand by her bed. After several seconds she worked the bottom hidden drawer open and pulled out her husband's cell phone. She stuffed it in her purse and grabbed a soda from the refrigerator, not to quench her thirst, hoping instead to fool anyone watching the house and questioning why she went back inside.

Amy Trujillo said goodbye to her two friends at Desert Ridge Middle School. Her friends turned right without even looking, heading for the front buses. Their driver had a thing for always arriving early so her bus could be first in line. Being second bus had been the farthest back she had ever been.

Amy searched for her driver, Cheryl, who liked to stand by the passenger side door to greet the kids as they climbed aboard.

"Excuse me," a man said.

When Amy looked she saw a middle-aged white man, clean-shaven, with short dark hair, wearing a dark suit, a white shirt and red tie. She felt a lump in her throat and her hands started to shake, thinking he was one of the new administrators, or possibly campus security.

"We didn't do anything. We were trying to smoke a cigarette Jeanette stole from her mom, but we couldn't even get it lit."

The man laughed. "I'm not with the school, you can relax."

Amy closed her eyes and took a deep breath, helping the lump to go away, but not the shaking. She could hear her heart thumping in her ears.

"I've been trying to reach your mom, but she's never answered. I'm sure she's busy. She really wanted this packet so she could look it over tonight. I have to head back to Santa Fe. Can you take it to her for me?"

Amy was so happy not to be in trouble she did not ask any questions. "Sure. I gotta go catch my bus." She reached out and yanked the large manila envelope out of the man's hand without looking up at his face again, and raced to the bus as if it was about to take off without her.

Cheryl's shoulders straightened and pulled back slightly, her eyes widened and her mouth hung open after Amy ran past her getting onto her bus. She looked over at the man in the suit, who grinned and shrugged before casually walking between a couple buses towards the parking lot.

CHAPTER EIGHTEEN

When Celia pulled onto Constitution Avenue she noticed a patrol car following her two car-lengths back. It followed her for several miles on Constitution and into the left turn lane at Juan Tabo Boulevard. Celia started to pull her phone out to text she was being followed when she saw in her rearview mirror the cop hit his steering wheel.

He turned on his emergency lights and siren, pulled out around her on her right, made a U-turn, and sped off west on Constitution Avenue. Celia checked her mirrors to make sure there were no others. Although she felt reasonably certain she was no longer being trailed, she could not help but drive slowly and scan everywhere until she arrived at her meeting place.

After pulling into the parking lot at the Flying Star Café, she sat in her car for ten minutes. She took note of every car pulling in from Juan Tabo Boulevard. Only after Celia felt relatively certain nobody else tailed her did she get out of the car and walk inside the restaurant.

"Are you okay?" I asked.

"Not really," Celia muttered, putting her purse and keys on a chair.

"Try to relax, when you're ready tell me what happened."

The waitress set down the coffee Celia had requested and took two sips before scanning the room.

"I asked to sit back here so nobody would be close to us. I'll let you know if anyone comes this way."

She looked at me, took another sip, and set her cup down. Her fingertips subconsciously rotated the cup slowly, again and again.

"Somebody got in my house."

My eyes narrowed, already concerned for their safety. I stayed silent, not wanting to derail her.

"It had to be the police." Celia took another sip and went back to rotating her cup. "So far, the only things taken as far as I can tell were my laptop, the computer from the office, and the three thumb drives from the top desk drawer."

"Nothing else?"

"No. I don't think so. I had cash out on the dresser, along with several pieces of pretty nice jewelry. They weren't touched. The laptop had been on my bed...I'm on it too often anymore when sleep evades me."

I felt for her, knowing exactly what she was going through. The basics of eating and sleeping do not seem important after a personal, tragic loss.

"It didn't seem like anything else had been touched in my room. In fact, the office was the only room ransacked."

"It's been almost, what, six months since Peter was killed? Something's up, otherwise they would have done this before."

"Didn't you say they were watching the house when you visited?"

"Yes. I'm sure they recognized I'm a cop, or used to be. It's possible they could be thinking I'm going to pick up where Peter left off. In fact, I would bet they think I'm an Albuquerque officer."

Celia's eyes widened, looking at her coffee cup and leaning it up on the bottom edge. She fidgeted, never taking her eyes off the cup. It did not take a detective to realize she was afraid to say whatever was about to come next.

"I've got something to tell you. Maybe I should have told you earlier, but Peter made me promise to only tell someone I trusted."

I nodded, a quiet *thank you* so as not to distract her.

"Peter told me about a week before he died not to throw away his phone. He said if something happened, give his phone to the person I decided to trust. The strange part was he said to tell the person to take the phone to the Sheriff's office hiring billboard on southbound I-25 south of Alameda Boulevard. When I asked him what it meant he refused to tell me. He said the less I knew the better."

"Did he give you any idea about the connection between the phone and the billboard? Or what the person was supposed to do with them?"

"He said hopefully they would know." She reached in her purse and pulled out Peter's iPhone with the white charging cord wrapped around it. She set it on the table, her fingertips lightly touching it for several seconds before she slowly slid it towards me.

I gently put my hand on the end closest to me and understood the difficulty for her…it was like giving up a piece of Peter and I waited for her to relinquish it in her own time frame. When I picked it up I put it in my jacket pocket as Celia stood and raced toward the restroom. I walked over to the manager, making sure to look at her nametag.

"Roberta, can you do me a favor?"

"Sure. What is it?"

"I'm hoping you would be kind enough to let me call a friend of mine with your cell phone. Mine's having some problems."

Roberta stared at me for several seconds without blinking, probably trying to decide my sanity level.

"I promise it will be short."

"What do I get out of the deal?" She smiled.

I laughed. "How about twenty bucks for anything less than fifteen minutes. Fifty if it goes from fifteen to thirty."

"It's yours." She held the phone in her right hand, her left hand extended palm up.

After the exchange I returned to the table, surprised Celia was back. "Don't ask," I said, when Celia gave me her what-are-you-up-to face.

I sent a text from Roberta's phone and waited for a response. I got lucky…Kenny Love replied quickly. He was a great forensic computer investigator…if anyone could help me, he could. I called Kenny right back.

"I thought you were done with investigations," Kenny said.

"Me, too. Trying to help a friend."

"Must be serious if you are using a different phone."

"Kinda. I'll call you another time to lay it all out to you. Right now I got something I know nothing about."

"So what's new?" Kenny chuckled. "I got about ten minutes if you want to try now, otherwise late tonight."

"Now is fine. I have a cop here who was killed…I think by rogue cops. I'm thinking he might've had some dirt on them."

"Sounds interesting, except for the cop-killing-a-cop thing."

"Yeah, it stinks. The man left his wife a message to keep his phone and to only give it to someone she really trusts.

The part I don't get is he said to take the phone to a specific billboard."

"Ahh. He's pretty sharp. What he's done is not have anything in an easy file somewhere for them to find."

"Makes sense. Their home was broken into today and the computers and thumb drives were the only things taken."

"Figures. They're looking for the info he has on them. He buried it though. He has to have a special app on his phone. When you get to the billboard and point the phone at it, the app will let you see his info."

Kenny did not have much time so we agreed I'd text him all of the apps on the phone and he'd be able to tell me which one to use.

I returned Roberta's phone and gave her another twenty for good measure. When I returned to the table I made sure I had Celia's full attention.

"Listen, you and Brooke might want to think about leaving the area for a while. Is there someplace you can go?"

"It crossed my mind, but it would be unfair to Brooke. It's not much but she has her competition coming up in Denver, so at least we will get away for a couple of days."

"I'll work on this while you're gone. Please let me know where you're at every couple of hours. I'll know something's up if you don't text."

We walked to the parking lot chatting about Brooke and the upcoming competition. Celia pushed the unlock button on her key fob and I started to head to my car several spaces down.

"AJ," she called out. "Thank you for what you did for Brooke. They rushed over to tell me as soon as you and Mac left the other night. I know they weren't supposed to say anything, so please don't be upset with them. They all thought it was so generous…and so do I."

Looking toward her, I smiled. "Don't worry, I'm not upset. I kind of knew they would tell you. I only wanted to be gone when they did, so they didn't make a big deal out of it."

"Well, it *is* a big deal, especially to Brooke. She couldn't stop talking about it the rest of the night at home. She wanted to call to thank you and I told her she could thank you the next time she sees you. Of course, she then wanted to know how long it would be."

We laughed.

Nice to see, her possibly moving forward even if it were only a small sign.

Celia walked over and gave me a hug and with her head on my shoulder, she said, "Thank you, AJ, for everything." She turned and got in her car.

CHAPTER NINETEEN

Emilio was surprised to see the Tahoe sitting at the park down the street from his house. He crossed the park wondering if anyone was in the vehicle. The sergeant had not contacted him regarding the second half of his payment, so he thought they might be in his neighborhood for something else—until the front passenger door opened. The sergeant waved him over as he began walking towards Emilio.

"Emilio, good to see you," Gyrene said.

"Thank you, Sergeant. Good to see you, too. I'm a little surprised, usually you text me to come meet you."

"I know…this was kind of last second. We were in the area doing something else. Thought I'd see if you were around. I'll walk with you to your place, don't really want to be seen giving you money out here."

Emilio felt uncomfortable with the suggestion since they had never been to his place. His need for the cash they owed him overrode his concerns, so he bit his tongue and nodded.

Gyrene thanked Emilio for his help, promising his crew would take care of him. He had done them a favor so they would make sure to do the same for him.

Emilio relaxed while they walked the block to his duplex. The streetlight three duplexes down gave enough ambient light to see Emilio's place looked like bachelors lived in it.

Once inside, Gyrene stopped in the entry to send a text. Emilio walked into the living room trying to clean it up, realizing he did not have enough time to clear all the trash and felt embarrassed.

Gyrene finished his text and walked further inside. He'd been in hundreds of homes where cleanliness had not ranked high on the priority list, although his sense of being orderly always left him shaking his head. He walked to a table against the west wall with three chairs around it. Pulling out the chair on the end, he sat sideways with his back against the wall.

"Relax, Emilio. We don't care what your place looks like."

Emilio jerked his head to the right when he heard the double rap on the front door. The officer walking in with a six-pack of beer caught him totally off guard and he could not move, other than looking back and forth from one officer to the other.

"Emilio, what's up man?" Sly asked, closing the door and turning right into the galley kitchen.

"Pull up a chair Emilio," Gyrene said, slightly pulling out the one in the middle facing the wall. Emilio shuffled over, choosing to sit across from the sergeant instead. He set himself up to be able to look past the sergeant over the bar counter and into the kitchen.

"Emilio, you need to chill man," Gyrene said. "We just finished our shift, thought we'd have a beer with you while we talked to you about some other things we could use your help on."

Emilio did not say a word, although he smiled hearing the guy in the kitchen opening three cans.

Sly walked over and gave the other two a beer, returning to the kitchen to retrieve his. Returning he pulled out the middle chair even further to make sure he gave himself room to stretch out his legs before he took a seat.

Gyrene reached between his equipment vest and his uniform top, pulling out a plastic bag with a wad of cash. He threw it on the table towards Emilio…"Gave you a little bonus, kid. You did great."

"Emilio, we have a tradition," Sly said. "We always chug the first one after a successful mission, then we slowly enjoy the second one."

Emilio hesitated until he saw the two men chugging. He decided he really could relax and did the same.

Sly stood, patted Emilio on the shoulder, and went to the kitchen for the next beers. Unlike the first set, he brought three cans out and each man had to open their own, a fact lost to Emilio.

Gyrene and Sly started joking about the look on the councilwoman's face when she first saw Emilio. Gradually, Emilio started joking with them, feeling like he was almost one of the guys. By the time Emilio finished the second beer his face flushed and his dry mouth made him keep smacking his lips, along with having difficulty staying up with the conversation. A few minutes later his head dropped to the table.

Sly waived in the new guy, Shooter, waiting on the small back patio. Gyrene put the money back in his vest before cleaning up the beer cans to take with them. He grabbed a towel and wiped down everything, despite none of them taking off their thin black gloves. He pushed the chairs in, hung the towel back up on the kitchen hook, and went to the bedroom.

Sly and Shooter had the parachute cord in place and Emilio naked on the floor.

"How many heroine pills did you give him?" Shooter asked.

"Three," Sly said matter-of-factly.

"Shit, that could be enough to waste him right there," Shooter said as he searched the room for any DVDs.

"Wanted to make sure. I didn't know how much would stay in the can after he chugged it even though I smashed them up."

"Oh, he got enough, for sure," Shooter said, wide-eyed and shaking his head looking at Emilio. "He must use video streaming because I don't see any DVDs. Good thing we brought several."

Gyrene threw five of the X-rated DVDs on the bed and put the raunchiest one in the computer and got the movie started. Sly and Shooter lifted Emilio by his armpits, dragged him over to the closet door and held him while Gyrene slid the loop around Emilio's neck. When they let go, gravity and Emilio's weight put all the pressure on his neck, cutting off blood flow to his brain. After they positioned the computer on the floor in front of Emilio, the two gave each other a high five.

Stone faced, Gyrene, turned to get the trash box with the cans. Stepping onto the front porch first, he scanned for any activity before he took off for the Tahoe, followed by the other two, a few minutes separation between each.

"I kinda liked the kid," Gyrene commented when Sly and Shooter got inside in the Tahoe.

"You gotta know the kid would have rolled if they ever got him in an interrogation room," Shooter reminded everyone. "I mean, he always had a scared-shitless look on his face. No way he could've stayed strong to not say anything and keep his mouth *shut*."

"I gotta agree," Sly added with a quick glance over at Gyrene.

"You're right. Let's get the hell outta here."

CHAPTER TWENTY

Lisa Stevens walked out of her house at ten minutes after five preferring to get a good run in before she headed to the office, never knowing if she would end up spending hours in front of a computer. Lisa liked carrying her phone and using standard earplugs to hear her music. She had received informational texts, tweets and email at the weirdest hours, especially now with the story of corruption bringing people out of hiding. Having her phone always made her feel more accessible.

Lisa had three basic routes between which she alternated. She pressed the button on her watch to start the timer and headed west on El Pueblo Drive, right onto Rio Grand Boulevard and then the short distance to the bicycle/running path on the south side of El Paseo Drive. Lisa crossed the road and headed west on the running path. Caught up in her music she never looked to the east before getting on the path.

Rook had been given the assignment to follow Lisa Stevens in case *The Syndicate* needed to take action. When Gyrene remembered Rook liked to run, he became the natural choice. So, Rook tailed Lisa on several occasions during her early morning runs. He felt certain she had a pattern. Even though he had not followed her for several days, he decided to test his theory. If correct, Lisa would turn left off Rio Grand Boulevard to head west on the running path next to El Paseo Drive.

Rook positioned himself east of Rio Grand Boulevard at ten after five in the a.m. and waited. Lisa usually started her runs before a quarter after five, so Rook acted as if he was stretching his hamstrings in case other runners went by. Nine minutes later he spotted her…Lisa never looked in his direction and turned west on the running path. Rook smiled broadly at the same time he did a fist pump. He took off running, wanting to see if her turn around spot remained the same as the other two times he followed her.

As usual, Mac headed to the office at 5:00 a.m. hoping to get some of the items on his list accomplished before his first conference. The quiet time in the morning before Alex arrived had always been productive for him. The entire legal community knew Mac arrived for work at zero-dark-thirty, well before any of them even had a legal thought in their brains. Nobody ever infringed on Mac's privacy. Alex's arrival had long been the unofficial opening for business in Mac's office and most mornings it meant lawyers standing in line asking for, "just a minute of the judge's time."

Mac settled into his chair and reached for his cold diet soda. He relished the first drink while he pulled out his cell phone to text Lisa.

> *Hope your run went well. Looking forward to seeing you tonight.*

> *If you get the chance we can go to dinner and you can meet AJ.*
> *He would be very interested to hear about your story. Love you!*

LISA'S PACE SLOWED WHILE SHE READ THE TEXT. SMILING, her head bobbed slightly side-to-side as she thought about her uncertainty having time to meet with AJ.

I'll try to, Babe, she thought. *No promises though. I'll let him know later.*

Her thoughts returned to her run and made her realize she had passed her turn around point. Turning, she ran a little faster than normal to make up for having gone too far. She approached a young man in a white shirt and black shorts going the opposite way and paid no attention to what he looked like. Her mind locked into getting back on pace as she raised her left hand in a feeble acknowledgement of runner to runner.

CHAPTER TWENTY-ONE

After Mac left for work I went on a run in his neighborhood. The five-thousand-foot difference in altitude from my runs in California always added a level of difficulty when I visited Albuquerque. Normally I'd set a time and distance as a goal so I could fight through the difficulty breathing. Today, I set my mind on learning the area around Mac's house, streets leading in or out of his neighborhood, and the front of the neighbor's houses behind his. The overall appearance left me feeling comfortable because his neighborhood appeared to be upper middle class residents who cared about the appearance of their homes. None of them sent off any negative vibes as if they would be willing to keep tabs on Mac for dirty cops. Of course, money talks, and dirty cops know where to come up with it. I did not expect problems at Mac's house specifically, but I didn't want to be caught off guard.

My sister had picked a small restaurant on Coors Boulevard for our breakfast. I arrived thirty minutes early and read a couple articles in the paper. One of the articles in particular caught my attention claiming officers did not have to do a chokehold on an intoxicated fifty-nine-year-old man, tragically ending in his death. A male attorney, Aaron

Vasquez, had been hired by the grieving widow, who along with her children were not shy in their comments about the police department in general nor the officers specifically.

I heard the bell on top of the front door ring and looked up to see my sister, Jo. Wearing a smile from ear-to-ear and walking at a quick pace, already ten feet in front of her husband who we called Abe because of his similarity to the President. Abe wore a tiny grin as he ambled at his normal pace, never in a hurry to get anywhere. He was the calm in Jo's storm of needing to always hurry and get things done. He knew he would get his bacon and eggs, even if he were fifteen seconds behind Jo in getting to the table.

We greeted and hugged like loving family members do. No kisses on the cheeks like our family in Italy practiced, but good hugs nonetheless. We spent the first fifteen minutes catching up on all of the standard things like work, children, grandchildren and what projects they had going on. Jo was several years older than me and Abe had her by the same amount.

We stopped to order after the waitress appeared a second time, standing with the pen in her hand and her pad raised, the look of determination to wait us out if need be to get our order going.

We relented and ordered.

"So, when's the last time you guys went to your cabin in the Pecos Wilderness?" I asked.

Jo's high cheeks and squinted eyes said it all, followed by the two of them looking at each other as if I had to be on drugs. My segue into finding out if they still had a cabin in the mountains to go to for safety did not start out the way I wanted.

"You can stop looking at me like I'm crazy. I'm not. I guess I should have asked if you still have the cabin."

"Yes, why?" Jo asked. Their smiles disappeared as they now stared at me with somber faces.

I figured I might as well say it.

"Truthfully, I had this thought I could gradually get around to telling you some stuff and working your cabin into the whole thing. Obviously, I did not do so well." I paused, hoping for something from them. The most I got was Abe taking another sip of coffee before he sat back, crossed his legs and set his crossed hands on his lap.

"Mac called me to ask for my help. I can't talk about specifics, but I can say he might be in some danger. The thought running through my mind…if I start to help him and someone ultimately identifies me, there is the chance you guys living here may be someone they target."

"Who might target us?" Abe asked.

I sighed, not wanting to say some of my brethren who were wearing a badge for all the wrong reasons.

"The cops."

Jo started to say something when I held up my hand, seeing the waitress approaching with our food. When she had gotten out of earshot I nodded to Jo.

"For you to be here telling us this…for Mac to call you for help…are our grandchildren in danger?"

"No, no, no. Relax. I don't really think anything is going to happen, seriously. I just didn't want to have to explain everything to you at the last second while I was trying to tell you to get out of town if I had to. What I wanted to do was to give you guys some time to process this, and then to start being observant about who is around you, or if you are being followed. You understand, right?"

"Do they know you're here, in Albuquerque I mean?" Abe asked.

"They know someone is here. They have not done anything yet as far as I know to figure out who I am. Everything will change if stuff starts happening, but not right now."

"Can you tell us anything?" Jo asked.

"Yeah, some. Mac has received some threats, basically to cooperate or people would get hurt. One guy in a recent lawsuit against the city cannot be found and Mac had the guy's case in his courtroom. Plus, you may remember someone murdered an officer a few months ago while he drove home from work. I have reason to believe it was a hit because he had gathered a fair amount of information about some dirty cops."

They looked at each other, then back at me, their eyes shifting down to their plates.

"What? What is it you're not saying?"

Abe slowly rolled his hand down his bearded chin. "Christian has been telling us about some things for a couple months now."

Christian, their second oldest, had a bit of an unsavory past connected with some shady characters. His personality being what it was, he could get along with almost anyone and everyone relaxed around him. He knew a lot of people, and more importantly, the information from those people about what was happening on the streets.

Abe continued, "We have had some conversations about how the DOJ investigation a few years back did not stop the rogue unit in the PD. Christian said he hasn't heard a new name for them, but I guess they used to be ROP, but he knows they drive unmarked black Chevy Tahoes, at least two of them."

I continued to talk with Abe while we ate. Jo held onto her coffee cup, her legs crossed, never touching her breakfast. She listened intently, and it was apparent my sister had other things on her mind…the safety of her kids I presumed.

We ended with them agreeing to grab everyone and head to their cabin if I called and gave them the password we agreed on, *green chili.* I knew they would go home and pack their fifth wheel trailer so they would be ready to go.

CHAPTER TWENTY-TWO

Senior Deputy District Attorney Andrea Colson arrived in Judge McDunn's office ten minutes early and Mac overheard Andrea and Alex talking. He smiled knowing DDA Misha Hanson had experienced enough embarrassment in his chambers she probably begged Andrea to take over for her. When he heard Gordon Rogers' voice in the outer office he punched Alex's line to have them come into his office and get started.

"Senior DDA Andrea Colson, how are you?" Mac asked.

"I'm well, Judge," she said with a smile.

"I hope everything is okay with Ms. Hanson," Mac said, always concerned about not destroying a young attorney's confidence.

"She's fine, Your Honor. Based on your parting comment in the last meeting, the DA and I decided it best for me to be here today."

"Very well. Gordon, you ready to go?"

"I'm fine, Judge. Thanks for asking," Gordon said, a huge grin on his face. The other two laughed.

"Ms. Colson, I presume you are fully briefed as to where we stand on this matter in the *People v. Sandoval* case. Please tell me you have good news."

"I believe so, Judge. One of our investigators, Jason Hepner, I believe you know him, called the security camera company located in Kansas City. We are prepared to bring one of their technicians in to testify about the cameras, Techs at the police department never switched the cameras to Mountain Standard Time and we are prepared to put every one of them on the stand if we must. Therefore, we would argue we have sufficiently met the burden set before us in the last meeting."

While Mac pondered Andrea's statement, his eyes did not focus on anything. Without realizing it, Mac's little fingers did their own little dance around each other. Both Andrea and Gordon knew Mac well enough to recognize his finger cue meant he was deep in thought and it was not a good time to interrupt him. Both waited.

"Gordon?"

"Andrea knows full well the overall integrity of the police department was put into question by the DOJ investigation not so long ago. She also knows the investigators on this homicide do not now, nor will they ever, in my humble opinion, have the great reputation of some of the more experienced and thorough homicide investigators in the police department. The time zone can obviously be altered, and returned to the original time zone just as easily. Ms. Colson is a good attorney, and we know if she could have produced a forensic analysis of the camera to verify the time zone had never been changed, she would have done so in a heartbeat. I've never been afraid to tell one of my clients to plead out when a good investigation has been done and the facts are stacked against them. This…this is a witch hunt Your Honor, not by the prosecutor's office, although I must say, I am disappointed in the DA who more and more is becoming a puppet of the police department."

"Enough political rhetoric, Gordon," Mac said, holding up his palm.

Gordon Rogers sat tall in his chair, nodding out of respect for Mac before turning to stare at Andrea. She glanced over at his stare and crossed her legs to turn slightly away from him. Both looked at Mac, silently hoping his opinion would side with them.

Mac portrayed a self-confident posture while contemplating his decision. Inwardly, he could only feel apprehension and he had spent time thinking about the slippery slope of his decision. Not from a legal position, but from a personal one. Denying the motion meant going against everything he knew to be good sound legal reasoning. Upholding the motion meant whatever group had threatened him before would now have a real reason to up the stakes. Not one second of his time had been wasted on worrying about his own safety, but they had proven with Viktor they were not afraid to take out their ire on someone else.

"Andrea, you make a compelling argument, one which, on its face makes me consider the merit of denying the motion to suppress. However, taking into consideration the totality of the blunders and failure to adequately answer why the misconduct, not to mention my concern for the integrity of some of the investigators, I am going to uphold the motion to suppress the search."

"Can't say I'm surprised, Judge. Had to give it a shot though. In light of your decision, I will be asking for a continuance after we put everything on record in the courtroom."

"What will be your basis for the continuance?"

"Mr. Sandoval waived his right to a speedy trial and is already out on bail, so we are not in any rush to have to make decisions regarding his freedom. This search played a significant role, not only in the investigation, but in the preparation for trial, Your Honor. We need the time to properly and thoroughly decide first of all if there is enough evidence to continue with prosecution. And, you know me, Judge. To be quite honest, I feel I need to do an in-depth analysis of the investigation and the personnel. Of course, I would not dare make such a comment on the record."

"Mr. Rogers, any problem with a continuance?"

"No. Andrea's trying to do the right thing and there is no detriment to my client right now."

"All right, I'll see you both in my courtroom in about ten minutes."

CHAPTER TWENTY-THREE

Sitting in the courtroom and seeing Mac on the bench brought me a sense of happiness, knowing he had reached a level he wanted since we were young. He looked comfortable and in his element...with the exception of his eyes glancing past the attorneys several times, almost scanning the audience. When I did the same, his reasoning became evident.

I sat in the back row on the left giving me a pretty good view of the entire courtroom. Two groups of officers were in the courtroom sitting on either side of the center aisle. Mac's expression seemed sincere and respectful when his eyes panned past the group on my right. The same could not be said for the other group in front of me. His eyes narrowed slightly and his cheeks lowered to a more neutral position. He had always had a good relationship with the majority of the officers, but it appeared something about the DOJ investigation had fractured the department. Seconds prior to *People v. Sandoval* resuming and going on record, the doors to my right opened when several officers in nearly dress uniform walked in, standing in the aisle rather than taking a seat.

All the officers looked back, and not surprisingly the ones in front of me were smiling. The Chief of Police, Dick Baylor, stood military straight, his hat under his left arm with his right hand holding the hat's bill.

A temporary hush went over the room lasting nearly three seconds. I saw Mac give a professional nod to the Chief who stood dead still, not returning the respect. For the Chief to show up seconds before Mac was to put on record his decision on a motion to suppress the search of Mr. Sandoval's home gave me an eerie feeling. The Chief had to have gotten word from the District Attorney's Office about the way their morning meeting went in Mac's chambers, and he had to have been prepared to be in the courtroom if the decision were not favorable.

I followed the Chief and his entourage out of the courtroom the instant Mac gave his ruling upholding his earlier decision to grant the motion to suppress. The Chief was met by a slew of reporters on the front steps of the Second Judicial District Court building, another pre-planned event I presumed. I followed behind and drifted right to hear the statement. The Chief had softened his tactics about specifically attacking Mac, referring only to the justice system getting in the way of good officers trying their best to find actual justice for people like the O'Briens. The hair on the back of my neck raised when the entire statement was over and the Chief had not mentioned Mac's name once, a tactical move on his part for deniability for what likely was to be coming soon.

When the reporters began to disperse one of the officers with the Chief walked over. I read his shiny metal name tag…Chamberlain. He had his own fair share of rank and years in service based on all the extra fluff on his arm sleeves and his epaulettes.

"You got some ID?" Chamberlain asked.

I hesitated, looking at the small group of reporters talking amongst themselves. "My name is AJ Conti," I said, followed by my date of birth.

"I want your ID," Chamberlain repeated, his tone becoming distinctly authoritative. At the same time the Chief and the other officer walked over by Chamberlain.

"What's up, Freddy?" the Chief asked.

"This guy was in the courtroom. He followed us out here. Says his name is AJ Conti. I've asked him twice to produce ID. I'm not going to ask a third time."

The Chief looked from Chamberlain to me, canting his head slightly as if to say...*we're waiting*.

"Nasty scar on your face, Mr. Conti," Chief Baylor commented. "You get that from confronting the police elsewhere?"

"No. Quite the contrary, I'm surprised that would be your first presumption. I'd expect that out of Chamberlain here," I pointed at him with my thumb, "but you...?" I held my stare into the Chief's eyes. "You're about to make a big mistake," I intentionally looked at the Chief's nametag, "Chief Baylor."

"Oh really, and why so? Enlighten me." He looked at Chamberlain who could barely contain his anger. "Well, Mr. Conti, I'm waiting."

"Let's start with case law which says I have identified myself, based on the presumption not every person always has identification to hand to a police officer, therefore, properly identifying oneself verbally, so long as it is true and accurate, is considered sufficient. I wouldn't expect a pencil pusher like Chamberlain to understand case law though, so let's give you another reason."

Chamberlain's face instantly turned red, his lips pushed out and he started to step towards me. The Chief stuck out his arm in front of Chamberlain, forcing him to stop.

"I would say you got your ass handed to you in the

courtroom and I would bet your investigators on the case, whatever it is, probably subscribe to the same school of, '*we do things our own way, not the lawful way*',…you know, the same one Mr. Chamberlain here does. And lastly, the most important one for you Chief is, in a matter of seconds I can get the attention of the reporters down there who are watching us like hawks, and share with them how my constitutional rights are about to be violated by some pretty high brass in the Albuquerque Police Department. If you want to make those reporter's day, be my guest. I can call the defense attorney, what's his name, the one who is always kicking your ass in court? I'm sure he'd love to make a little more money off the department. I'm going to give you some sound advice. Take your goons and walk away before I scream and get the reporters over here."

To Chief Baylor's credit he never showed any anger or contempt, although the corners of his lips almost curled up as he nodded twice. "Gentlemen, let's leave Mr. Conti to be on his way." The Chief turned and Chamberlain scowled at me before he followed.

CHAPTER TWENTY-FOUR

Ralph Lorenzo, Aaron Vasquez's PI, believed every word of Simeon's statement about his drugs being ripped off by cops. Aaron had told him of an earlier client, Hector Sanchez, a man he helped sue the city of Albuquerque and their police department. He received a little over a million-dollar settlement due to a strike to his head with an asp, a quite effective extendable metal baton. Not only did he have to have numerous stitches to his head, two officers were caught on camera by an independent bystander punching Hector after he was handcuffed.

Ralph had no idea what kind of reception he would get from Hector's wife, Katrina. She had refused to talk with Aaron on the phone on two different occasions after Hector's death. Aaron told Ralph how Hector and Katrina had moved to Holbrook, Arizona, shortly after the settlement. Hector wanted to get away from Albuquerque because he did not trust the police there. He got a job as a short order cook, not wanting to use the four hundred thousand dollars he put in the bank after paying Aaron's legal fees and the taxes.

According to Aaron, Hector had been on a fishing trip to Fool Hollow Lake near Show Low when his trailer exploded around two in the morning leaving little of Hector for the medical examiner to inspect. Sheriff's deputies told Aaron they were confident the explosion was caused by Hector cooking meth and closed out their investigation in less than forty-eight hours. Aaron had tried to convince the Navajo County Sheriff's Department they were mistaken...Hector never used meth, much less cooked it. The death was ruled an accident and Aaron ultimately gave up on the case.

Ralph arrived at Katrina's moderate adobe style home in Holbrook around 10 a.m. He hated wearing suits, but he put on his nicest blue one, trying to look professional, hoping she would be more apt to speak with him. He slid his pen in his breast pocket, grabbed his professional padfolio, adjusted his tie, and headed across the street. He had seen Katrina walk by the kitchen window facing the street right after he parked. Taking a deep breath, he knocked on the door.

"I don't want to buy whatever it is you're selling," Katrina said, after she opened the door one-third of the way.

"I'm not a salesman. My name is Ralph Lorenzo. I'm an investigator, for Aaron Vasquez in Albuquerque."

Ralph watched her turn pale in front of him, her head looking up and down the street as if she was afraid someone might be watching. He needed to say something or he'd lose her.

"I came yesterday and stayed in the Holiday Inn Express. I drove around for thirty minutes this morning to make sure nobody followed me."

Katrina looked both ways, opened the door wider and stepped back to let Ralph inside. Closing the door behind him, Katrina turned the deadbolt after she locked the handle.

"You trying to get me killed?" she asked, her hands flaring out to the sides.

"No, of course not. I'm…."

"What the hell makes you think you can put me and my child in danger like this?"

"You're already in danger, Katrina, why do you think I'm here?" He could see the hesitation by her head tilt and scrunched eyes. "We want to put an end to the terror caused by the corruption within the Albuquerque Police Department. You're not alone. We don't need you to testify or anything, but we need to try and figure out what they're doing to those who sue them and win."

Katrina kept quiet and gestured toward the living room. Ralph took the opening and went straight to a corner chair. Not expecting to get inside the house, he said a silent amen before opening up the padfolio.

"No tape recorder, and call me Trina," she said softly.

Ralph put his palms up facing her to let her know he would do whatever she wanted.

"Let me start with, do you think someone murdered your husband?"

"*Hell* yes."

Ralph stared at her, pen in hand waiting for more.

"They came into the house the same morning around four a.m. They had on those caps with the eyes and nose cut out, but I could see they were all white guys. They told me they 'took care of Hector,' and then they threatened to kill my baby if I did not do what they said."

"What did they want?"

"They wanted all the money we got in the settlement against the police department."

Ralph held his question afraid he might derail Trina.

"They got pissed when I told them we didn't have it all. One of the guys slapped me a couple of times, and I think he enjoyed it. One of the other guys told him to stop…like gave him an order."

"What had you spent money on?"

"Hector put a hundred grand on this place. He could have paid cash for it all, but he wanted to put money away and not touch it. He thought our daughter would need college money. The only thing he splurged on was the fifth-wheel they killed him in. He always worked so hard, you know…I wanted him to do it so he could go fishing and relax. I don't remember the exact cost, but I think it was almost fifty thousand."

When Trina started to cry, she bolted from the room. Coming back, she brought a box of tissues and set it on the table near her when she sat down.

"They made me go to the bank and wire transfer the money to an account number they gave me. Two of them stayed in my house with my baby and one of them followed me. He took off the cap, but stayed far enough back so I couldn't see his face. They ordered me to bring back the slip of paper with the account number, then they burned it in front of me."

"Have you ever seen them again?"

"No. But every few months, and on the anniversary of Hector's death, they send me photos. They obviously follow me because the photos are always of recent events, or some of my girlfriends coming over. It's creepy. There's also a typed note every time reminding me they will kill us if I go to the police."

She wiped the corners of her eyes with the backs of her fingers.

"Now it's my turn. Why are you really here?"

Ralph took a deep breath. He looked Trina directly in the eyes, hoping she sensed he would be up front with her.

"Another one of Aaron Vasquez's clients is missing. We think he's dead. Now, I'm pretty certain they're recouping some of the money by threatening people, and then killing them afterward. In your case, I think they figured they could threaten you easier than Hector. I have no idea what they do with the money they get back, but it can't go back to the city in any way. Somebody is probably lining their pockets would be my best guess."

"How do I know I can trust you?"

"You already did, something told you to let me come inside." Ralph moved to the front of the chair and interlocked his fingers.

"Look, we help people who have been screwed…you know that. I'm here because I care. Hell, they might try to kill me, too, if they find out I'm snooping around. I promise you, I want to put a stop to this so you can quit looking over your shoulder."

When Ralph prepared to leave, Trina took her daughter outside and started watering the potted plants. After being satisfied no one was watching she nodded. Ralph walked out the front door straight to his car and started punching in a text message before he got to the end of the block. He paused before hitting send, deciding it would be easier to wait until he got back instead of trying to answer the many questions Aaron would be asking.

CHAPTER TWENTY-FIVE

I had charged Peter's iPhone earlier in the day and waited on the front porch for Mac. Before he could pull into the driveway, I walked out to the road to meet him. Opening the passenger door, I jumped inside.

"Let's go," I said, putting on my seat belt.

"Where to?" Mac asked, obviously caught off guard.

"Head over to Alameda Boulevard and go west."

While driving Mac said he heard how someone, who happened to be in his courtroom earlier, followed the Chief of Police outside.

I did not acknowledge his inquiring statement.

"After I-25 get on the Pan American Freeway going south."

Mac shook his head. "You confronted him, didn't you?"

"No. Some guy named Chamberlain confronted me. Wanted ID."

"They walked away angry from what Lisa's coworkers are telling her. Especially Chamberlain. He's one of the deputy chiefs."

"*Ooh*, a deputy chief." I smiled and looked at Mac who stared, obviously not in a mood for joking. "Good for him. He got upset when I gave him my name, but not any ID, and even more when I told the chief why he should call Chamberlain off before he made a mistake."

"Did you have to? Now, they are going to start figuring out who you are."

"I wasn't trying to create problems, I only wanted to hear the Chief's speech to the press." I didn't lie, but I also wanted to change the subject. "For him to never mention your name once is not good."

"Why?"

"Because, if he mentions you specifically and then they do something more to you, it looks as if he is coming after you. If he only mentions the system letting the O'Briens down and something happens to you, it's considered unfortunate, but not him targeting you. Besides, they are going to turn up the heat. There's no way he's not going to send you another message after what happened in court today."

"So you felt you needed to add to it?"

"Mac, I had no intention to do anything. Chamberlain slid over while I was listening to the speech…he caught me off guard. There was nothing I could do then, they were going to know my name one way or the other. I could be on the defensive having to put up with Chamberlain bullying me and trying to intimidate me by asking any number of questions, or I could put them on the defensive and buy a little time before they figured everything out about me. So I did. I decided I'd make them think twice before doing something else. Turn left here. When you pass Wilshire Avenue stop in front of the Sheriff's office hiring billboard."

When Mac stopped I pulled out Peter's phone.

"Mac, you ever heard of an augmented reality app for your phone?"

"No. What is it?"

"My friend, Kenny Love, he was like our hi-tech guru at the department, I called him about it when Celia explained how Peter told her to give his phone to someone she trusted. When I told Kenny all of the apps on Peter's phone, he told me which one was an augmented reality app.

"Then he told me to go to this YouTube site for *19 Crimes and App*. When I pulled it up I couldn't believe what I saw. There was a person holding their cell phone pointing the camera at a *19 Crimes* bottle of wine. You see the wine bottle in the background with a still picture of a person on the label. But, the same person talks to you in the phone. It's really weird how you can see a still picture, while at the same time you can hear the voice of the person in the picture talking to you through your phone."

"Okay, so why are you telling me this?"

"Because, I'm going to bring up an app on Peter's phone and point the camera at the Sheriff's office hiring billboard. One of the four cops on the billboard is going to talk to us, exactly like the person on the wine bottle in the YouTube video."

I touched the app on Peter's phone and pointed the camera towards the billboard. The officer in a SWAT uniform started talking to us on the phone's screen, even though the billboard had four still pictures of officers.

Peter relayed to us how a hidden wireless hard drive existed in his garage and to first access a file he labeled DOJ with a specific password. He also gave us the login and password info to a Dropbox.com on the hard drive.

Mac's head shifted back and forth between the two several times.

"I hope you got the information, I kept looking at the billboard to see if the cop was talking," Mac said.

"I did the same thing the first time I watched the YouTube video with the wine bottle. Welcome to augmented reality, my friend. It's no longer only in the movies. We're just not up with the tech world like my buddy, Kenny."

"So what do we do now?"

"We go to their house while Brooke is at gymnastics. If I had to guess, the cops know where she is, so they aren't watching the house."

The drive seemed to take longer than either of us expected. We were trying not to expect too much, but the reality Peter had some serious information seemed possible. He had been murdered and his house trashed, at least the dirtbag cops believed he must have something.

"How are we getting in the garage?"

"We don't need to. Park in front of the house. It's like accessing your home Wi-Fi on your phone when you're in the neighbor's backyard, instead of having to get their password to access their network."

I looked at my watch figuring we had twenty minutes max before the risk of Celia and Brooke returning home, and most likely being followed. Celia had told me their router had not been taken, and according to Kenny the wireless network should be able to bridge off the home network. I used the password we were given by the billboard cop to the file on the hidden hard drive. Soon…we heard Peter Howard speaking from the dead.

> *'If you are watching this then things must have gone bad. I can only hope Celia led you to this because you are on the correct side of justice. I have a pretty in-depth investigation into some of the corruption going on within the department. To begin with the Chief and Mayor want to move into higher political positions. They have started the unit known as*

SDM, short for Syndicato De Muerte, or Syndicate of Death. They strategically used SDM based on the closeness to SNM, Syndicato Nuevo Mexico, the largest gang in the state. Their belief was people would automatically think of SNM if initials were thrown around regarding someone being killed. They are basically enforcers sometimes referred to as The Syndicate, although I call them The Syndicate of Death because they have killed for the top Brass already, and more will die if they are not stopped. You will find some surreptitious recordings attached implicating those guys and I received some threats, those are attached as well. I also have the names of those involved in The Syndicate. You'll find everything in Dropbox. Be careful, there are several administrators who subscribe to Chief Baylor's way of thinking, even though most rank and file do not. Whoever you are, please take care of my wife and daughter. Thank you. Godspeed.'

We were running out of time. "Get ready to leave. I'm shutting this down."

"Where we going?"

"Kenny told me we can access the Dropbox account anywhere and on any device, so long as we have the login and account numbers. He said we need to make sure we go to someplace like a library, preferably out of town. Dropbox captures and stores the IP address, so we do not want to use our own devices."

"Got it. We'll jump on the freeway to go to Rio Rancho this time. I used to live out there so I can easily get us there," Mac said.

We left with five minutes to spare, parking a block down from Celia's house so we could watch in the mirrors. Less than forty seconds after Celia pulled into the driveway a patrol car drove by the front of her house, barely moving at five miles per hour. The officer almost stopped as he watched Celia and Brooke go into the house, definitely not trying to hide anything.

Thankfully the patrol car turned east on Meylert Road, so we went the opposite direction out to Lomas Boulevard to leave the area. Their attempts at gradually unnerving her were working. I was glad Celia and Brooke would be getting out of town for a couple days to Denver for the gymnastics competition.

CHAPTER TWENTY-SIX

Lisa met us for dinner at a bistro in a Menaul Boulevard strip mall. Mac obviously ate there often since they had his table in the back waiting for him. Cops are not the only ones who want their backs to a wall and their eyes on the door. With as many bad asses as Mac sent to prison, I understood why he chose the same.

"So, AJ, I hear tell you went toe-to-toe with Deputy Chief Chamberlain," Lisa had a sly smile on her face.

I shrugged as my hands flew open, knowing I could not get past an explanation, even if only a little one. "Off the record," I paused, getting a grin out of Lisa, "I informed DC Chamberlain, via Chief Baylor, he was about to violate my constitutional rights by forcing me to produce ID, after I had adequately identified myself verbally. He didn't take too kindly to my comments. The chief on the other hand, he gauged me the whole time and realized they would lose the battle with so many of your colleagues watching."

I looked over at Mac. "According to Peter, the chief has higher aspirations, but Chamberlain is the one I'm worried about."

"Why?" Lisa asked, looking at me, then Mac, then back at me.

"Peter said there is a new rogue group of cops, known as The Syndicate," Mac spoke up. "He referred to them as enforcers. I would guess AJ sees them getting their directions from Chamberlain. He probably sees the chief's job as his when Baylor moves on."

"I see," Lisa said. "Not to change the subject or anything, I'm meeting Aaron later tonight. He has some more information for me and he seemed a little nervous, which is not like him."

"You both need to be careful," Mac said, reaching his hand out and placing it on Lisa's. "Where are you meeting?"

"I love it when you worry about me," Lisa said, reaching up and touching Mac's cheek. "The park at Comanche and Moon at nine."

"Do you think he would talk with me?" I asked.

"Maybe," Lisa said. "I'll ask him tonight. Don't be surprised if he wants you to meet with Ralph first, his investigator. He'd size you up…see if he trusts you first."

"Whatever he wants, I'm good with it."

"How's your story coming?" Mac asked.

"Pretty good. I don't think I can hold off putting it in print much longer. My editor is getting antsy and I have a couple of sources in the police department, but they're starting to get nervous. One is assigned to headquarters and is around the brass. He told me another dirty cop had recently been added to, what did Peter call it, The Syndicate? My guy said the person had been in the news a lot lately, used to be part of the ROP team."

"Kyle Lansing, possibly?" I asked. "Peter's file will tell us the names of the players, but if Kyle was added since they killed Peter he won't be there."

Mac and Lisa looked at each other. "That's a pretty good guess," Mac said. "What made you think of him?"

"I heard about him on the radio station the other day. Something about shooting an undocumented Mexican man."

Lisa became quiet, her eyes drifted down, not really appearing fixated on anything and when I looked at Mac he raised his brows. I figured if he did not interrupt her train of thought, keeping my mouth shut might be the best thing to do. We waited.

"It all makes sense," Lisa said. Her entire posture went from relaxed to focused. Looking at Mac, she asked, "Remember several years ago when they hired those cops who had all been fired from other agencies? What administrator promised the public they would not get weapons, they were going to help in other ways?"

"Chamberlain," Mac said. "Damn, you're right. Kyle Lansing was one of them. Not only did he get back on patrol, he got put on the ROP team. He's been on admin leave for a year waiting for Hildebrand to decide whether or not to prosecute, so they got used to him not being in patrol. It would be perfect timing for him to go straight to The Syndicate since he recently went back to work after Hildebrand wussed out."

"Exactly, I got to go," Lisa said.

"What about dinner?" Mac asked.

"I'll have them throw mine in a to-go container." Lisa got up, gave Mac a quick kiss and me a wave.

"She'd make a great detective," I said.

"Yeah, she's tenacious. When she's into something she won't stop."

"Do I detect a hint of concern?"

Mac nodded as he watched her walk out the door.

"When she gets like this, she doesn't think about her own safety. This one has me worried, AJ, and she only sees it as more of a reason to dig deeper to expose the truth."

The grave look on Mac's face spoke of his unease for her wellbeing.

AARON VASQUEZ HAD BEEN SEATED AT A BOOTH INSIDE Scarpa's, one of his favorite restaurants close to his home. He had nearly emptied his Cabernet when Ralph slid across from him.

"I'll have a Bud Lite please," Ralph said to a young waitress passing by. He did not care if she was their server or not, he needed a beer sooner than later.

Looking over at Aaron, he said, "Long day going to Holbrook and back."

"How the heck did you get Trina to talk to you?" Aaron asked

"I lied to her, told her I had spent the night in a hotel there. Made it sound like I had been overly cautious about being followed and other lives were at stake."

"I'm totally surprised. How long were you there?"

"Fifteen minutes max. She got really nervous about me being there, scared almost."

"So, what did she say?"

"The bottom line is, they went to her home hours after they killed Hector. She had to learn of his death from those assholes when they barged into her home. They threatened to kill her baby if she didn't give them the cash Hector got in the settlement against APD. Made her leave the baby with a couple of them, while they followed her to the bank after giving her an account number so she could transfer the funds. She told me they send her stuff in the mail like pictures of her or the baby, a little girl now, just to remind her how they're still keeping an eye on her."

"I always knew they killed Hector. He didn't have anything to do with meth, much less being a dealer. Nobody at the Sheriff's office would listen to me. They closed the case as fast as they could."

"I have no idea where Viktor is, but I'm pretty certain he's dead."

"Hmm. Up until now I've been unwilling to admit it, actually more like hoping he wasn't. I told him to be careful, but he blew me off."

Ralph took a long drink of his beer, waiting for Aaron to process the likelihood of his comment.

"I'm meeting Lisa tonight at nine…but at a park. I've been kind of paranoid lately, I feel like someone's been, I don't know… watching me."

"You want me to come over after we eat to make sure there aren't any bugs in your house?"

"Nah, it's been a long day and I don't think anyone's been in my house. I don't know, maybe tomorrow night. I haven't felt like anyone's bugged my house or phone, it's more like a feeling someone is staring at me sometimes. I'll be okay."

"Aaron, what are you going to tell her?"

"I think I need to tell her everything."

MAC AND I ARRIVED AT HIS HOUSE AROUND 8 P.M. WE had been discussing Lisa's story when we rounded the corner to head for the front door. A covered front patio had metal grating going from the cement to the patio roof, and someone had taped a neatly folded white piece of printer paper to the metal screen door. Mac stopped dead in his tracks, staring at the paper. We knew who put it there; the repercussion I told him about earlier had arrived. I took it by the corners with my fingertips to minimize my prints and opened it enough to see typed words looking to be at least a twenty font. Without reading it I looked at Mac, still in the same spot. He nodded slowly so I walked over next to him, warily opening it so we could read it.

> *You don't get it.*
> *We make the rules now.*
> *If you don't want to play, then people have to pay.*

Mac looked at me and without a word we turned and headed to his car.

"You armed?" I asked, already knowing the answer.

"In here," he said, lifting his left crutch with the well-worn leather handled briefcase hanging from it.

CHAPTER TWENTY-SEVEN

Mac drove closer to the speed limit than I would have. I could only presume he knew we would be early and he didn't want to draw any undue attention. He had always been a good chess player, able to read potential moves well in advance. Stakeouts and trailing people often require those skills.

I sat back and watched.

We approached from the south, dead ending into Loma Del Rey Park. As parks go, it seemed like a small one, making it easy to watch at first glance. The main road on the south side of the park has the potential to be busy, so seeing a couple of police cars go by would not be a surprise. We were looking more for the undercover, or special ops types.

Mac drove around the area, approaching the park from all angles until he felt comfortable we had not seen any obvious stakeout vehicles. Shortly before nine he parked in front of a home on the northeast corner of the park. The number of large trees at night had the potential to make it difficult to see activity. There were a few streetlights, but nothing to light up the cement walking path and I changed my mind about how easy it would be to watch. It was one of those times when I hoped the people in the neighborhood stayed true to my belief about most people being oblivious to what goes on around them and didn't pay attention to us.

Lisa arrived first parking six houses from us. She got out and walked to one of the benches close to the walking path across from her car and sat. Within a couple of minutes we saw a man walking on the path closest to her. Mac mumbled he had Aaron's walk and size. Sure enough, he rounded the path by the main road and walked up the side closest to Lisa. When Lisa stood, they hugged before sitting down and getting into a discussion. Lisa's habit of talking with her hands rapidly moving made her easy to identify, even in the dark.

Given Mac's crutches and unique walk, I went alone to check the area. Walking at a less than casual pace, I rounded a corner and ducked in behind two large trees rather than heading down the same path Aaron followed. I had no interest in their conversation since my gut told me they were being watched by someone other than us…and my intuition kept my full attention.

Something caught my eye near the T-intersection where Mac first drove in. It looked like an all-black SUV parking on the west side facing away from the park. A quick risk-benefit analysis had me assessing the risk of being seen once I left the cover of the large trees. Would it be worth getting closer to the car? I watched the brake lights go off, but no interior light came on and no doors opened. I took off from behind the tree toward the next closest tree a good seventy-five feet away. I had not made twenty-five feet before the brake lights came on and the SUV took off without headlights.

Not wanting to walk any further towards the two, I pulled out my phone acting like I received a call, turned around, and began walking back the way I came. Turning on the street across from Mac's car, I walked four houses up before I crossed over and made my way back to his car.

"Did you see the dark car parked over where we came in?"

Mac nodded. "I have a straight shot at the intersection. Was it them?"

"I can't say for sure. Dark SUV, probably a Tahoe if my nephew's information is correct. Pretty strange though, nobody got out, and the instant I started walking out from under cover of the big trees, they took off. Another reason I think it might have been them is they drove past several houses without headlights; something all cops are used to doing. You learn to drive without lights while working graves if you want to catch people in the act."

"We need to follow Lisa home, make sure no one else follows her."

"I agree." I knew the danger to her had intensified based on the note Mac received.

"I called my brother and sister while you were out there sneaking around," Mac said. "There's nothing saying they might not go after my family."

"Good," I said, not really believing the threat to be to his direct family. The concern in his voice told me now was not the time to voice my opinion. Besides, I knew his brother Sam was a black belt in Karate and he had his own arsenal of weapons, while Mary and her husband Phil were both quite proficient with the shotgun and the 9mm they owned.

Lisa and Aaron prepared to leave the park close to ten. Mac turned right before Lisa took off since she would be heading straight towards us. He went a short distance and made a U-turn, and by the time we got back to the intersection we saw Lisa's car stopped in front of us and Aaron getting out of the passenger seat. Once they both drove away, we looked for anything suspicious before we started moving. Neither of us saw any black vehicles looking like what I had seen earlier and Mac headed toward Lisa's house.

After a couple of hours Mac felt pretty convinced no suspicious vehicles were in the area around Lisa's home, so we took off.

CHAPTER TWENTY-EIGHT

Aaron turned onto Red Yucca Avenue and the feeling of despair returned. His divorce necessitated him selling the home of his dreams. While this new home was beautiful, the pang of remorse existed even after a year. Turning onto his street, he pushed the garage remote and waited for the door to roll up. He drove in slowly until the hanging tennis ball touched his windshield before pushing the button again and getting out of his car.

When he walked into his house the neon blue clock on the stove read ten thirty. He felt good about sharing his information with Lisa knowing her article would be coming out soon and maybe the police department would see the likes, and wrath, of DOJ once again. Leaning over his computer desk, Aaron reached beyond the bottom of the short middle drawer. He pushed up with his fingers in several spots until the hidden drawer popped open. His hand felt around and pulled out the solid black SanDisk Flash Drive. Aaron inserted it into the USB port and pulled up the APD corruption file. He entered all the information Ralph had shared with him and included some of what Aaron had shared. Thirty minutes later he closed out the program and put the flash drive back in its hiding spot.

At three in the morning Rook turned left off High Desert Place onto Red Yucca Avenue. He drove past Copper Rose Street and turned left on the next cul-de-sac. He dumped the headlights and drove to the end, made a U-turn in the cul-de-sac, and pulled over to the curb at the open lot directly behind Aaron's house. Sly and Shooter got out without saying a word, both dressed in all black fatigues. Neither had their duty weapons, but Shooter brought a Sig Sauer 9mm, with a noise suppressor, both without any identification markings. Their plan was not to use the gun unless all hell broke loose.

They had been watching Aaron for several days and they knew the layout of the house, along with the three locations for shutting off the alarms. On the videos they took of him they had watched enough at high resolution and slow motion to have his five-digit key code. When they scouted the house earlier in the evening they discovered the side garage door unlocked and not part of the alarm system.

Before going to the side garage door, Shooter moved up to the sliding glass door on the back patio, finding the lock engaged. He put his head up to the window without touching it, put his cupped hands on the sides of his eyes, and scanned inside the house. The darkness prevented him from seeing much, but something across the room caught his attention.

He turned and tapped Sly on the shoulder, who'd been scanning the surrounding houses checking for onlookers. Shooter pointed to his eyes with his first two fingers of his right hand, then to the house. When he pointed across the room, Sly scanned the inside area and smiled when he came across the green alarm light.

They moved to the side of the house and entered the garage, leaving it open behind them. Sly checked the inner garage door to the house, but the knob would not turn. With a mag lite, he saw the dead bolt had not been turned into the door frame. He used a knife to pop open the door and saw the green light on the control box, and he paused to listen for movement on the second floor. Feeling comfortable, they began to remove the listening devices and cameras they planted a couple weeks before, then prepared to set everything up they would need to complete their mission.

AARON ROSE OUT OF BED AT FOUR FEELING GOOD FOR only getting five hours of sleep. He hurried into his workout clothes so he would be at the gym by a quarter after five to meet his workout partner. Brushing his hair, he wondered why he got along so well with Enrique, a sergeant with Albuquerque PD. Aaron generally did not have a great deal of respect for cops, believing most let the power of the badge go to their head. Enrique acted like a down-to-earth man and appeared to really care about people. He had approached Aaron a year earlier during one of his workouts and offered to help when he had incorrectly performed an exercise. He knew he really liked Enrique when he met his wife a couple weeks later and how he still doted over her after eighteen years of marriage.

Aaron hurried down the stairs and out of habit went to the alarm box nearest the garage. The system being unarmed surprised him but he dismissed it to his forgetting to arm it the night before; something he often did. Reminding himself to get better at locking doors and using the alarm, he went to his desk.

Grabbing his laptop because he often stopped at a coffee shop after his workout and knocked out work, he walked briskly to the counter for his gym bag and a bottle of water from the fridge.

While putting the bottle in his left hand, he began to close the door. As it passed in front of him a large man pulled one of his shoulders and struck the other one. He spun Aaron around before his mind registered the man's presence. He had his arm around Aaron's throat with his elbow directly in front of his chin.

Aaron dropped the bottle as he instinctively reached up with his hands to pull his arm away. The laptop fell to the floor but he had not let the gym bag slide off his arm before reaching up. Aaron's mind vacillated between getting the man's arm away and getting the bag off his own arm so he could fight better. Strangely, the last thought passing through his head before he slipped into unconsciousness was the realization the man had been trained on how to perform a choke hold.

Once he passed out, Sly felt Aaron's dead weight of one hundred and forty pounds pulling down on his arm. He laid him on the tile floor as Shooter knelt beside him wearing a rubber glove on his right hand holding a rag and a brownish bottle in his left hand. Shooter poured enough fluid on the rag to soak it before he held it over Aaron's nose and mouth.

"Don't kill him with that shit," Sly warned.

"I'm not, I'm not. This gives us time to get him set up in the garage is all."

Shooter made sure Aaron kept breathing, albeit shallow and slapped his face a few times to check. When he did not move, they picked him up and took him into the garage. For ventilation they raised the main door up a couple of inches along with the side door which remained open from earlier. They laid Aaron on the cement and put a jerry-rigged chemical weapons mask over his face. The mask had a hose attached to the front with duct tape, and ran to the exhaust pipe of the car. One of the few times Sly felt Rook had made himself useful was when he spliced several different hose sizes together and made one end large enough to slip over the end of the car exhaust pipe and the other end small enough to fit on the mask.

Sly started the car and pushed the buttons for all four windows to roll down completely. Aaron received large amounts of exhaust fumes directly to his mask. Somehow Rook knew to have enough ventilation so the car would not shut off, while at the same time the majority would go to the mask.

While they waited, Shooter picked up Aaron's laptop and put it in his backpack. He searched the remainder of the house while Sly went to the desk and moved the chair so he could crawl under the middle drawer. Lighting up the area with his mag lite, he spotted the hidden compartment door. Aaron had a few items hidden inside besides the flash drive. All he wanted was the flash drive and the money. He left everything else and closed the drawer.

Shooter came downstairs with a second laptop and put it with the first. He patted the left pocket of his pants where he put the wad of cash he found stashed under the mattress.

An hour later, when Shooter checked for a pulse…none existed. Sly, choking from fumes, reached over and turned off the car. They removed the mask, placed Aaron in the driver's seat slumped over to the middle and set his water bottle in the drink holder. Tossing the gym bag on the passenger floor, they closed the main garage door. They rolled up the hose, secured it with a bungee cord and gave each other high fives.

The Syndicate knew from previous surveillance only one person in the area around his home stirred early in the morning. Sly radioed Rook who said the guy had left his house ten minutes earlier. They walked out the side garage door with the backpack, the hose and mask, and all their equipment. In less than two minutes they had everything in the back of the Tahoe.

"I'm starving," Sly said. "Denny's, I'll buy."

CHAPTER TWENTY-NINE

When Police Chief Dick Baylor woke up at ten minutes before six he checked his cell phone and saw the red number one on the text icon. Opening the message, he saw the big thumbs up next to a sleeping face emoji and smiled. Putting on his gym shorts, tennis shoes and t-shirt, he headed downstairs and climbed on his stationary bike in the spare bedroom. He knew the mayor would want to hear the good news, but the Police Chief decided to make him wait.

Baylor got lost in his ride, going almost fifteen extra minutes. He had not paid attention to the speed nor the distance, but Dick Baylor didn't really care. He had thoughts about how things would become so much smoother with two cogs in the wheel eliminated…less lawsuits and at least one more positive vote on the city council. With the councilwoman and the lawyer settled, he only had one more item to deal with to complete the trifecta, and then smooth sailing to becoming the Cabinet Secretary of Public Safety.

Sitting on his back porch, Dick enjoyed a fresh cup of coffee. At seven o'clock he grabbed his cell phone and brought up Paul Mullins number. The time had come for him to get a recall on the favor owed to him.

"Hello, Dick," Paul said, none too cheerfully.

"Paul, you don't sound like you're happy to hear my voice."

"Sorry. Just had to clean up a mess the dog made," he lied. "What's up?"

"How's your son doing at Rutgers? What is it, his junior year?"

Paul knew this day would come, despite his constant prayers to keep Dick from ever getting the opportunity to put him in this position. He could feel the color in his face slowly draining. He pulled up a chair before he fell down.

"Your office might get a call today about a well-known man, a certain gay legal professional. I would prefer you handle it, I'm not saying any of the other ME's in your office aren't capable, of course. It's just, you know, it would really be nice for you to take special care of it. And Paul, stick to the obvious."

"Dick, I'm not sure. It's not like I work alone. It's not as easy as it looks."

"You know, Paul, the funny thing about the statute of limitations, going off to college doesn't make it go away. You owe me, Paul, or did you forget? We will be square after this...your son can go on with his life and you can quit looking over your shoulder. Hell, it won't even be difficult, you'll see."

Paul heard the call ending beeps—his arm dropped and rested on his thighs as his eyes followed the phone, staring at it for a good fifteen seconds. He had always considered himself a good person. Paul knew he was not the most devout Christian, but he tried to do the right thing. Surprisingly, he didn't have any anger towards Dick, a man who simply expected something for something; a barter if you will. Paul could almost respect him for it, especially since he initially approached Dick with his son's issue.

He could not say the same about his wife. Paul hated her for forcing him to contact Dick...their son needed help. . .not to believe he got away with what he did to the young girl. And not believe all would be well after he got into such a prestigious university. Paul had been around law enforcement enough to know his son would not stop until he got caught or got help. He prayed every night, asking God to steer his son away from other possible victims and for him to find the strength to leave his wife and not care about the money she'd get or the drop in lifestyle he would endure. Each morning he knew neither prayer would be answered. His son could not quit his deplorable actions any more than he could find the inner strength to leave his wife. Paul hated himself almost as much as he did his wife. And after today. . .maybe more.

DICK BAYLOR CONSIDERED RAYMOND SAMPSON A MEANS to an end. They had like minds in many ways, especially when it came to getting what you want regardless of the cost. He knew his promotion would come when Ray became the governor. Right now, they were so close to accomplishing that goal, he had no choice but to put up with Ray's condescending comments about him, always behind closed doors. But Dick got his payback digs in. . .carefully. Ray would be his gravy train, fair enough, but it did not mean he had to accept being crapped on. When he became the Cabinet Secretary, his direct dealing with Ray would be much less considering the governor would be traveling all over the state putting out fires, schmoozing people, and basically trying to get re-elected, while Dick would be going all over the state dealing with the varying law enforcement and corrections leaders. Smiling, Dick decided he made Ray wait long enough. He pushed the call button.

"What the hell took you so long?" Mayor Sampson asked, a hushed anger in his tone. "Did it go off okay? Did they have problems?"

"Relax Ray, everything is fine. It took some time to make sure the rest would fall in place like we talked about, is all." He never mentioned when he got his text, otherwise there would have been a slew of additional questions. Dick knew Ray well enough to know he'd immediately start thinking about other things—and Dick was right.

"When should I expect to be called out there? I don't want to be so involved in anything I can't get there."

"Ray, we need to let things happen naturally. Besides, who cares what time it is, I'm sure you can find a way to excuse yourself for some important breaking news like you've done before. Speaking of issues, how's our city council doing?" Dick wanted to change the topic, steering Ray's mind in a different direction.

"One of the members could not make the last closed-door meeting, I hear she did not feel well. Something tells me there might be a change of direction, thankfully."

"Let me know. I think adequate steps have been taken to ensure cooperation, but trust me, they would not have a problem with doing a little more. Gotta go, Ray. Keep your phone close."

CHAPTER THIRTY

Nearly a week had passed since Anita's attack. She laid low for some time, never leaving her house, even staying away from City Council duties. Despite the difficulty she tried not to cry when her husband or daughter were around, but sobbed uncontrollably when they were gone. This was the first morning she felt somewhat rested.

Anita sipped her coffee sitting on her back porch. Her husband had left early as always, and Amy was primping like normal. Anita felt she needed to make an appearance downtown so she showered and got ready.

Hearing Amy in the kitchen, Anita went inside. "You got everything ready, little girl?"

"*Mom*, I'm not little anymore. I'm a teenager. And yes, I do."

Anita smiled, remembering how she too wanted to act grown up when she had been Amy's age.

Amy started putting things in her backpack when she saw the packet she had received. She pulled it out and laid it on the table, while her mother rinsed out the dishes. Amy zipped her backpack compartments, slung it over her shoulder, and gave her mom a kiss on the cheek.

"Oh, mom, the packet on the table is for you," she said, walking toward the door. "Some guy in a suit gave it to me at school and asked me to give it to you. Sorry." The front door closed and Amy jogged to catch up to her friends.

Anita looked over at the packet as she dried her hands, again and again. She moved to the table and stood looking at it, her hands clasped tightly in front of her. Part of her wanted to rip it open, while the fear of what she would find caused her to turn and walk away, grabbing the newspaper off the counter before going back outside. She attempted to read a couple of articles but stopped, unable to focus. Trying to keep her mind on anything but the packet, she continued to make her way through reading headlines.

Anita turned to the obituaries, something her father taught her to do years ago. He had always told her she should know if someone in her community passed away in case she came across a surviving family member, so she would be able to give her condolences. Even though she no longer lived in a small community, she seldom made her way through a paper without going through the obits. The third picture on the page displayed a young Mexican male adult. Her eyes scanned passed him to the woman's picture next to him. Suddenly it registered and her eyes darted back to his picture. Anita gasped, her left hand covering her mouth.

"Dios mío," she cried as tears filled her eyes. The young man had tried to calm her while the incriminating pictures were being taken. He kept telling her they wouldn't kill her if she cooperated. In his own way he had provided her the strength to get through what happened, at least temporarily.

Anita let the paper fall on the table and went inside, grabbed a tissue then went to the kitchen table. She held her breath and her hands shook as she undid the clasp on the manila packet and grabbed the papers inside. As she sat on the chair, her knees followed the rhythmic shaking of her hands. She closed her eyes, said a silent prayer, counted to three and opened her eyes when she yanked out the items.

One picture showed her husband, Jeremy walking out of a convenience store with his morning coffee as he did every day. The other showed Amy at her bus stop laughing with her friends. She pulled the white printer paper from the back and read the large font, bold-faced message, *Your choice*. No other words were on the paper.

Anita felt the nausea coming, dropped the paper, and got to the sink. When she finished heaving, she put cool water on her face and held the towel tightly for several seconds.

Sitting on the back patio with her legs drawn up in the chair, Anita drank coffee and smoked cigarettes for the next two hours. She had tried to quit knowing her family hated it, but she always kept a pack hidden for difficult times. She read the young man's obituary over and over, hoping to find something suggesting he died accidentally. Unfortunately, the article was the initial generic type right after the death, sometimes followed by a more in-depth article after information had been gathered from the family.

While she sat Anita tried to rationalize her options. Something told her the young man had been killed for being a witness. What she could not figure out was why they did not kill her instead of all the scare tactics. Anita wished she had taken more time to befriend some of the officers at Albuquerque Police Department. Taking a long and deep drag, she realized she didn't have anybody there to turn to for help.

The buzz on her cell phone snapped her out of her deep thoughts. The message had been sent by another councilmember who thought like she did. Anita tapped the green icon and read the shocking news.

Aaron Vasquez is dead. Suicide? In his car…in the garage.

"No, No, No!" The tears Anita thought she ran out of began to run down her cheeks.

CHAPTER THIRTY-ONE

Mac went to his office around ten thirty for a short recess and was drying his hands when Alex popped his head in the office.

"Mac, you got a call waiting, it's Ralph Lorenzo. He sounds upset."

Mac opened the door and made his way toward the desk. Alex shrugged, his face warning Mac it might not be good.

"Ralph, you okay?"

"It's Aaron. He never showed up at the office. He's not answering his phone. The new girl in the office already called the PD to have someone go check his house. I'm headed over there now."

"I'm going to have a former cop, good friend of the family, meet you there. What are you wearing?"

"Uh, I'm, I'm wearing jeans, black polo shirt, and a tan blazer."

Mac heard the familiar three hang-up beeps in the phone and quickly located AJ's number in his call history and tapped.

"Hey, I'm going through the files…"

"AJ, I think something's happened to Aaron, the attorney Lisa met last night."

"Yeah, the one I want to meet."

"Start heading to Tramway Boulevard–I'll text you the

address. His investigator, Ralph Lorenzo is going to be there. I told him you would hook up with him. I'll text you what he's wearing."

Mac hung up not waiting for a response. "Alex."

"I got it, Mac. I'll use my phone and text AJ. What are you going to do?"

"Go on record and say an emergency came up. No way can I listen to attorneys questioning prospective jurors. I wouldn't hear a word they said."

One thing was certain, The Syndicate followed through on their messages. I had not yet figured out how we might get ahead of them much less have an idea of who they were targeting at any given time. Without hesitation I became resolved to no longer waiting around for their next move. The time had come for us to take the fight to them.

As much as I wanted to drive as if my car had emergency lights I could not afford to be pulled over. It took me fifteen minutes to get in the area. I saw the police cars to my left in front of the second house on the east side of the street. I drove past and went two blocks, made a couple of right turns and circled back around on the same road the cop cars were parked. I pulled to the curb a block away and stopped.

I watched for five minutes to make sure nobody outside was filming people in the area. APD would know my car soon enough, no need to help them know it sooner.

I spotted Ralph across the street, catty-corner to the patrol cars, leaning against a tree in the front yard of the corner house.

Ralph looked my way after I crossed the street and I saw him use the back of his wrist to wipe his eyes.

This isn't good!

We shook hands without introduction. When I put my hand on Ralph's shoulder he started to cry as he laid his arm across the tree and leaned into his forearm. Looking past Ralph, I saw a woman standing by the front door as she clutched a red coffee cup with both hands, her arms drawn into her chest. Her shoulder length hair seemed a shade lighter than the red of her cup, but it definitely stood out. I knew it would only be a matter of time before the police video cameras came out and neither Ralph nor I needed to be in their evidence collection. It had been my experience red heads were not the kind of woman you wanted to upset. I could only hope she would understand.

"Excuse me, Ma'am."

She looked at me, her lower lip starting to quiver.

"My name is AJ Conti. My friend over there, his name is Ralph Lorenzo. I was wondering…?"

"He's…Aaron's…investigator," she enunciated slowly, separating her words.

"Yes, Ma'am. He's pretty broken up, and I really don't want the television cameras capturing him all distraught, but I can't get him to leave."

"Liz."

"Excuse me?"

"My name, my name is Liz. Go get Ralph and come in my house. I'll fix you both a coffee, or something stronger if he needs it." When Liz walked in the house, the screen door closed behind her, but she left the front door open.

I walked at a slightly faster than normal pace over to Ralph, putting my arm around his shoulder and guiding him to walk with me. We went into the house and I closed the front door. I could hear sniffling coming from the kitchen area...Liz's I hoped. *The less people aware of us being in the house the better.*

I grabbed one of the dining room chairs and took it into the living room, setting it in front of the large window so Ralph could sit and watch. He still had not said a word.

When I walked into the kitchen Liz looked over her shoulder at me, ripped a paper towel off and dabbed her eyes.

"I'm sorry about balling like this."

"Liz, nothing to be sorry about. This is a sad situation. Did you know Aaron well?"

"The first six months he lived there, not at all. I think he realized I was alone over here like he was over there. He finally came over and introduced himself. We had husbands who cheated on us, then tried to leave with all the money. A sad thing to have in common, but it gave us something to talk about in the beginning."

Liz had made a pot of coffee, a relaxing aroma for me.

"Ralph, would you like a cup of coffee," I asked. When he shook his head I did the same to Liz. She grabbed one more cup and poured for the two of us.

I followed her into the front room where she sat on the couch a little behind Ralph's right shoulder, so she could look out the window. I sat in the chair near her, looking out over Ralph.

In the time it took us in the kitchen to have a conversation while getting coffee, the crowd outside of Aaron's house had tripled. I didn't know many people in the area any longer, having been gone almost as long as I lived there as a kid. Still, I did not have to live there to know over half the crowd going under the crime scene tape were cops, with the rest of them looking like politicians.

Even from across the street the violations of proper protocol, regardless of jurisdiction, jumped out. The large garage door had been opened and all of the "officials" seemed to be walking to the car to take a look. I had worked several cases of victims in a car in their own garage, leaving one of two choices over ninety-five percent of the time. I could already see it coming—suicide, according to the way APD trampled the scene.

I looked at Liz, who again had her cup gripped and arms drawn up against her chest. Only this time, she had her legs pulled up on the couch in front of her and the fact she rocked back and forth in a tight little ball told me there was more to her than her red hair.

"You know, my good friend, Judge McDunn, he's received several threats lately. He's the reason why I'm here."

Liz stopped rocking, her large eyes staring straight at me. I noticed Ralph slowly looked over his shoulder at Liz.

"What all did Aaron tell you?" I asked. Ralph turned further, now looking at me, his brows scrunched together. "Liz, I think we all know what happened here." I waited, knowing she needed time to process everything. Her tears were for Aaron, her friend. The look of fear on her face had to do with her realization she might be in danger, too, simply for being his friend.

"He…he told me he thought the cops…the bad ones… were going to come after him someday. Aaron always made sure to say most of them were good, honest people. The bad ones though, he told me there were more here than I would believe."

I stole a look at Ralph who had turned to face Liz. He looked at me and nodded and Liz's credibility slowly increased.

"Would there be any reason you could think of to maybe cause Aaron to want to take his own life?"

Ralph's head snapped in my direction—a hatred in his eyes. I raised an index finger and bowed my head. Ralph hesitated, then turned to look at Liz.

"*No*, no way. He had been talking about his vacation in a couple weeks to go see his new grandbaby. He was so excited. Plus he talked about expanding his practice, maybe bringing another lawyer in with a couple more paralegals. No, I'm positive…there's no way!"

Liz's tone had been one of irritation, almost bordering on anger, for my asking the question. Those were signs I had hoped for, signs telling me her answer was honest and heartfelt.

"Aaron told me three days ago to tell Ralph he has a hidden compartment under his roll top desk, behind the small center drawer. You know, if something happened to him." Liz took off running to the hallway and we heard a door slam.

"They're going to pay for this, AJ," Ralph said, his first words to me.

I nodded.

Justice is a funny word, with varying philosophical definitions throughout the centuries. Somehow we needed to get on the offensive, but carefully. Vigilante justice for a guy like Leroy Jethro Gibbs on NCIS seemed acceptable to millions of viewers, but it had never reached the same level of tolerance in the real world. We needed patience, a solid plan, and most importantly, for the sake of future innocent victims, we needed to make sure we didn't get dead.

CHAPTER THIRTY-TWO

Chief Baylor's driver pulled alongside the patrol cars in front of the house. After Baylor exited, his driver went to park. Baylor lifted the crime scene tape and walked under as the patrol supervisor, Sergeant Hopkins, walked to greet him.

"Where's he at?" Chief Baylor asked.

"In the car, Sir."

The chief took off walking toward the garage. There were five officers, two with significant rank, standing in the garage, laughing and carrying on. The first officer to spot the chief snapped to attention, when he did not need to. Not surprisingly, the others followed suit. Chief Baylor shook his head at the follow-the-leader mentality. Although he recognized the irony of his wanting officers to be confident on one hand, while needing the *follower's mentality* they displayed for him to reach his goal.

Baylor stood at the open driver's door, his left hand resting on the frame above the window. Always cognizant of stray, unwanted pictures, he held back his smile. He bent over to stick his head inside the car. Using the steering wheel and headrest for support he mumbled, "Not gonna sue us anymore, are you asshole?"

When he stood up, Mayor Sampson was nearly prancing up the driveway. He did not have the same fear of pictures, a huge smile with his white teeth showing, plastered across his face.

"Gentlemen, great to see you today," Mayor Sampson said to the officers scattering from the garage. "Chief, is it true?" He asked, feigning ignorance.

"Yes, I'm afraid it is. Aaron Vasquez took his own life, Mr. Mayor."

Mayor Sampson looked inside the car, his right hand resting on the metal frame between the front and rear doors. He stood up, the same smile still on his face.

"Great day, Dick. A great day."

"Jesus Christ, Ray, do you have to act so damn happy?"

"Dick," Sampson said, patting him on the shoulder, "I've waited quite a while for this. He's been nothing but a thorn in my side. Not anymore." Not waiting for a response, he took off walking into the house, curious to see how the attorney who took their money lived.

DC Chamberlain walked up about the time the mayor strolled in the house. He didn't care for the mayor, who in his opinion was nothing more than a weasel getting them to do his dirty work. Chamberlain didn't need the mayor to become governor for him to get what he wanted, the chief's job. He was willing to go elsewhere if need be, but his preference had always been to stay right there. With the assistant chief burning his last bit of vacation time before he retired, Freddy felt he had played his cards right. Mayor Sampson had no say in whom the city council might replace Chief Baylor with after they moved on to governor and cabinet secretary of public safety.

"Does the weasel have to go around smiling like he's happy the guy's dead?" Chamberlain asked.

"I tried talking to him, he doesn't listen. You know Ray."

"Prick."

"I'll second it."

Chamberlain almost grinned knowing Dick seldom said a bad word about the mayor.

"We may have a problem."

"What now?" Dick asked, his scrunched brows showing his concern.

"Investigator Sara Gray is the lead on this case. I can't believe Sergeant Montez didn't assign it to one of the others who thinks like we do. She's already pitching a bitch about all the people in the crime scene."

"She has a point, unfortunately. Can't reel it in now, it would look even worse. All the press people over there would have a field day pointing out how we screwed up this crime scene and then tried to fix it. We are better off making a statement about how all of the evidence immediately led us to the conclusion Mr. Vasquez committed suicide."

"What about her?" Freddy asked, nodding toward Gray.

"I'll talk to her."

"Are you sure, Chief?"

"She's not even a senior field investigator. You think the chief of police talking to her won't be enough? Really?"

Chamberlain nodded before he headed inside the house to see what the weasel was doing.

Investigator Sara Gray had never spoken to the chief. He had not been the chief when she graduated from the academy, and there were enough layers of brass between them for her not to have had an opportunity.

Sara had been voicing her displeasure to Sergeant Hopkins about the number of people traipsing around the crime scene from the time she arrived. He told her his original officers tried to maintain a solid perimeter by standing at the crime scene tape at first. When lieutenants and captains started showing up they walked under the tape and ignored the officers. Hopkins knew he lost control and backed his officers off trying to stop people. He apologized to Sara for letting the scene become as contaminated as it had.

"Now the chief's here," Sara growled.

Sergeant Hopkins could see the anger in her eyes and her jaw clenching.

"You stay here, I'll go talk to him."

Sara watched Chief Baylor go into the garage and lean inside the car, touching things like he had never been on a crime scene before. What made it worse was when she saw Mayor Sampson walk under the crime scene tape like he owned the scene, wearing a wide eerie grin on his face. When he went to the driver's door and leaned in, placing his hands all over the car, she came close to losing it. Sara slammed her notebook cover closed and threw it on the gravel front yard. She took off walking around the south side of the house, hoping it would be hidden enough for her to blow off some steam.

Sara took out a new toothpick and spit out the old one she had about chewed into little pieces. She had long ago figured out chewing on toothpicks helped relieve stress, the same as smoking did for some of her peers. The difference was she did not have to walk outside to a designated smoking area and waste time to get her relief.

After several deep breaths she walked back to her notebook. Bending to pick it up, she saw a pair of black dress shoes come up to her. She straightened up and the chief stood directly in front of her.

"Um, Chief Baylor, I'm Investigator Sara Gray." She put the notebook in her left hand and extended her right.

Chief Baylor hesitated, looking down at her hand. He canted his head as his eyes went from her hand, to her eyes, and back to her hand.

Sara looked at her hand, noticing the blood for the first time. She withdrew her hand and felt her face flush. "I'm sorry, Chief..."

"What happened to your hand?"

Sara had never been one to hide from the truth. "I punched the wall, Sir."

Chief Baylor stared, intentionally trying to make her feel uncomfortable.

Sara broke the silence, "This crime scene has become a travesty. There's no evidence preservation protocol taught anywhere in the United States, which hasn't been trampled on here, today, and I suspect you know it."

Baylor looked over his shoulder and saw the chief medical examiner going under the crime scene tape. He looked at Sara and said, "Excuse me for a second," and took two steps towards the driveway.

"Paul, it's good to see you." Baylor lifted his chin to suggest Paul Mullins walk over to him. Baylor put his hand on Mullins shoulder and leaned in close.

Sara saw the chief's head nod causing Mullins to change direction. She took three steps toward them, opened up her notebook, and wrote down the time the medical examiner arrived. She feigned writing more notes while turning sideways hoping to better hear their conversation.

"Remember what I told you this morning," Chief Baylor said to Paul. "This is really straightforward—suicide by carbon monoxide. Don't stray...then you and I are even."

He patted Paul on the shoulder twice and both men turned in opposite directions.

Oh my God, Sara thought. When she saw the chief pat the medical examiner on the shoulder she turned, putting her back towards them. She felt a tap on her shoulder and turned to face Chief Baylor again.

"Investigator Gray, let me say I've heard some pretty good things about you and your work," Baylor lied. "I understand how you feel. Now, let's talk about your future. I think a person with your skills and work ethic could go a long way in this department. I believe you will best serve the department by grabbing your gear and heading back to the office. I'm sure you have some unsolved cases you could better use your time to focus on."

"Chief, with all due respect, this is my crime scene."

"No, Investigator, it's not. I have put Deputy Chief Chamberlain in charge of this crime scene. You are to leave, period. You are not filing any reports and you have no responsibilities here. Do you understand?"

"I understand, *Chief*. This is wrong on so many levels, and you know it. I'll grab my bag in the house and follow your direct order, *Sir*."

Sara could see people all around, cops and civilians alike, watching the exchange they just had. She knew the best thing to do was to leave, but she made sure to log in her mind the number of people who did not belong inside the crime scene tape. She had counted thirty before she walked past the ripped tape on the ground, heading towards her car on the opposite side of the street.

A small crowd followed her to her car. She had no idea what news outlet they reported to, but everyone held a pad and pen or a tape recorder. Not airing dirty laundry to the press was taught to all police officers, and most adhered to the concept. Sara chose to follow suit and repeated, "No comment," again and again until the crowd of reporters headed back across the street.

Sara opened her trunk to put her bag inside and when she turned to look over, she saw the chief and the deputy chief talking in the driveway. Sara closed the trunk and went to the driver's door.

When Sara started to enter the car, for some reason she looked over at the front door of the house directly across from Aaron's house. She recognized the man on the porch now looking at her as Aaron Vasquez's investigator, although she had no idea what his name might be. She tried to be coy when she looked back at the scene once more in time to see the two administrators walking toward the garage. She looked back at the man on the porch and with her index finger close to her body, she pointed at herself, then at the man, and finished with a one hundred and eighty degree swirl. The man nodded and opened the screen door to step inside as she got into her car.

Ralph had read her sign language perfectly.

CHAPTER THIRTY-THREE

Ralph said he needed fresh air, but I sensed he wanted to get a better look. I was pleased he stayed on the front porch and figured it was a good time to call Mac since Liz had not come out of her bedroom.

"One second," Alex said when he answered, followed by silence except for the sound of the phone being put down on a hard surface.

"AJ, I put you on speaker phone, it's only Mac and me in his office," Alex said. "The doors are closed."

"Mac, I'm so sorry…this is not good. Obviously I cannot get too close, but his neighbor directly across the street, Liz, let Ralph and me come into her house. We've been watching through the window. If I had to guess I would say they made it look like carbon monoxide poisoning. He's in his car inside the garage and it's either total incompetence, or one of the best intentional squashing of evidence cases I've seen. Dozens of people, and I mean dozens, have gone past the crime scene tape, and now it's not up anymore, so civilians are gradually making their way into the driveway."

The door opened and Ralph looked me in the eye, a purpose in his eyes instead of tears.

"We need to go out back and hop the wall," Ralph said.

I didn't need further explanation, Ralph was on to something and I didn't want to interrupt.

"Mac, Alex, I got to go. I'll call you with an update when I can."

"Ralph, what's up?" I asked.

"Some investigator chick, she was taking notes, the chief goes over to her and then she grabs her shit and leaves," Ralph said. "At her car she sees me looking at her and motions to go around to the back of the house."

The cop in Ralph did a quick peek over the fence. He saw the Dodge the investigator drove, so despite his bad leg he hopped the brick wall. I followed. The front passenger window was down and the woman inside seemed nervous, not taking any time for small talk.

"IHOP, Wyoming and Paseo Del Norte," she said, followed by kicking up the gravel in the gutter as she accelerated.

We were about to leave when we heard a voice over the wall—Liz.

"Look, we need to go," I said, though I could not see her over the wall. "Liz, thank you for your hospitality. If you have somewhere to go for a couple days you might want to leave the area." I threw one of my old business cards over the wall. "My cell is on the card. Call if you see anything suspicious or you receive any threats. Thanks again."

Through sniffling we heard, "You're welcome."

We walked around the corner and headed to my car. We started to cross Red Yucca Avenue when Ralph backhanded my left shoulder to stop me. He pointed with his index finger and a head nod to the woman standing behind the same tree where I first saw him. She had all the appearance of someone who did not want to be seen, standing directly behind the trunk and only peeking around the side. Ralph said nothing and started walking toward her. Something in my gut said we needed to go, but Ralph's walk spoke of a man on a mission. I went the opposite way to my car so we could get out of there as soon as he finished.

The instant I saw Ralph's shoulders turn my way I drove forward. I turned left on Red Yucca and went the fifty feet before stopping at the stop sign, certain I would be out of direct sight of anyone in Aaron's yard or house. I pushed the unlock button and the passenger door opened. Ralph had the lever on the side of the seat lifted and the seatback laid down before I realized what he was doing. A Hispanic woman with swollen red eyes climbed in the back, followed by Ralph throwing the seatback up and almost jumping in.

"Let's go," Ralph said.

No time for questions, I thought as I got us out of there in a hurry.

THE INVESTIGATOR HAD LEFT INSTRUCTIONS AT THE IHOP front desk, so the hostess motioned us to follow her. We went to the back area partitioned off from the rest of the place with a half-wall and windows to the ceiling. Not the most secure place but at least we were away from other people. We got through the introductions fine, although one cop and two former ones, all from different jurisdictions, led to quite a bit of sizing up for the all-important question, *can I trust him or her*.

"Look, you don't know me from Adam, so I'm going to cut through the BS and say it straight," I said.

"It's the best method as far as I'm concerned," Sara said.

"First of all, we have a lady in the car with a story you might want to hear, and I don't think she will impede anything we are about to do here."

Sara squinted, her lips pushed out, and she turned her

head. Despite being an investigator, her body language told me everything I needed to know. She would say yes, but she needed to come to the conclusion in her own way. When she finally nodded, Ralph headed for the door.

"I'm a good friend of Judge McDunn...he's received several threats and some defendants in recent lawsuits against the APD are dead. We think all of this has to do with another rogue unit, kind of like ROP, but worse."

"And Aaron Vasquez?" asked Sara.

"I didn't get close enough to look at any evidence before the chief and his cronies allowed everything to be trampled. Still, I can say I'm almost certain Aaron did not kill himself. In fact, he warned the neighbor, Liz, you know, the house we were at, he warned her something might happen and told her where he hid a flash drive for Ralph. I suspect it's not there."

"On the underside of the oak desk, no, it isn't. I saw Deputy Chief Chamberlain reaching under there like he knew what he was after when he thought I wasn't watching."

Ralph and the woman walked up and sat, he next to the wall by Sara, the woman next to the wall by me. I could see Sara recognized the woman immediately as silence filled our space once again. Laying oneself out is risky, doubly so when we all believed Aaron Vasquez had been murdered.

I'd had enough. "Sara, meet Councilwoman Anita Trujillo. Anita, this is Field Investigator Sara Gray." Neither extended a hand to shake, but both gave a respectful mini-smile and head dip. I repeated everything I'd told Sara, hoping my openness would get the ball rolling toward establishing a rapport. Ralph went next, explaining everything he had found out about Hector and Viktor. After another round of silence, Anita finally cleared her throat.

She described everything…what had happened to her, how her daughter had been given a packet to bring to her, and how they were trying to intimidate her with death threats attached to current pictures of her husband and daughter.

The closest Ralph or I had gotten to proving the guys we were after were cops came from Simeon's description of being driven in a Chevy Tahoe with all the equipment of a police vehicle, along with the men all having on gun belts and bullet proof vests though the insignias were removed. Simeon's credibility grew when Anita changed the playing field with her account of being pulled over by a cop car and her description matching the vehicles and uniforms Simeon provided.

Sara had not asked a question nor said a word. I could see she would probably be a good investigator, if she were not already, by the way she took in all the information and used good listening skills, along with the fact she knew her talking meant others may not keep talking. Something about her grew on me as we continued to share information.

"I'm not sure how many of you knew Sergeant Peter Howard, he was killed a few months ago driving home from work," I said. All three nodded enough I could tell they were at least familiar with the name and the story. "I don't want to get into all the backstory about how I got this information, although I am not beyond sharing it with any of you as we continue to build a trust factor here. Suffice it to say, Peter was probably killed for collecting information on this rogue group, known in their little circle of dirtbag cops as SDM, or Sindicato de la Muerte, Syndicate of Death. They intentionally chose it to create confusion with the Mexican gang, SNM."

I could see Anita's hands start shaking and tears forming in her eyes so I laid my hand on top of hers.

"I read in the paper this morning the young man they made lay beside me for the blackmail pictures is dead…why didn't they kill me? They're going to…aren't they?"

"No, Anita, I'm pretty sure they won't," I said.

I looked at Sara and Ralph, both staring like I was full of crap.

"No, seriously, they could have killed you like they did the guy they made lay down next to you. If they wanted to kill you, they would have. They're not afraid of killing anyone."

"So why not then?" she asked, her voice quivering.

"You're a valuable asset. If they shut you up, change how you vote for things surrounding the police department, and threaten to blackmail you with pictures, there's no need to kill you. As for Judge McDunn, I feel they are not ready to execute a person in somewhat of a powerful position. In their own way it's like they are trying to control the chess board."

CHAPTER THIRTY-FOUR

Lisa's pale face and red eyes told Mac she already heard about Aaron as her coworkers trying to comfort her stepped back and made their way to their desks. When Lisa saw Mac the crying started all over. Mike Sanders stepped out of his office and with a sweep of his hand suggested they come to his office.

"This morning Lisa told me about her meeting yesterday with Mr. Vasquez," Mike said. "Given the circumstances, I can't help but believe we need to either run with the story now, or we need to cool our jets. I think Lisa needs to lay low for a while, I mean, she could be in real danger here."

"I agree, we probably need to get her somewhere safe," Mac said.

Lisa reached out and grabbed a napkin from Mike's cluttered desk, wiped her eyes and blew her nose. "Quit talking about me like I'm not here and I don't have a say in the matter."

"Okay, then weigh in," Mike said.

Lisa said, "Reporters all over the world are in danger at various points in their career. You were in danger before, weren't you?" She paused momentarily waiting for his reaction. "Exactly. Did you run and hide from it? No, of course not." She turned to face Mac. "And you, you've received credible threats from these assholes, but you haven't crawled in a hole."

The men looked at each other, neither having a reasonable rebuttal not based on emotion.

"What do you propose then?" Mike asked.

Lisa didn't answer but looked at Mac, knowing he wanted her to stop. "Didn't you say AJ got the names of the rogue officers?"

"Yes, but do you really have enough to name them right now?"

"No. Not yet. I think we could break up the article. It would give us time to see what else AJ can dig up."

"It's a safe approach," Mike said. "We need to make sure we have enough information before we name individual cops."

"What about Kyle Lansing?" Mac asked. "He was never supposed to hit the streets, much less be part of ROP. Now, he's on special assignment again. Deputy Chief Chamberlain is behind it all."

"I like it…and naming him under those circumstances doesn't bother me. So, Lisa…put together the first part of the article, including the Lansing info. We can probably get the article in tomorrow's addition, day after at the latest. In the meantime, you need to be careful."

Mac mouthed, "Thank you." He knew Lisa was too headstrong to listen to only one of them, but both telling her to be careful had a chance.

MAYOR SAMPSON ASKED, "ARE YOU GUYS GOING TO MAKE sure this plays out like it's supposed to?"

"Why are you concerning yourself with it?" Chamberlain asked.

"Because it's my career on the line, too. Answer the damn question."

The two glared at each other.

"Relax gentleman," Chief Baylor said. "We've got the ME in our corner. Don't ask me how, you're better off not knowing."

"Fine. Keep me posted." Sampson turned, left the garage and headed for the sidewalk, waving his hand to get his drivers attention.

Baylor did not want to hear anymore complaining about the mayor so he changed the topic. "I'm not sure about the investigator, what's her name, Gray?"

"We can keep an eye on her," Chamberlain said. "I'll have Sergeant Montez bury her with work, she won't have time to think about this case. Besides, we need to be careful not to do too much. The more they kill, the more risk there is and it could all fall apart."

"You're probably right. Do me a favor, keep an eye on her."

"I will. Remember the guy I confronted at the courthouse the other day? I got the information back on him. I started coming over here to tell you before the fricking mayor came over."

"Really? What did you find out?"

"Conti went to the police academy when he was twenty-one and worked for the same police agency in central California for sixteen years. Colorful career, several shootings, almost died when he got that scar on his face. He'd been a homicide detective but recently gave it all up.

"The interesting thing is he grew up here in Albuquerque. Guess who he grew up next to?" Chamberlain figured the chief would have gotten it easily. Instead, all he got was a blank stare. "He grew up next door to Judge McDunn."

"I don't like where this might be headed. It's possible Conti came into town just to visit, but I doubt it. The timing…it's no coincidence."

"I don't think so either. Now you know why I don't want to get all wrapped up about Sara Gray."

"Yeah. Between McDunn's girlfriend working for The Journal, and now his detective friend shows up in town…we can't have them snooping around digging stuff up. I think we need to turn up the heat in their direction, don't you?"

"I think so. I've been waiting for your blessing, Chief."

"You got any ideas in mind?"

Chamberlain smiled, the evil in his eyes jumping out at Baylor.

The chief liked having Freddy in his corner for his cunning schemes, not to mention he hated the thought of having him as an enemy.

"I have a couple," Chamberlain said, rubbing his hands.

"You wanted it, you got it. I approve."

CHAPTER THIRTY-FIVE

Brett Metzger could not believe what he heard. In his position as a drug rehab counselor he'd heard some off-the-wall stories. Some true, some not so much. He usually did not pay attention since many stories were attached to excuses why someone had fallen off the wagon…again. Now, it was different. A twelve-year-old boy was the one telling him, not Brett's client, the boy's father.

The father had once told Brett he and his family did not live in the best neighborhood…they lived in Syndicato Nuevo Mexico gang territory. When the boy told how he heard of a hit supposedly going to happen, Brett's ears perked up. He expected the boy to say SNM would do the job. To his surprise, they wanted nothing to do with it when they learned the hit would be on a judge.

Brett asked the boy if he knew which judge and the boy said he heard them say the judge walked on crutches. Brett had heard many times from older SNM members they had been represented by Judge McDunn when he worked at the Public Defender's office. They often spoke of McDunn treating them with respect, and they appreciated his speaking Spanish, especially to their mothers.

When the father and son left, Brett closed the door. He picked up his cell to call the one guy who had his finger on the pulse of street life.

"Brett, long time no talk."

"I'm sorry, Casino. Hey man, I need to find out if something is true."

"You got it, Bro. What is it?

"I heard a hit has been put out on a judge, but SNM wouldn't take it. Can you find out about it and get back to me?"

"I'll let you know." Casino hung up.

While Brett dealt with his next two clients, time seemed to stand still. He had faith in Casino, but it had never taken him so long to get back to him. On the other hand, asking about a judge getting whacked never happened before. While finishing up paperwork, his cell vibrated.

"Probably couldn't find anything out, could you?"

"No. Just the opposite, dude. Like always, you never heard this from me."

"I never do, Casino. You know me."

"I know, I know. Sorry. So, it's true man, SNM turned it down, you already know why. Apparently, the Asian Killa's are going to do it. Those Vietnamese boys are violent, and true to their gang moniker, the AK-47, is what they like to drill people with. I guess they think it sets them apart."

"Thanks, Casino."

"Hey, I'm not done. I think they're gonna do a drive-by tonight at the judge's house. Here's the bad shit, it was paid for by some dirty fucking cops."

Brett's mouth fell open.

"Dude, you there?"

"Yeah, Casino, I'm here. It's a lot to take in."

"I know, man, some sick shit. Gotta go, later."

Brett heard the three beeps and set the phone on his desk. His head landed in his hands as his elbows planted on his old military metal desk.

Brett's thoughts drifted to several years before when he ended up in front of Judge McDunn for possession of heroin. His lawyer told him to expect to be returned to prison as a habitual offender, and Brett knew most judges would have sent him back. Instead, Judge McDunn told him he saw something in Brett, saying he would take a risk on him. Brett remembered how good he felt when someone, who was someone, believed in him and was willing to take a chance on him. McDunn waived the extra year for Brett being a habitual offender, so he was not locked into giving a mandatory prison sentence. The Judge could send him to a drug rehab program.

Brett could not believe he made it through each of the three phases of the program, but he knew McDunn being there every step of the way providing mentorship and encouragement was the reason why.

Brett grabbed his phone, brought up McDunn's name and texted nine-one-one. Less than two minutes later they were having a conversation, Brett laying out everything he learned and how he verified it without mentioning Casino by name.

"Judge, I know those cops have been ripping off drug dealers for a while now, but *this*?"

"It's getting out of control, Brett. They've already killed several people."

"Judge, you don't think they had anything to do with Aaron Vasquez's death?"

The phone became quiet and Brett thought he heard

McDunn getting choked up. "You *do*. Holy crap Judge, you need to get outta there."

"Thanks for the heads up, Brett. I'm proud of you, keep up the good work, you're saving lives."

Brett heard the familiar sounds ending the call and pulled his phone away from his ear, staring at the blank screen. Judge McDunn's avoidance of the danger he was in and his lack of commitment to leaving had Brett concerned.

I CAME OUT OF THE HALLWAY BATHROOM IN TIME TO SEE Mac tap the screen on his phone and toss it on his bed. He unlocked the wheels on his wheelchair and paused, grabbed the phone and put it on the seat between his legs. He leaned his crutches on the foot pedals and up against his chest, popped a wheelie and followed me to the living room.

"I heard you talking on the phone, everything okay?" I asked.

The pinched look on Mac's face showed he might be caught somewhere between concerned and determined.

"Those thoughts you had before about them not attacking a judge, you're only somewhat correct now."

Mac laid his crutches against the couch, bent over and grabbed his Springfield 9mm off the coffee table. He did a slight pull on the slide for a quick check of the round in the chamber and followed it with a palm slap at the base of the grip to make sure the magazine was seated.

I watched closely waiting for an answer I knew would come once he felt secure. Mac put his phone on the table and the Springfield on the seat between his legs. I had seen him with one of his many weapons stuffed there before, so my concern had nothing to do with the weapon. When he finally looked at me I raised my brows and flared my hands, my best rendition of asking… *Well?* without saying it.

"We are going to be attacked by a relatively violent Vietnamese gang here in town. My source says it's gonna happen tonight and their weapons of choice are AK-47s."

"*Seriously*?"

"Yes. Here's the kicker, they're being funded by The Syndicate."

"So, what do you want to do?"

The look on his face reminded me of when we were younger and I asked one of my many stupid questions. The memory made me smile.

CHAPTER THIRTY-SIX

I had to make a few arrangements for a welcoming committee for the Asian Killas. Figuring Ralph would want to help me host the party, I grabbed my phone and punched in his number.

"Hey, you wanna come play in our reindeer games?"

"What the hell you talking about?"

"We received good intel, the Asian Killas will be doing a drive-by at Mac's house tonight."

"I'm in." Ralph enjoyed a small chuckle.

"Good. Leave your weapons at home. Mac has a mini-arsenal here and we want to keep our traceable weapons for later."

After giving Ralph the address to Mac's house, I told him to park in the driveway on the east side of the judge's address. I envisioned dirty investigators taking our cars if we had them in the firefight zone.

Hanging up with Ralph, I asked the judge for Brett Metzger's phone number. Mac wanted to know why, so I told him I wanted to ask Brett for some help and it was best he did not hear what the favor would be.

Once outside, I dialed Brett's number.

"Brett, my name is AJ. Judge McDunn gave me your number." I then explained some of the background as to why I was in Albuquerque.

"Is the judge leaving his house?"

"When you called him, did you expect him to run and hide?"

"Not really."

"There's the answer then. The reason I called is going to sound strange, so you may not want to help, which is okay. I need some assistance in getting a couple of unmarked weapons. I'm hoping you may know someone I could contact."

"For *tonight*?" Brett asked, his voice full of disbelief.

"No. I'd need them tomorrow. We're good for tonight."

Other than my nephew, who I didn't want digging up illegal guns, I gave him the time he needed.

"Look, I've got to go. Think about it…you have my number. If I don't get a text by eight in the morning, I'll know you were unable to help out."

Brett seemed comfortable with the arrangement and hung up.

I put my gun and magazines in the trunk of my Mustang after I parked it beside Ralph's car and went inside to start gathering the weapons we'd need. With the sun setting, my gut told me we didn't have much time.

Ralph and I went to Mac's driveway to assess AKs likely approach. His house sat in the miniature cul-de-sac where the L-shaped street changed directions. From the right his street was straight and long with neighbor's trees blocking the view of his house. More importantly, if AK approached from the right the driver's side would be facing the house, leaving only one passenger window from which to shoot. We agreed a car full of AKs would have a better line of sight to Mac's house from the other direction and figured they'd probably wait for confirmation Mac was home by watching from somewhere near the intersection.

Logic dictated the AKs would turn onto the short portion of road, which only covered three house lengths before it turned into the long straight section, allowing them to start shooting the instant they turned onto the road with Mac's house right in front of them. After they opened fire they could leave eastbound on the long straight street and the neighbor's trees would protect them—if they could get far enough away.

Ralph positioned himself on the east side of Mac's house against the wall a few feet in front of the backyard gate. He had one of Mac's four AR-15s, along with Ralph's weapon of choice, a Glock 23, and four additional magazines.

Mac switched wheelchairs to the one with a holster attached to the frame off his right leg to hold his Springfield 9mm. He also had his fully-automatic MP5, and positioned his chair in a room at the front of the house. Two narrow floor-to-ceiling windows were located on the wall looking out to the front yard and the intersection where we expected to first see the Asian Killas car. The wall between the two windows had thick rock facing on the exterior, providing Mac some semblance of cover. My goal was to draw the initial firing at me, leaving Mac and Ralph to return fire with minimal shots at them.

Mac's house was a simple L-shape with the front of the garage and the front of the room Mac was in basically even. To get to the front door a sidewalk rounded the corner of the room Mac was in and the door was twenty feet away.

A mound of rocks and plants in the front yard hid the AR-15 I planned to use, along with one of Mac's other Springfield 9mms and three additional magazines. I sat in his second wheelchair on the porch, the front door open behind me, *waiting*. Seeing a guy in a wheelchair on the front walkway at night would be what they would focus on, not what the guy looked like.

Ralph saw the car first as it pulled up to the curb shy of the intersection in front of us. One guy got out of the back passenger side and ran up behind a tree on the corner lot. When Ralph signaled me with a short whistle I said a silent prayer and turned on the porch and driveway lights.

I gradually rolled down the sidewalk in the wheelchair to the corner of the house parallel to Mac and I saw the guy run back to the car. I heard the car start and saw it slowly turn the corner to come right at us...their headlights came on as it picked up speed.

Bailing out of the chair, I ran for the mound of rocks. The sound of gunfire erupted as rounds kept hitting Mac's house as they tried to shoot me. They fired what seemed like a dozen rounds in a split second…all behind me as I ran. Enough rounds were fired for me to know they were committed.

I heard Ralph's AR-15, followed by the automatic fire from Mac's MP5. Diving behind the rocks, my hand grabbed the Springfield and I started to return fire. I saw muzzle flash from both passenger windows closest to us, as well as over the top of the car from a guy hanging out the left rear passenger window.

The passengers on the right side were taking rounds, their bodies lurching with each hit. I fired a volley of three rounds at the guy shooting over the top. His body pitched backward…*strangely reminiscent of JFK.*

I heard the wheels scratching as if the driver tried to punch it to get out of there. Before the wheels grabbed,

Ralph put rounds in the driver's head and chest. His foot must have slipped off the accelerator because the car drifted at an angle through Mac's driveway and stopped when the bumper shook the forty-foot pine tree in the neighbor's yard.

I jumped up and headed for the car, the smell of gunpowder not enough to mask the distinct odor in the air of burning rubber. Two shots rang out. *Ralph*, I thought, expecting to see him on the ground. I rounded the corner in time to see Ralph put two more rounds into the left rear passenger.

We carefully made our way to the car to find all four males were dead. Not one of them looked to be over eighteen.

Ralph held his position on the slim chance one of them might move a muscle. He was prepared to make sure it would be their last twitch.

Returning to my mound, I retrieved the cold AR-15 never fired and walked through the front door. I could see Mac was not injured, unlike the many items in his house. His questioning eyes were locked on me and I nodded to let him know they were all dead. We all knew from our varying courtroom experiences a dead man has less to say than one who survives and gets on the stand full of lies and prepared answers.

I grabbed the Army canvas bag with six handguns, a Mac-10 with a suppressor along with two shotguns, not to mention a few hundred rounds. I unzipped the bag to put in my AR-15, then zipped it closed. Walking out to the backyard and over to the east wall, I had a challenge with the bag's weight. Still, I got it over and to the driveway where I parked the Mustang. Closing the trunk, it locked just as I heard the sirens in the background.

Mac had folded the wheelchair I used and put it in the pool table room up against the wall. With everything in its place, we headed outside.

Mac stayed in his chair. Ralph shook his head when we rounded the corner to tell me they were all dead. I felt bad for the four young men, who gave up their lives. Their destiny had been determined when they bragged about taking the contract from the Syndicato De Muerte.

We lined up side-by-side in the driveway, Mac still in his wheelchair, the weapons we used lying on the cement twenty feet in front of us. When we saw the emergency lights we all raised our hands, palms forward.

CHAPTER THIRTY-SEVEN

I did not enjoy lying on the driveway with cops pointing their weapons at us, but I expected it. Still, expectation did nothing to ease my fear one of them might get an itchy trigger finger.

One of the two young officers was yelling at Mac to get out of his wheelchair and lay on the pavement. Mac calmly tried to explain how it wasn't possible without him plopping out of the chair, nothing to support him as he went down. Not surprisingly, his effort was met with another round of yelling.

"I'm a homicide detective," I stretched the truth, "and you're about to make a big mistake."

For the first time since they arrived there was silence. *I've got them thinking, I need to seize the opportunity before they open their mouths again.*

"You have two cops and a District Court judge here with a car full of Asian Killas over there." I pointed with a head nod. "We will cooperate, we all understand you have a job to do. But making the judge flop on the ground because you do not want to take into account his disability won't look good on the ten o'clock news, not to mention for your careers."

The sirens meant more coming, so I needed to get these two in our corner before they were bombarded with other cops telling them what to do.

"One of you can cuff me and the other guy on the ground while the second one keeps a weapon trained on all of us. Then cuff the judge with his hands in the front sitting in his chair."

Seconds before the next patrol car slid around the corner, one of them finished the cuffing. I got lucky, the officers arriving took cover with their weapons on us, but they let the original two continue with their plan.

The first patrol sergeant wisely had officers take us to the backyard, out of sight of the cameras, cell phones and professional news media, about the time the television crews were pulling up. By the look on her face something told me she had already assessed we were probably the good guys and the four dead in the car brought the trouble to us.

"Your Honor, we have detectives in route," the sergeant said. "I'm sorry, but we need to leave you cuffed until then."

"Not a problem, Sergeant. Thank you for getting my friends chairs to sit on. At their ages they'd need help getting up if you made them sit on the ground."

Laughing, she said, "Yeah, it wasn't easy picking them up off the driveway, but at least they weren't dead weight," she winked at Mac.

She went inside the house, leaving the one officer who barely looked old enough to shave. He watched us from the sliding glass doorway.

"Smooth move," Ralph smiled.

"Thanks. She's on our side, at least for now."

"Let's hope we get a decent detective or two," I said. "Otherwise, we might all be spending the night in jail."

AN HOUR LATER WE SAW THREE PLAIN CLOTHES DETECTIVES walking towards us.

"Here we go, gentlemen." I said. "I'll see you when I see you. Best of luck."

I recognized the third one through the door. The instant Sara Gray saw me she tapped the shoulder of the guy in the middle, pointed at me and whispered something to him. When the guy nodded, Sara came over.

"I'll take this one inside," Sara said over her shoulder. She did not look for his approval, but grabbed the crook of my arm and directed me to stand. With her hand on my arm, she walked me to the bedroom in the corner only partially visible from the living room. After a patrol officer brought a couple of chairs she sat me in one with my back towards the open bedroom door while she sat facing me. We sat off to the side so she could look out into the living room.

Sara started off professionally, asking all the right questions while gauging the likelihood of someone coming in the room. After about fifteen minutes she stopped, leaned forward and said, "Okay, what's the *story*?"

Hesitating for a second, I processed our earlier meeting with how she was acting now. My gut told me she was on our side, so I went with it. I explained what I knew the other two would tell their interviewers…we had agreed to say I went outside after I turned on the lights and saw furtive movement by the tree. When I saw a guy run back to the car, I raced to the front door and yelled for them to take cover. We knew we'd be questioned on how I knew something was about to happen, so they'd answer with the fact I just knew, like all good cops who have been in several shooting situations. It put the onus on me since we could easily say they only responded to the danger I said existed—no prior planning on their part.

We figured most detectives would buy into it, at least for the initial interview. We also decided if it went to further questioning, I'd be the best candidate to hold my own in an interrogation. I had done dozens of major interviews, not to mention being questioned about my prior shooting incidents.

Our plan was to play off Mac having received threatening notes, leaving all of us on edge, especially since Viktor Laine had yet to be found. I brought a grin to Sara's face when I told her we had agreed to throw Detective Sergeant Montez under the bus by mentioning him telling Mac the notes were nothing.

Had Mac not received the threats we would not have been prepared, and would most likely been overtaken and killed. The notes and threats were the sole reasons we had guns in strategic places. Each of us would mention how those poor young men probably never expected Mac to have a fully-automatic MP5, much less two cops with him, who between them, had survived several firefights.

The corners of Sara's lips relaxed and almost rose to a smile. She looked at me straight in the eyes before sitting back in her chair. Putting away her pen, she crossed her legs, and relaxed her arms on her lap.

"I don't suppose you want to tell me what really happened," she said, although the hint of her desire to hear more lingered in the air.

I looked over my shoulder to make sure no one was within earshot. "You're not recording this, you're not taking notes, you're not going to use this statement in any way against any of us, and this is one hundred percent off the record."

"I agree. I guess you have to decide if you trust me."

"Sara, I trusted you the instant I met you. I knew you believed in doing the right thing. So, before you ask why I said those other things and made you agree to them, I'll tell you why. I've done hundreds of interviews, and even though I'm not in your chair, I wanted to read your body language. Suffice it to say, you passed the test." I grinned.

Sara's cheeks started to rise as she gave me a tiny nod before her facial expression returned to stoic as her eyes shifted past me to the doorway.

"You about done," some male voice behind me asked.

"Just finishing up. Be right out," Sara replied.

When she nodded at me again I laid out the quick version for her. The pleasant expression on her face did not last long when I said The Syndicate paid for the Asian Killas hit on Mac…her expression turned to worry, her jaw muscles tightened and she squirmed in her chair.

Sara's eyes darted past me again. She tilted her head up before she stood. I knew our interview was over and we were about to find out where we would spend the night. Sara directed me out into the living room, her hand still in the crook of my arm. I saw Mac and Ralph first, and then the familiar face came into view off to my left.

"Ah, we meet again, Mr. Conti," Chief Baylor almost smiled.

"So we do, Chief. Funny how those things happen, isn't it?"

What little smile he had quickly departed. "Un-cuff them," he ordered in a deeper, more assertive tone. Three different officers removed our handcuffs at the same time.

"Regardless of what you all say, this looks like a setup," Chief Baylor said, making sure to slowly examine each one of us as if we were bugs under glass. "You can rest assured we will dig deeper into this, and if we find anything that does not line up...we'll be back to arrest all of you."

He started to leave, but turned around to stare at us. Looking at us but talking to his officers he said, "Make sure you take all the weapons in this house...for safe keeping, of course." His eyes stayed on Mac for several seconds. "Too bad you won't get any of the guns back you used to *defend* yourselves, your Honor. This is a homicide scene; they'll remain in evidence for ninety-nine years, as I'm sure you're aware."

He took a step toward the door before he looked back over his shoulder at Mac once more. "And by the way, you might expect contact from the Judicial Disciplinary Board when we are done explaining to them what we found." His shoulders pulled back as he stood tall in time to walk outside for the cameras.

Sadness was written on Mac's face. Preponderance of evidence by a board is a much lower threshold than beyond a reasonable doubt in a courtroom. Dirty politics has a way of infiltrating all levels, and Mac's face told me he knew he may have spent his last day on the bench.

Sara slipped a wadded-up piece of paper into my palm as she slid behind me to leave. After all of the weapons had been removed and officers had gone out front to watch the evidence collection, I opened it. There were seven numbers and the word *personal* written on it. The way things were headed I figured I might have to actually call it.

As I put the number into my cellphone directory, I used the name of a well-known female Israeli Mossad agent on television whom Sara resembled.

CHAPTER THIRTY-EIGHT

The three of us went out by the pool in Mac's backyard. We were in for a long night given the amount of brass being picked up for evidence from all the guns utilized. Ralph and I did not want to go to our cars parked in the neighbor's driveway for fear some detective or prosecutor would argue we moved our cars in preparation—a true statement. By waiting out the investigation, we could effectively avoid the issue. What they did not know would not hurt us.

Peter Howard told us from the grave most of the rank and file of the department did not agree with Chief Baylor's methodology. With that in mind, I pulled out my cell to start looking on the internet.

"What are you doing?" Mac asked as I punched in numbers.

"Ordering pizza for the people out there working the scene. I know what it's like to have a crime scene from hell with evidence in every nook and cranny. It takes time, so I figured I'd make sure they have some food."

"Really? Nothing else, I mean I can't buy into relieving their hunger is your only goal."

I smiled. "Peter said most of them are good people… hell, you've said it too, so I take it to mean they wouldn't support what The Syndicate is doing, or the top brass approving of it. You never know when we might need some help. I feel good about relieving their hunger. Besides, I'm hungry, too."

"You can think about eating at a time like this?"

The sad fact about becoming callous after killing several people was not something most could comprehend, including the eighty percent of police officers in the nation who never fire their weapon outside of the range. The soldiers coming home from Afghanistan were more likely to understand. There was no explanation I could give Mac to help him see, so I chose not to answer.

I pushed the green icon on my screen, ultimately asking for the manager so I could explain the situation. I ordered fifteen pizzas along with several liters of soda, with a promise of a twenty dollar tip for the delivery person. Ralph and I grabbed Mac's six-foot centerfold table from the garage, took it out front and found an area where the techs did not need to work. Sara looked over, wondering what we were doing and all I could do was roll my shoulders.

Walking to the neighbor's driveway I pulled out my phone to call my brother-in-law. After our talking the other day about *green chili* my needing to explain myself would be minimal. When he answered, I carried on a conversation about what might be a good Mexican restaurant, one that served spicy *green chili*. I figured his pause was due to him needing a few seconds in order to come to grips with what I told him. He did a great job by continuing the conversation as if we were really discussing restaurants.

When it was time to hang up he said, "Hey, good luck."

I feigned a laugh. "You, too. Be safe." After he hung up I felt bad for the fear I injected into their lives. Still, I balanced it with knowing I made the right move to get them out of town sooner than later.

When Mac and Ralph came over, Ralph took a seat on the curb, resting his arms on his legs. His stare told me he was thinking about Aaron. Although being a bodyguard was not part of his job, I sensed he felt he let him down. Having gone through a similar situation with Bethany being murdered I knew mentally he could acknowledge there was nothing he could have done, while internally he'd need time to get past the real feeling of guilt he was experiencing.

"I called my brother and sister," Mac said. "They thanked me, but neither gave me the impression they would leave."

"We do think a lot alike. I called my brother-in-law, too. We had already agreed if I used a certain code word they'd pack up everyone in the fifth wheel and go to their cabin until I called them to return. I would bet they already had it packed and are driving out of town as we speak."

Mac's far off stare showed he didn't hear a word I said. I could see him clenching his jaw, sensing his concern for his siblings, but I could tell it went far beyond them.

"Have you contacted Lisa?"

He nodded. "I sent her a text to let her know I was okay. She's probably in shock at how far this has gone with The Syndicate. I kinda feel she's running on adrenaline, as if her article out will help solve things. In truth, I think she believes her article will do something for Aaron. Unfortunately, her judgment is a little clouded since we know there is nothing we can do to turn around their claim of it being a suicide."

"We won't get outta here till sometime tomorrow. Is she going to be safe?"

"I believe so. I think I convinced her to stay at the office and not leave without someone else being with her."

The car with the pizza company sign turned the corner,

but came to a stop in the middle of the road due to the crime scene tape. I waved and started walking toward it as the driver got out. His eyes widened as he looked around at the activity in Mac's driveway. I smiled, realizing the driver wanted to ask what happened but could not bring himself to do it.

Ralph and I got everything to the table, grabbing one of the boxes and a liter of soda for us to take inside the house. Knowing the common thread running throughout all police agencies...*no gratuities for their employees*, we did not say a word to the crime scene personnel...we simply left the food and drinks on the table for them, but leaving them to say...*they never knew who paid for it.*

Entering the house, I looked back and saw Sara with a faint grin on her face. With a slight nod she thanked me for looking out for them.

CHAPTER THIRTY-NINE

Shortly before 10 p.m. Ralph still sat in the backyard staring into the pool...his world had been turned upside down so we gave him the space he needed.

We stayed busy in the kitchen making pots of coffee and putting it in a few carafes to leave out front with disposable cups. We decided to stay and watch the activity sitting at the corner of the house.

Mac received a short, to the point, anonymous text message and showed it to me. The message told Mac *they* were a friend and as a friend, they asked if we were okay. We had recently finished a conversation about friends and how we wished we had more people we could count on to help us. The look on Mac's face told me he would be inclined to respond despite knowing the risk. The sender might be part of SDM looking for info to set us up again.

"Maybe get the person to authenticate who they are," I said.

"What do you mean?" Mac asked.

"They probably won't tell you their name, but they might give you some information to help you verify you know them. Think of it like leading a witness on the stand right where you want them to go."

Mac paused to reflect, readying himself for the conversation.

"*Still a little shocked, being attacked in my house,*" Mac texted.

"*Glad you're okay,*" they responded.

"*Friend? Help me to understand how,*" Mac wrote back.

"*Word is traveling fast in our community. Lots of us upset, more than you know.*"

"*Last time we spoke?*" Mac asked a pertinent question.

"*Six months, mutual friend, where the deer and the antelope play.*"

Mac smiled at me and mouthed, "Friend of Peter's, met on the range." I nodded and rolled my index finger to let Mac know to continue the conversation, hoping we could get something substantive…even if the person wanted only to check on Mac's welfare.

"*Feelings about the ph imbalance?*" Mac asked.

"*Lasted for a while. Very acidic, scary. Some believe it could rebound.*"

"*Imps create acid, need to locate their dens or the acidity remains,*" Mac replied.

Mac looked at me and I nodded. "It seems there are a lot of good officers out there who don't support the current regime; the fact cops killed Peter Howard has them scared."

"I agree," Mac said. "I was hoping we might get some help, but I doubt anything will come of their text conversation beyond them supporting our belief, not after what happened to Peter."

Sara came walking toward us, a deadpan look on her face.

"Mac, this is Investigator Sara Gray…Sara this is Judge McDunn."

"We've met for a couple of search warrants." Mac remembered.

"Your Honor, sorry to meet again under these circumstances," she said shaking Mac's hand.

"So, the lone detective left surrounded by a group of work ants diligently digging up evidence," I said. "Let me guess, you had the least seniority?"

When Sara smiled, my guess was confirmed.

Sara slid over to the right of Mac and leaned against the wall. Typical cop move, put yourself in a position to see as much as possible, including watching the worker ants in front to see if any would be interested in where she had moved off to in order to rat her out when beneficial to one or more of them.

"No one seems to have noticed you are over here, much less care," I said.

Sara's head whipped around, eyes narrowing as she processed it all, and me too most likely. Turning back, she kept an eye on the technicians. Talking above a whisper she said, "The consensus of the three of us who did the interviews is admin will let it stand. It would look too much like a witch hunt if they reassigned it or brought you in when everything points to an attempted hit on a judge." Sara glanced at us, then back to the action. "Everybody else believes you must have said or done something offensive to one of the high-ranking AKs in court for them to put a hit on you. I didn't add to their conversation, figuring if everyone is going to believe that story then admin can't screw with you again, at least not on this case."

Pushing away from the wall, Sara looked at us as if she did not care if anyone else might be watching.

"You know they'll try again, right? Probably not with a gang but they have unfinished business. Your Honor, you're clearly a threat to them. You need to take a sabbatical, or whatever the hell you call it...you need to get out of town at least for a while."

The look on Sara's face showed she genuinely cared about Mac's well-being and I could tell Mac saw it, too. He responded in typical Mac fashion. He looked directly into Sara's eyes as his fingertips touched her elbow.

"Detective, thank you. I appreciate your comments. Truly I do. But...I can't. Not after what they did to my colleague...and dear friend, Aaron Vasquez."

He withdrew his hand and looked at me. "My brother, AJ, here," his eyes looked back to Sara, "he says 'right is right and wrong is wrong,' so regardless of what happens now, we're trying to do right by the people of this city."

Sara's eyes pleaded with me to weigh in and support her suggestion.

As much as I knew her caring for Mac's safety to be genuine, I couldn't side with her. "Bad things have been happening for a while now, Sara," I said. "Greed is a funny thing, it's almost cancerous in its own way. If they can kill one of their own, kill a lawyer, attack councilmembers, and put a hit on a sitting judge? Their greed will fester. They won't be satisfied. They'll want more. Somebody has to try, Sara."

Closing her eyes she nodded. Opening her eyes, she took a deep breath.

I thought she would walk away. I could not have been more wrong.

"This is probably going to cost me my career, but it's not much of a career when I feel like I've been sentenced to support a value system so unlike who I am. I've watched for a while now...good cops slowly crossing the line as they see this administration back improper and illegal tactics. I can't do it anymore."

Sara paused. Mac looked at me with the same questioning look on his face as I no doubt had. *Where's she going with this?*

"Judge, I hope I can count on you to write a nice recommendation letter," Sara said. "I'm all in. How can I help?"

CHAPTER FORTY

Deputy Chief Chamberlain pulled the metal door behind him doing nothing to stop it from slamming shut. All eyes turned in his direction, but none of The Syndicate seemed overly bothered by his appearance. After all, they didn't screw up the hit.

"DC Chamberlain," Gyrene said, extending his hand.

Chamberlain swooshed his hand through the air like he was swatting at a fly, walking right past Gyrene.

Gyrene believed deeply in the structure, something instilled in him by the Marine Corps. He had been to battle with leaders, some good, some not so good. The wave off by Chamberlain amounted to pure, unadulterated disrespect. Gyrene had enough. He started to curl his fingers and raise his hand, stopping short of flipping off the DC. A quick glance at his men told him none of them saw it, their eyes were following the DC.

Patience Marine, patience, the repetitive words rolled through his head.

Gyrene's mind drifted to seeing Emilio, walking with him to his apartment. He recalled the internal struggle he had, knowing where they were going and what lay ahead for Emilio, while at the same time hating the whole concept. He liked Emilio and wanted to help him. Instead, like a good Marine, when he received an order from the DC, he followed it. Strangely the words from an old movie popped into his head. *Your son is dead for only one reason. I wasn't strong enough to stop it.*

"Sergeant," Chamberlain barked again, "*Sergeant.*"

Gyrene appeared caught-off-guard. His eyes located Sly, who did a quick head nod toward the DC. Gyrene's eyes followed.

"Yes, Sir."

"I don't know whose idea it was to use a second-rate gang like the AKs to do a hit, when it's obvious we should've used Syndicato Nuevo Mexico."

"They wouldn't take the contract," Gyrene spoke up.

"What the hell do you mean they wouldn't take the contract?"

"Many of their upper echelon would not agree to it. Apparently they have a respect for Judge McDunn, which some of us wouldn't understand, Sir."

"Respect my ass."

Exactly my point, asshole, Gyrene almost smiled listening to his thought.

"Whatever. Now we need to clean up the mess, and we damn well better get our money back from the AKs. If they don't want to give it back we will do a full-court press and kill as many as we can in a morning raid. We'll look like the good guys for going after the gang who went after a judge. On second thought, when I go back, I'll start working on a plan to use SWAT teams to do just that, and keep you guys out of it."

Chamberlain pulled out his cell phone and typed notes to himself.

"Since we did not get the outcome we wanted, we need to look elsewhere. We can't attack the judge directly any time soon so find others to go after. We need him to raise the white flag by stepping down."

"What are you saying?" Gyrene asked.

"Find other people to take out. Go after his girlfriend, go after his administrative assistant, hell I don't care who it is. All I care about is the judge mentally surrendering and realizing we won."

After Chamberlain left, Gyrene went to the coffee pot. He no longer wanted to be part of SDM. Still, he knew what would happen to him if anyone found out. He took his time with the coffee, making sure to calm himself down. He needed the time to prepare a face to show he was ready to get down to business.

"Okay gentlemen, you heard the man," Gyrene said. "I'm of the opinion if we go after Judge McDunn's family members we will draw excessive heat. Whereas, if we do like the boss suggested, maybe not. We can send some of us after the judge's admin assistant at the same time some go after his girlfriend, especially since she's been digging around trying to get dirt on us. If we take her out, we send a message not only to the judge, we also send one to all the filth out there as to how we will take care of any snitch wanting to give info to the likes of her."

"I'll take care of her," OM volunteered, the corners of his lips turning up in an evil smile. A few laughed knowing OM's love for hurting females.

"I get the impression it wouldn't be quick and painless," Shooter said.

"Oh, hell no," OM replied. "There would be pain involved."

"Rook, you've been following her the most. What are your thoughts on how we do it?" Gyrene asked.

Caught off guard, Rook's eyes jetted around the room. They had never asked his opinion about anything, much less the best way to go about attacking someone. He took a second to clear his throat.

"She goes for a run dang near every day at the same time…early morning. If we attack her in her house it kind of looks obvious. If we do it while she runs it could look like some hiding-in-the-bush rapist tried to get at her. We make it look like she gets killed trying to fight off a sexual attack."

"Damn, I like it!" Sly smiled at Rook. "I'm really impressed." Sly's eyes wandered over to see how OM was taking the new suggestion?

OM did not appear to be pleased.

"Man, I know you wanted to bring her back here to torture her, but the kid's got a pretty good plan, especially since it could be any attacker."

OM grunted walking toward the coffee pot. He kept shaking his head as if he could not believe they were going to defer to a snot-nosed rookie over him.

"Does she ever run anywhere remote or is it all on the roads?" Sly asked.

"Oh yeah, going or coming, and sometimes both, she uses a canal bank near her home," Rook elaborated. "Lots of trees and brush, plus those are mini-ranches so the houses are not right next to the canal."

"Wait a second," Sly put up his hand. All eyes were on him while he paced, something he did when he started conniving. "I think we can kill two birds with one stone, so to speak. I got a connection at UNM hospital. This might work." Sly smiled, making sure he had everyone's attention before he swaggered over to the white board to spell out his plan.

CHAPTER FORTY-ONE

When Lisa heard about the shooting, she wanted to drop what she was doing and race over to Mac's house. She did not do it, knowing she would only get as far as the rest of the press, no closer. For the first couple of hours she was beside herself, using every contact she had to see if anyone had information on whether Mac or his friend were shot, taken to the hospital, locked up in jail, anything? She tried calling his phone several times, only to get his voicemail.

Finally, she got a patrol sergeant who was one of her informants to tell her detectives had three guys in the house being questioned, but none of them had been shot. A short time later she received a text from Mac telling her he was okay. For the first time she was able to relax. Although Lisa felt she had to see for herself despite telling Mac she would not leave her office alone.

When she arrived there, the road was still blocked off and officers would not let her pass the crime scene tape. Looking down the road, the gravity of the shooting started to become reality. The front of Mac's house had numerous pockmarks from bullets and the long narrow front windows were gone. The number of yellow evidence cones caught her attention. There were more than she had ever seen at a crime scene.

Lisa called her editor to tell Mike she could not get back to the office in time to put the finishing touches on her article before the printing deadline. Mike said not to worry; they'd run it the following day if necessary. After some hesitation he suggested she try to keep her ears open to determine if there would be any way a sufficient connection could be made for her to add it to her article.

After Mac was done speaking with Sara, he spotted Lisa talking on her phone, pacing next to the crime scene tape. He had been instructed to stay close to the house, but after some sweet talking with one of the sergeants he rolled out in his wheelchair, going left away from his driveway. When he explained to the young officer standing guard how Lisa was his girlfriend, the officer allowed Lisa to go under the tape. They went to the closest driveway to get away from people so they could talk, with Mac's promise to the officer Lisa would not get any closer.

"Oh my God, are you okay?" Lisa said, tears rolling down her face as she clasped Mac's cheeks.

"We're all fine, thanks to a guy I helped years ago."

Lisa dropped to her knees and laid her head on Mac's lap. Tears took over. He stroked her hair, his eyes watering from appreciation, *I could have easily been in one of the body bags getting ready to head to the morgue.*

When Lisa lifted her head wiping her eyes with her shirt, she said, "I'm sorry, I didn't mean to cause a scene."

Mac looked into her eyes and touched her cheek.

"First Aaron…now this…I'm scared Mac."

"Me, too." Mac looked around to assess people's proximity and whether they were being watched. Once he was comfortable he lowered his voice and said, "The Syndicate put a hit out on me. SNM would not take it…in a nutshell due to the respect I showed them. Respect is everything to them. The AK's took the contract…if they had not started bragging about it and just came over they would have had us."

"So there is no way to prove The Syndicate wanted it done?"

By the look in Lisa's eyes Mac could tell she had transitioned from his emotional love to thinking like a reporter—he didn't care.

"Not really, all four are dead," he said nodding his head toward his driveway. "I'm sure the detectives could get somebody to squeal for the right incentive, but we're hearing the Chief wants the investigation to focus on us for murder and for ambushing them. AJ thinks the detectives won't work it up the way the Chief wants, but they'll have to be careful."

"Did you? Ambush them I mean."

Mac knew Lisa wanted an answer, but he also knew she wasn't his wife so she could be forced to testify. He wanted her to have plausible deniability so he sat quietly, looking into her bloodshot eyes.

"I'm glad," she said, before she laid her head back on his lap.

Lisa stayed with Mac long enough to know he was safe and she was back in control of her emotions. She kissed him goodbye and walked to her car around the corner. Pausing for a second to make sure no eyes were watching, she pulled out her phone to dial her editor.

"Is everything okay," Mike asked.

"Yes and no. None of them got shot…this time. I'm

scared for him, Mike."

Neither said anything for several seconds, the reality of the next time lingering in both of their minds.

"I've decided you're right. You have enough to get the first article out tomorrow on Kyle Lansing and Deputy Chief Chamberlain lying to the public about Lansing never hitting the streets. If you're okay with it I'm going to go try to grab a few hours of sleep. I'll come in early to put the finishing touches on the follow-up article for the next day."

"I'm good with it. But Lisa, I think we ought to get someone to stay with you…for protection."

"Thanks, Mike, but that's not happening. You know how I feel about special treatment. Besides, they're after Mac, not me. I'll just grab a couple hours of sleep and I'll be in the office where you can keep an eye on me," she said, feigning a chuckle.

"I'm serious, please be careful. Who knows what those assholes will do."

"I will, Mike. I promise."

Mike's words resonated with Lisa all the way home. She drove slower, changed her route and constantly checked her mirrors. Feeling certain she was not being followed, she turned onto her street and crept along well under the speed limit, scanning all the driveways and cars to make sure they belonged. Convinced nothing was out of place, she pulled into her driveway. Lisa texted Mike to let him know she made it home before she went inside. In less than ten minutes she was lying in bed, physically, mentally and emotionally drained. Sleep arrived almost the instant she closed her eyes.

CHAPTER FORTY-TWO

It was close to three-thirty in the morning when the last of the evidence technicians drove away from Mac's house. Overcome with sadness by the murder of a good friend, Ralph had drifted to being alone with his thoughts as the evening drew on. Not surprisingly he didn't waste any time heading to his car in the neighbor's driveway.

Mac wanted to make the judicial commission come after him, unwilling to roll over to make their decision easier. He decided to go to work with confidence, to show not only the commission, but the justice system and all who were watching he had done nothing beyond defend himself and his property within his constitutional right to do so. He knew there would be future fallout with decisions to be made on how the system would proceed, especially with regards toward defendants belonging to the AKs. All of it would happen in due time, for now he simply wanted to get to the office.

While Mac went through the arduous task of bathing and preparing for a day of work, I paced. I felt reasonably certain the AKs would not simply roll over and accept the death of four of their brothers without wanting retribution. What I counted on was the likelihood they would not do anything foolish so soon. I believed they would react like a fighter who had been knocked down. Everyone knows the fighter will get up to try again. What is often lost is the reality of how the fighter must shake off the cobwebs first.

Asian Killas needed time.

I had moved through front yards in the neighborhood, moving from shadow to shadow, pausing to make sure I was not being watched. It was my belief SDM would stop at nothing and it had been solidified by their willingness to do whatever it took to keep control, along with greasing the political futures of those giving the orders.

My phone dinged with a text.

> *You up for coffee? Same place we met after the non-suicide?*

My curiosity was piqued, and not only for fresh brewed coffee.

I knew Mac would be leaving for the office in about ten minutes. Once I made sure he was comfortable going alone we agreed to stay in touch with a text every hour.

Returning to my phone I answered the text with a thumbs up emoji.

Walking into the restaurant, there was hardly anyone there. The number of servers to customers seemed to be two to one. Not that I was complaining since it usually meant fresh coffee at least until they started getting busy. I spotted Sara in a booth along the back wall, as far away from the front door as they would let her get.

When she turned to look at me, her face appeared expressionless. I thought I saw a hint of a smile, or maybe I was just being hopeful. *I wonder if she's changed her mind.*

"I can tell by your grin you're happy to see me," I said.

Except for the raising of one eyebrow her lack of expression barely changed. *Maybe I needed to try something else?*

"I didn't see your detective car outside. Did you park it in front of one of the stores?"

"I drove my own," she said. "I'm off duty today."

The waitress came up with a fresh pot of coffee, the steam still wafting out the top as I flipped over my cup. When I made eye contact with her, I double pumped my brows like something was seductive, making sure I let her try to figure out if it was her, the coffee, or both. The waitress grinned before she turned to leave.

Sara's lips turned up in a slight smile, even though she shook her head at me. I grinned back before I savored my first sip of morning coffee. There's something about the first sip of any drink, which feels like you've rewarded your own body, or at least your taste buds.

"I thought you could take your work vehicles everywhere, even on days off?"

"We can. If you do then you have to be available if needed. My being available to them is diminishing."

"Hmm. I thought you wanted to meet so you could tell me you changed your mind."

"No…not at all. I knew I wouldn't be able to sleep, plus I know how much you like your coffee."

"Ahh, good use of your trained observer skills." I followed the quip by pretending to take an overdramatic whiff of my coffee before I took another sip.

When Sara chuckled, I felt better. Her decision to help us seemed to be weighing heavy on her heart. Anything I could do to lighten up her mood I considered a plus.

"I have something for you." She reached into her leather folder on the seat and pulled out a sheet of paper. Glancing to her left, she made sure no eyes were watching as she handed it to me.

In one quick scan I could see two capitalized boldfaced initials, followed by an address. I counted a total of five sets of initials, the exact number of dirty cops in SDM. Folding the sheet in half, I laid it on the table close to the wall before taking another sip from my cup. Considering I did not have the names Peter gave us readily available, I felt good with a second set. Plus, the current listing included the name Kyle Lansing.

"I'm not sure what your plan is, or if you even have one. Thought we might need those at some point. I didn't put the top dogs down since they have bodyguards and chauffeurs," Sara said.

"Are you thinking any of The Syndicate might crack if we apply pressure?"

"I don't know what I'm thinking to be quite honest with you. Something told me you might want those names is all."

"I appreciate it. I can see us using the information. In your opinion, if there would be one who might give in, turn on the others, who would it be?"

Sara thought for some time while I waited sipping coffee.

"The youngest one of the group hasn't been a cop for long, he might not be as ingrained in illegality as the others. The problem with him is DC Chamberlain is his uncle and I'm pretty certain the connection is the only reason he's part of them. All the other guys have at least ten years of experience on him. Besides him, I'm really not sure."

"You realize, one way or the other, this whole thing will be over in probably seventy-two hours. Maybe less."

She nodded, turning her head to look out the window.

"You know, you don't have to do this. We have no choice,

they put a target on Mac's back. You could probably lay low for a while, let it all blow over, save your career."

Sara took more time and never looked at the waitress who returned and poured more coffee. I figured Sara was thinking about backing out. Instead, she went where I wasn't expecting.

"I've done a little digging on you, AJ. It's a little hypocritical for you to tell me I can bow out gracefully, when everything I read or heard about you would indicate you would not hesitate to do what's right regardless of the cost. In fact, you have...several times."

I leaned back into the seat, holding my hot cup in both hands, trying to take in what Sara said. I had no idea why a detective checking on my background would surprise me, but it did.

"You're right. I apologize. From now on I'll assume you are all in unless you say otherwise." I hesitated long enough to see the appreciation in her eyes.

"As a side note, Sara, I'll be picking up some guns this morning. If you plan on working with us you'll probably need one or two. The last thing you want to do is use your gun and have it traced back to you."

"You've been busy, haven't you, finding a way to get what I'm presuming are unmarked guns, in a city you are unfamiliar with," she said, with a grin.

"I've pretty much found throughout my career there are times when doing things by the book doesn't always work. I'd lump this group of cops in that category. Dirtbags... they don't generally follow the book. It's kinda like asking someone to please sit down on a search warrant when they drop the F-bomb every third word. Telling them to sit the F down works, always has, always will, even though it violates police department policies."

Sara laughed…the kind of hearty laugh sounding as if she had been transported to a real situation and she knew exactly what I was talking about.

"Now, before we go pick up those tools of the trade, I suggest we eat. Who knows when we might get the chance again?"

CHAPTER FORTY-THREE

Rook hated the idea OM would be the one hiding in the bushes on her route. It was one thing to hurt her and send her to the hospital, but as much as OM liked to rough up women, and her being the judge's girlfriend, Rook feared OM would go too far. The more Rook followed her the more he began to admire her.

Something about her told him she was strong and self-confident. He loved the fact she liked to run with her pace nearly matching his. Her strong workout ethic surpassed him since she would not miss a run in the morning regardless of how little sleep she had the night before. Rook regretted he had ever said anything to the group weeks before about her never missing a run. Thanks to Sly's memory, they were now in place…waiting for her.

Rook wished he was not so transparent. He had a feeling Sly did not trust him, as if Sly sensed Rook might be tempted to warn the woman about the impending attack. Sly had not directly said anything, but when the two of them were sitting in the car instead of one being with OM because it was technically a two-person job, Rook knew.

They parked on the same side of the road as Lisa's house, four houses down. The dirt canal she would take, if she stayed on her running schedule, started two houses west of hers. OM was in place behind a large tree less than fifty yards from the road.

Like clockwork, they saw Lisa step onto her front patio at seven minutes past five. She took a couple of minutes to get her iPhone set, her earbuds in place, and do a little stretching. She walked to the dirt shoulder of the roadway without ever looking to her left, exactly the way Rook had laid it out. They counted on her being a creature of habit.

When she took off running, Sly tapped the send button on his phone to let OM know the plan was in motion.

OM took stock of everything one last time. His dark sweats an attempt to look like a runner only proved he had no clue what runners wore that time of year. He specifically did not want to have anything extra, like a radio to weigh him down, if for some reason he would have to run to get away from some would-be hero.

Sly started the engine, creeping forward to follow her. When Lisa reached the canal she turned right heading north toward OM. Sly tapped Rook's shoulder with the back of his hand and smiled, nodding his approval of Rook's intelligence gathering. Sly sped up, then stopped on the opposite side of the entrance to the canal, leaving the engine running.

OM had positioned himself behind the tree to be able to see with one eye down the canal toward the road after he received the text message. When he saw her turn, he started moving behind the tree like a boxer getting ready to shadow box. He never got into any of the martial arts like many of his peers, all he wanted to do was punch things, preferably people's faces.

Watching Lisa progress towards him, OM realized she was making his job easy by staring down at the dirt path in front of her instead of scanning ahead. He stepped out on the path with perfect timing, startling her. Her head flew up while her hands instinctively came up in front of her as if she was going to stop something. OM threw his first punch as her eyes widened. The punch landed somewhere around the bottom of her nose, splattering blood as her head jerked back, followed by her body falling back and hitting the ground.

OM could see he stunned her as her eyes searched for focus, lacking recognition and her hands moved wildly around her face. When he started to kick her in the ribs, he failed to account for the softness of the dirt on the bank of the canal. His foot slipped causing his kick to hit her square in the hip. He had never kicked anyone wearing cheap canvas tennis shoes. The pain from his big toe breaking shot through him, almost doubling him over.

He never planned on getting hurt. His mind raced between hardly being able to stand because of the agonizing pain and finishing the job without getting caught. Finally, he focused on one thought, *Get her off the path.*

Grabbing her hair he started to drag her, the imbalance of not putting full pressure on his injured foot made it more difficult. He became aware of time, the rushed feeling inside knowing he was taking longer than anticipated. Sweat began to run from his fear, the foot injury, and the hoodie over his head. It rolled down his face settling in his eyes. He had to let go of her hair. Grabbing his hoodie with both hands, he yanked it off his head and wiped his face. He looked down to see her stirring and grabbed handfuls of her hair again and slammed her head to the ground one last time.

OM dragged her another ten feet into the shin high grass. There, he ripped away her iPhone and earbuds stuffing them in his sweatpants pocket. He grabbed her right hand and began to squeeze tightly, smiling when he could feel the breaking of bones in her fingers. Anger replaced his foot pain. He punched her in the face with both hands several more times.

The pressure of time reminded him he had to go and he started to make his way to the path. Out of pure anger, as if it were her fault his toe was throbbing, he raised his good foot and slammed the heel down on her knee. The sound of bones cracking brought another smile to his face.

He started to hobble down the path as fast as he could and stopped shy of the road, where he tried to walk straight so as not to draw attention. Opening the back door of the Tahoe, he dove in headfirst cursing and screaming.

"I broke my fucking toe."

"Close the door," Sly yelled.

"I broke my fucking toe!" OM whined again, not moving from his lying position.

Sly gave Rook a quick nod toward the back door and Rook understood. Moving forward too fast caused his seatbelt to lock up tight against his chest. He fumbled with it as panic began to build in all three of them.

"Hurry it up," Sly yelled even louder.

Rook finally got the belt unlatched, pushed open the door and stood in one fluid motion. At the same time OM half sat up, grabbed the back door and pulled it closed. Rook barely got back in his seat before Sly hit the gas and started the car rolling.

Sly kept repeating in his head to drive slowly to counter his desire to punch it, wanting to get as far away as possible. He knew they were in a portion of county territory where the Sheriff's officers loved to stop drivers who ignored the speed bumps and the flashing yellow lights. He set the cruise control at twenty-five to keep from getting in trouble.

"What the hell took you so long?" Sly asked OM.

"Are you fucking deaf? I broke my toe, Asshole."

"Did you kill her?"

"I wanted to, but I didn't. Broke a few bones since she broke my toe."

Rook did everything in his power to keep a solemn face. If Sly would look at him and catch him laughing, OM would beat the hell out of him. He breathed a sigh of relief, believing OM had killed her when he took so long.

"I'm impressed," Sly smiled as he looked at OM in the rearview mirror.

OM saw Sly's eyes in the mirror, so he yanked his head up once instead of asking why.

"First of all you didn't kill her, which I think all of us kind of expected you couldn't stop from doing. More importantly, your planning skills are fantastic."

"What the hell are you saying?" OM said, rocking in the backseat trying to stop the pain.

"Now, we get to have a person on the inside of the emergency room as a lookout. Nobody will be the wiser, all thanks to your thinking ahead to break your toe." Sly and Rook busted up laughing.

OM never said a word. He let his extended middle finger do the talking.

Fifteen minutes later they pulled up to the University of New Mexico hospital to let OM get out of the vehicle. Sly told him to call if he saw anything suspicious, or when he got released. Without any of them saying it, they all expected him to be there for several hours.

Driving away Sly called Gyrene to let him know OM was at the emergency room. He knew the call would generate another call to get an ambulance headed for Lisa after

Gyrene drove far enough away from their warehouse to use a payphone outside of some packed convenience store dealing with the early morning rush. In the meantime, Sly needed to call their contact at the hospital to get him ready.

CHAPTER FORTY-FOUR

My phone dinged with a text at six a.m.

"This may be what I've been waiting for."

Sara looked at me with questions in her eyes.

I read the text:

> *It's been arranged. Casino parking lot, west of the city, south side of the road. Old, faded Chevy van, no windows on side or back. Forty-five minutes. More than ten minutes late the deal is off. All cash.*

The cash only I expected. The minimal time surprised me.

"Let's go. We don't have much time."

"Where are we going?" Sara asked.

"To the casino west of town. We have forty-five minutes to get there."

"Christ, AJ. I'm not sure we can make it."

I threw two twenties on the table to cover our meals, with a big tip since I didn't have time to wait for change.

"My car, in case something goes wrong," I said.

Sara seemed fine with it, not really wanting to put herself in the middle of questions as to why she would be speeding in her car if we got caught.

Neither of us said much until we started crossing the Rio Grande River on I-40. Sara could not stand the silence any longer.

"You're killing me, AJ. Talk to me."

When I looked over, her wide eyes stared at me.

I smiled.

"What's wrong? The cop in you can't stand not knowing every detail?"

Sara smacked my right arm and I grinned. There's a difference between a smack of anger or frustration as compared to being comfortable with the person to do so. Sara's happened to be the latter.

"Resorting to abusing an old former cop?"

"Yeah, right," she said. "From what I could tell last night, you're not old, at least not until you pass forty."

The tone in her voice sounded more matter-of-fact than complimentary. Still, I liked hearing it.

"So, when we get there, we're looking for an old Chevy van. I'll get out, you slide across to the driver's seat. If all hell breaks out, you punch it and get out of there. No questions asked. No sense in both of us dying."

"You expecting trouble?"

"No. Not really…guess I'm used to thinking of worst-case scenario. Then if worst-case doesn't happen…it's a positive outcome."

I looked over with a smile. Sara grinned, shaking her head.

We pulled into the casino parking lot with five minutes to spare. Right about then I appreciated the car I'd rented. We eyed the van in the northeast corner, the nearest car over half the parking lot away. I coasted to a stop a good fifty yards away and put the car in park, but left the engine running. One quick glance at Sara, followed by a deep breath, and I stepped from the car while Sara gracefully slid over the console before I closed the door.

Nobody occupied the front seats of the van, although I did pick up some movement in the back. Instinctively, my forearm touched my gun on my hip.

When I got within fifteen feet of the van the side door slid open and a male voice from inside spoke up, "Get in."

I moved more cautiously, out of instinct and training. He had the tactical advantage, looking from a dark van out into the morning light. The best I could tell he was alone… unless they were hugged up against the back-corner wall of the open side door.

At the door, I did one quick scan before I looked over my shoulder toward Sara. As I stepped inside, the guy slid the door closed behind me. He wore long cargo pants, a plain dark hoodie with it pulled up over his head, and some kind of dark bandana across his face. I could see he was a white guy or maybe a Mexican…definitely not black or oriental. I did not detect an accent hearing his few words. Although, I did detect his nervousness topping the charts.

"You have to know I'm a former cop, so why are you taking the risk?"

You could have heard a pin drop while the guy assessed it all in his mind, probably for the millionth time. We both knew if I did him *wrong* his new home would be at a federal prison till he was old and gray. Up to then he had not committed a crime that I knew of, and I had yet to see a weapon, outside of the crates at the very back of the van behind him.

"My reasons don't really matter now, do they? You fuck me and no prosecutor is going to give a second thought as to why I'm doing it. They'd still throw the book at me. Let's leave it at…the judge did me a solid once, so I figure if you are willing to take on The Syndicate as a former cop, the judge must mean something to you, too."

We weren't there to bro hug or share stories so nothing else needed to be said. We both knew we had one bit of common ground…Mac.

I showed him my left palm, then slowly reached inside my jacket trying to only use my thumb and forefinger. We may have come to a meeting of the minds, but any quick movement would no doubt result in a gunfight. I grabbed the cash, slowly pulling it out to show him.

"What all do you want…I ain't got nothing fancy?"

"I don't need fancy, I need dependable. Easy to hide, easy to toss if I have to. With two exceptions."

He turned his head, looking at me out of one squinted eye.

"First, I want a twelve-gauge pump shotgun…and second, I need any ammo you have for anything I purchase. The last thing I need is my face plastered on some video in a gun store buying ammo."

"Hell, if that's all your worried about I got you covered. As long as you got the cash."

Fifteen minutes later, I slid open the side door, hung out far enough to wave Sara to pull up. She brought the car up alongside the van and jumped out. Popping the trunk, she kept her head turned away from the van so the guy could not see her as he handed me the merchandise.

"Thanks for your help," I said, extending my hand.

He looked down at my hand for a good five seconds before he slowly grabbed my hand. The wariness for him to shake a cop's hand radiated through his grip.

"Don't like cops and despise dirty fucking cops. All's I can say…hope you kill the motherfuckers. Might help change my mind about some of you."

I doubt it. I gave one quick nod to acknowledge him.

He slid the door closed and drove the van away before I

closed the trunk. When Sara and I got inside, neither of us said a word for several minutes while I gave the guy time to get some distance between us.

CHAPTER FORTY-FIVE

Gerald Brownley had twice given *The Voice*, as he called it, information on drug dealers in exchange for cash. He and his wife were both trying to go straight, hoping they could get out from under the grasp of methamphetamine. Gerald never figured out how *The Voice* got their names or information. Although, he did wonder if it came from the one time they shared personal information at Narcotics Anonymous.

They had amassed a substantial debt when at its peak all their money went for meth. Neither of their parents would help them financially, fearing the money would somehow be used for more meth. Along with telling them no, they reminded them how they had been *raised better than that*. When the opportunity arose with *The Voice*, cash for information seemed like a no brainer.

As a nursing assistant at the University of New Mexico Hospital Emergency Room, Gerald had unofficial access to information by scanning a chart when no one was looking, or by listening to the medical staff talk to one another. He knew his job was in jeopardy for HIPAA violations if he ever shared the information improperly, but they needed the cash.

His wife was a cashier at a convenience store making almost as much money as Gerald, putting them at slightly above poverty level. They struggled month-to-month, even after *The Voice* paid them for their previous information and had been able to pay off one of the four credit cards they had maxed out. When payment was due, *The Voice* called Gerald, who would tell him where the envelope with cash would be hidden, along with a specific time to pick it up. *The Voice* made sure Gerald knew they were dead if they ever showed up early.

The ringtone of the TV singing competition for *The Voice* erupted on Gerald's phone.

"A woman's coming to the ER right now. Her name is Lisa Stevens, a reporter for the Journal. I'll pay you twenty-five grand if you get this right."

25Gs was more than the two previous payouts combined. "Holy crap," Gerald said. "I don't have to do anything illegal…do I?"

"No. Nothing! All you have to do is tell Sam McDunn, a physical therapist there, you think his brother's girlfriend is in the ER. Stay with him as he goes down there, make sure he calls his brother, Judge McDunn. When he starts to make the call, offer to meet the judge in the ER parking lot so he can go right in through the ambulance entrance with Sam while you park his car."

"That's it, nothing else?"

"One more thing, you park his car in one of the handicap spots since that's what he'd do. Listen closely, you make sure you do not, I repeat *do not lock it.* You go in the ER, you give one of them the keys then go about your business. Simple as that."

"What are you going to do with the car?" The words rolled out of Gerald's mouth before he could stop them. "Sorry, sorry, sorry, it's none of my business. I don't know why I asked. Really, I am sorry."

"You just lost five grand for stupidity. You ever ask a

question like that again we'll *Kill You!* You *got* that?"

"Yes, yes, it will never happen again." Gerald could feel his hands shaking.

"And, if we even think you might have shared any information with the wrong people, we'll make sure your eyes watch what we do to your crank whore wife while she begs for mercy before we kill the both of you."

Gerald heard the familiar sound ending the call. *Oh my God, what did I get us into*?

He went inside and tried to feign being busy, waiting for the ambulance. The sweat appearing on his forehead would not stop, no matter how many times he wiped it. When the ambulance arrived, the female was rushed in on a gurney along with the chaos when a serious case arrived. The commotion allowed Gerald the chance to race to the elevator. When he got off on the second floor, he hurried to find Sam.

Gerald had already thought about the risk of how he knew who Mac's girlfriend was, given they did not work in the same area. Blurting it out was his only choice, then pray for the *shock effect.*

"Sam, Sam, you need to get to the ER quick. The ambulance brought in a woman who the medics say works for the Journal. I think she might be the Judge's girlfriend."

Sam did not hesitate sprinting to the elevator. When he saw the car was sitting on Floor Five he raced to the stairwell and bounded down the staircase. They barely made it through the main hallway door when Gerald and Sam saw a group frantically working on a blond-haired woman in Trauma Room Two.

"It's her, isn't it?" Gerald turned to Sam.

When Sam nodded, his pale face told Gerald he was almost in shock.

"You need to call your brother," Gerald said, trying to act

like he somehow knew the two were dating. He was glad to see Sam frozen in shock, knowing his mind would focus on important things, not wonder how Gerald knew anything.

"Sam, you need to call your brother," Gerald repeated.

"You're right," Sam said, turning to head for the doors, pulling out his cell phone in the main hallway.

Gerald followed. "Tell him to pull up to the ambulance entrance, I'll wait for him there. He can go in and I'll park his car for him so it's easier. You can go inside and give them information about her to start the paperwork."

Sam zoned for three seconds before nodding. He touched the green icon on his phone screen to favorites and then his brother's name. Seconds later, he was speaking with Mac.

When Gerald heard Sam explain it exactly like Gerald did to him he closed his eyes. *Thank God!*

"He's in blue scrubs, my height, and has dark hair. He'll show you where to go," Sam explained. "Just get here, quick." Sam put his phone back in his pocket, took a deep breath, and turned to Gerald.

"He drives a Lexus SUV, beige…or tan…whatever." Sam turned, hustling back through the doors and into Emergency Room Two.

Gerald waited outside, knowing he had to be out of sight or someone from one of the trauma rooms would yank him inside to assist. Fortunately, he did not have to wait long before the tan Lexus stopped right in front of him. Gerald ran around the car as the driver's door flew open.

"Judge McDunn, I'm so sorry. You need to go through the automatic doors over there," he pointed. "The first double doors to your right will get you to the trauma center. She's in room two, it's on your right also."

"Thank you…?"

"Gerald."

"Thank you, Gerald," Mac began to swing his shorter leg so the brace would lock. He extended his crutches to intentionally increase his pace.

Gerald jumped in the driver's seat and drove through the covered area, his head turned away from the building in case someone might be watching. He turned left, went one block and parked in a handicap spot on the ground floor of the hospital's multi-story garage catty-corner to the emergency room.

Nearly done, his hands began shaking again as he sat in the car trying to gain control. He had *one more thing to do*. Taking two deep breaths he got out and made sure all doors were unlocked. He acted as if he only checked the door handles in case thieves lurked in the shadows.

The Voice will blame me if the damn car gets stolen. He tried to amble through the garage as if he belonged, but once outside he ran across to the ER.

Walking through the double doors, he saw the two brothers standing outside of Trauma Room Two.

When Sam saw him, Gerald walked over and handed the car keys to him. Gerald settled for placing his hand on Sam's shoulder instead of small talk. Sam nodded and turned back to the trauma room as Gerald took a few steps back, then nearly ran to the staff locker room area.

Pushing the door open, he dropped to his knees and threw up in the toilet. He got to the sink and splashed cold water on his face before staring at his reflection.

He felt disgusted with the person looking back at him. *How am I supposed to ever look Sam in the face again*?

CHAPTER FORTY-SIX

Sam, texted me to say Lisa had been attacked while running. She'd been taken to the emergency at UNM hospital where he worked, letting me know she looked bad and Mac had just arrived a few minutes ago.

"What's wrong?" Sara asked me.

When I didn't answer fast enough, she repeated, "AJ... what happened?"

"They attacked Mac's girlfriend. She's at the ER in bad shape."

When she said we should go there, I wondered if we should or not? It felt like an unanswerable question. "I don't think so. At least not directly to the emergency room."

"I don't get it, what are you saying?" Her eyebrows almost touched.

"I can't explain it. All I know is I have this terrible gut feeling. I'm sure they enjoyed hurting Lisa, but it feels as if she's only the bait...otherwise they would have killed her. Right?"

Her little nod told me she agreed, although she never said it.

"I don't have a feel for it yet...maybe she's the bait to see what kind of car I arrive in at the ER, or maybe to set up Mac... or both. I'm not sure, all I know is we need to be careful."

"Okay. So, if you're right we need to do some recon...take a look around. If we feel nothing's up...we go check on her."

I took a deep breath. "All right, if you were them and she is the bait, what would your next move be?"

She reflected for close to a minute, her eyes staring outside at nothing.

"It's pretty clear the judge is their priority, now that the attorney's been eliminated and the councilwoman silenced."

"Agreed, and…?"

"They have to know the judge will be at the hospital for a long time." She paused as if she needed to piece it together, so I waited.

She finally said, "I would look for his car."

"Okay, why?" I sensed we were thinking alike.

"It's not like they're beyond killing him, if last night is any indication. For some reason, they do not want to do it themselves."

I could see she seemed unsure…and she wanted to say something but at the same time she didn't. If my instincts were correct she hated the reality of what she needed to say. Most investigators who've done it long enough come across one dirty case where they must go after someone they knew or trusted. It is a sickening feeling at best.

"Sara, your skills as an investigator are exceptional. You're on to something here…trust your instincts."

Her lips flattened when she nodded. I saw the appreciation in her eyes.

"Last night, the Chief made a comment about the judicial commission, as if he would use them to silence Judge McDunn. Killing the judge so close to an attack would draw heat…silencing him through the commission wouldn't."

I smiled, appreciating a good investigative mind at work.

"What? Did I say something funny?"

"Not at all. I'm simply appreciating how you're working

through this. You're doing great, really, keep going."

"I'm thinking they know he'll be away from his car for quite a while. If I couldn't kill him I'd want to set him up… so I would do it with contraband. Then I could have any cop pull him over at my direction. It would lessen the attention on The Syndicate, along with bringing an immediate response from the commission."

"Sara, I'm impressed. Seriously."

Her smile and slight shrug told me she appreciated the compliment.

"Guess we should see if we can spot any black Tahoes near the hospital."

"One more thing," she stopped to make sure she had my attention. "You had a gut feeling, well so do I. Mine is, they are going to come after you to kill you, there's nothing political about you so they don't have to tip toe around. They could dump you out on the mesa when they're through with you."

I had to give her credit—she had no problem telling it like it is.

"Good thing we're going after them first," I said with a big smile hoping to relax her while at the same time hiding my own fear.

I listened to Sara's suggestions on the best way to remain stealth as we approached UNM Hospital ER. We parked the car two blocks south of Lomas Boulevard and gradually worked north towards the ambulance entrance. On opposite sides of the street we could look down to the reasonably heavy traffic flow on Lomas.

Sara spotted movement to her right on the ground floor of the hospital parking structure. She turned in time to see the front end of a black Tahoe exiting the covered area.

Letting out a low whistle, she ducked behind a parked car. When I looked her way, she put two fingers near her eyes and then pointed down to the garage.

When I saw the Tahoe, I knelt behind the parked car in front of me and watched as the dark vehicle slowly exited the parking area and went south. I felt certain they would not leave the general area, so we had to be careful. We stood and came together in the alcove of a door to a business.

"Where is handicapped parking in there?" I asked, pointing to the garage.

"First level, very close to where the Tahoe exited the garage."

"That's what I figured. Maybe we need to work our way into the parking garage, see if they are also watching his car from the inside."

"That might be tricky," Sara said. "We kind of have to expose ourselves walking in there and they'd spot your car approaching the entrance."

"I've got an idea."

CHAPTER FORTY-SEVEN

"I didn't think she'd go running this morning since she got home so late last night," Mac commented.

"You can't blame yourself," Sam said. "I can hear it in your voice."

Mac looked at his brother with tears in his eyes. He knew Sam was right, although it did nothing to ease the ache in his heart from feeling differently.

"I texted AJ but he never responded. I haven't called anyone yet. Is there someone you want me to get ahold of, while you stay here?"

"Mary will want to be here, and Alex…I left before he got to the office. Tell him his family could be in danger and to take them where we discussed." Mac stared into the room at Lisa while the frantic work kept going on around her now oblivious to him.

Sam turned to leave, pulling out his cell phone.

"Hey Sam," Mac called, still not taking his eyes off Lisa. "From your office phone, not your cell. Thank you."

Sam looked at Mac, his brows scrunched together. He shrugged, put his phone back in his pocket and walked through the door into the hallway.

Gyrene's phone rang as he shook his head seeing

Chamberlain's name on the cell screen. He let it ring five times before he answered, partially out of disgust for the caller, partially to get in a *dig.*

"What took you so long?" Chamberlain wanted to know.

Gyrene didn't answer.

"So, where are we? You haven't done anything yet, have you?"

"Yeah, she's been taken care of, she's in the ER at UNM."

"Shit! Don't you guys think for yourselves?" Chamberlain sounded disgusted.

Gyrene chose not to say a word, knowing if he did…it would lack any semblance of respect. The Marines taught him to bite his tongue when ranking officers were assholes.

"You haven't seen the paper this morning…have you?" Chamberlain asked, although it sounded as if he already knew the answer. "The bitch has an article, front page, directed at me for using guys like Kyle Lansing after I told the press we wouldn't."

What a dumb ass, Gyrene thought. *Good, I'm glad.*

"There are supposed to be follow-up articles she's written about police corruption…A Damn Series."

"Nothing we can do about it now," Gyrene's voice held a slight condescending tone.

"Bullshit! We need to lay low. If there is even a hint we had anything to do with putting her in the hospital we go down in flames. All of us."

He just admitted he would roll on us, Gyrene thought. *You fucking weasel.*

"They're going to print the rest of the stuff no matter what. Unless…"

"Unless?" Chamberlain blurted out, a ray of hope in his voice. "Tell me."

"I'm thinking we should let the whole thing go down with the judge. He gets popped by a patrol cop transporting the package, now she's the one having to justify stuff, given she's been sleeping with a dirty judge." He paused to the count of three for effect. "It would bring her credibility into question. Maybe they hold off printing the next article needing time to think about their trust issue with her."

The silence told him Chamberlain liked it, so he decided to take it further.

"This way, you only have to take on the one issue of putting veteran cops back on the streets, you know, for the public's safety after they proved they deserved another shot. Those follow-up articles might never be published if we kill the judge's credibility which kills hers."

"I think you're onto something here. I need some time to run through it all. He isn't going to leave anytime soon so I should have time." Chamberlain's tone changed back to being authoritative when he said, "If his car moves before I get back to you nothing happens without my authorization. You understand, Sergeant?"

"Got it," Gyrene said, intentionally not showing respect by calling him *Sir.*

The prick knows it's a good idea, he only wants time to make sure he can come out clean, Gyrene thought.

CHAPTER FORTY-EIGHT

I dialed Mac's sister home phone. I knew Mary would head to the hospital the instant she heard about Lisa, so hearing her answer the phone surprised me.

"Have you heard about Lisa?"

"Yes, Sam called. I'm getting ready to go there now."

"I'm wondering if you could do me a favor."

"Of course." She took me up on it without one second of hesitation. Mary would do almost anything to help someone in need; even if it were a little risky.

I explained the situation to her, along with Sara and me believing Mac may be getting set up. Even though Mary ranked in the top three most caring people I knew, she does not mess around when it comes to protecting family. I gave her the intersection and she agreed to be there in fifteen minutes.

When Mary arrived Sara sat up front and I sat in the back, although I positioned myself lying across the back seat. Mary handed each of us a ball cap to help hide our identity. She also had one of her husband's suit jackets on the back seat along with an old pair of reading glasses.

Mary drove around the corner, crossed Lomas Boulevard, heading to the main entrance. She parked, turned off the engine, and adjusted the rearview mirror so she could look at me.

"You're not going to do anything stupid are you, like get yourself killed?"

"I don't know…I do stupid pretty well."

"You always have," she said. "Good thing we were there for you when you were growing up to save you from yourself." She smiled as Sara chuckled.

"Love you, too," I said, knowing she did not want to let me know how frightened she really felt.

"Seriously, what are you going to do?"

"Look, you really don't want to know, please trust me on this. The last thing I would want is for you to have to get on the stand someday to tell them what I tell you. As far as you know I am simply borrowing your car."

"You're scaring me. Could you really be killed?"

I put my hand on her right shoulder and looked her in the eyes through the mirror.

"In case they have someone planted inside, we want them to think I'm gone. Make sure you speak in a normal tone when you tell your brothers I am at the airport ready to board a plane to Denver and won't be coming to the hospital. Then quietly get Mac to the side and tell him *not* to get into his car until he gets a call from an unknown number…I'll hang up on the second ring. Once he receives it, he must go to his car and drive toward his house."

A tear began to form in the corner of Mary's eye. I smiled, winked and gave her a little side nod, she understood. Opening her door, she stepped out.

I watched her wipe her eyes before she took off.

Sara had mapped out the locations where she would park to do surveillance on the parking garage. We figured we would try those first and then do a grid search if it didn't work. We had no clue what to expect, but we agreed neither of us would assign more than one car with a couple cops to watch in order for my car to arrive or Mac's car to leave.

We found the Tahoe in the third location Sara suggested. Mary had brought us a pair of binoculars her father owned. When I picked them up a strange flood of emotions overcame me.

"You all right?" Sara asked.

I nodded. "Just thinking about their dad. These were his, we used them on hikes when we were kids. My dad died when I was two…their dad treated me like one of his kids."

Sara cocked her head to the side and her cheeks raised. Neither of us said anything, although I sensed she had a new appreciation for why I'd be willing to do what had to be done.

We parked where we could peer inside the windshield since all the vehicles other windows had been tinted extremely dark.

Sara recognized the two occupants: Trevor Johnson, the DC's nephew in the passenger seat, and Jerry Bodner behind the wheel. She said Bodner had a reputation of messing with people he did not like, either physically, lying in a report, or planting evidence.

"Sounds like the perfect fit for a bunch hell-bent on corruption."

"Unfortunately!" Sara agreed.

"They look pretty kick back, as if they aren't expecting anything to happen anytime soon."

"So, now what?" Sara asked.

"Now we go park in the garage so we can do some recon, make sure nobody is inside watching Mac's car."

"That would be a waste of personnel, I mean, Mac would have to exit the one place they already have eyes on."

"You willing to go straight up to his car then?"

Sara thought for a second. "Maybe a quick scan."

I smiled, prompting her to hit my arm yet again.

After we parked on the third level, we made our way down the stairs to the ground floor. It didn't take long before we felt comfortable…nobody had been placed inside.

When we got to Mac's car, I couldn't see the flashing red light for the alarm, although I checked the driver's door and it was locked. Having been in Mac's car with him, I knew he always alarmed it so we started looking for anything out of place. Sara even got down to look underneath to make sure a bomb had not been planted. I looked through the front driver's window at about the same time Sara looked inside from the passenger side.

"AJ, down there," she pointed to the floorboard behind the front seats.

I walked to her side and sitting in plain sight was what looked like a brick of cocaine, directly behind the driver's seat. Easy to spot, more than enough probable cause to search the vehicle.

"The lame asses!" I shook my head.

Sara looked at me with wide eyes as if she had no clue what I meant.

"They obviously didn't spend any time evaluating and thoroughly understanding the subject of their mission."

"What the hell?" Sara said, shaking her head.

"They only thought about what they wanted to do, not about who they were doing it to. Mac uses crutches. If they had watched him at all they would know he needs to put his crutches somewhere when he gets into his car. He always sits, puts the crutches behind the driver's seat, and then swings his legs inside. He'd see the brick before he ever started the car. And since they're outside waiting for him to come out, Mac could have dumped it under a car in here. They're not thinkers…they're thugs."

"So, how do you really feel?" Sara asked, with a huge smile on her face.

"These boys need a taste of their own medicine." I took a deep breath to try to calm down before I looked at her. "Sara, I have to ask…."

Her hand shot up in front of my face. "I'm in, all the way. Quit asking."

CHAPTER FORTY-NINE

Sara and I crossed Lomas Boulevard, running hand-in-hand, like a couple hurrying to the emergency room to find out the bad news. Once inside the waiting room we shed the caps and stuffed them in my jacket pocket. We approached the guard at the door leading to the ER hallway and flashed our badges, making sure Sara took the lead so he would see the APD badge first and wave us through.

We walked through the double doors like all cops do when they work on follow up. Emergency rooms are usually so busy the doctors and nurses don't have time to check everyone. Acting like you know what you are doing, like you belong, usually draws a free pass.

Sam, Mac and Mary stood in front of us, all three hugged up next to the trauma room door to stay out of the way of personnel. My guess was Sam being an employee and Mac being a judge were the reasons they got to stand there instead of being told to stay in the waiting room.

When they saw me, I did a quick nod so they'd follow. We found a cubbyhole of space inside the empty casting room. Sara stood by the door acting as lookout while I explained the brick we found in Mac's car.

"That little weasel," Sam spoke up.

We all looked at him, none of us having any idea where his comment came from.

"Gerald Brownley…he wanted to help by parking Mac's car. He works here, he's the one who came to get me…told me Lisa had been brought in by ambulance."

"Now we know these guys have moles so we need to be careful. As far as the weasel goes, you need to let it go for now. We can bust his chops later, but for now, we need to go after the main players."

Sam shook his head in disgust, Gerald playing him the way he did. I figured Sam would put his black belt skills to use when the time came.

"AJ, take a look at this," Sara said.

When I walked up beside her she pointed to the patient status board on the wall across from us. The name in the slot for room four read BRSA.

"I overheard two people in scrubs mention the guy in that room was a cop with a broken big toe waiting for a surgeon. They were laughing about him doing it while he was out jogging."

"Sam, what does the BRSA mean?" I pointed at the board.

"Initials. First two of the first name and first two of the last name. It's a HIPAA violation to put names anymore."

I turned to Sara and asked, "What're the odds he's here by coincidence?"

When Sara shook her head I knew she agreed this was no coincidence.

Sam explained the information board as basically charting progression of care so any medical personnel could take a quick look and know the status of the patient. He explained to me Brody had some kind of a fracture to his big toe and he had an IV line in but he wasn't on a cardiac monitor. Sam said the IV most likely meant Brody had been given some pain medication, standard for the pain from a broken big toe. He also pointed out one of the surgeons had been notified for a consult on whether Sachs needed surgery or not. The surgeon hadn't arrived yet so Sachs sat in a holding pattern, likely enjoying his pain meds.

"Can you get me a lab jacket and a large syringe?" I asked Sam. When they all looked at each other I could see the questions were about to come racing at me.

"Don't ask, Sam. If you're uncomfortable with this I understand. I can go find them on my own."

Sam looked over at Mac and Mary and said, "Be back in a second."

I convinced Mac and Mary to go back to where they had been standing and not to leave. Mac handed his car keys to Sara before they left. I spotted latex glove packs on the wall, grabbed a pair and put them on before stuffing several other pairs in my pockets. Sara and I formulated a plan before Sam got back so he didn't hear any of it. Returning, he handed over the items and went back to stand by his siblings.

I slipped the lab coat over my suit jacket, put the reading glasses on the tip of my nose and walked towards BRSA's room.

His eyes were closed at first. When he did open them, I could see he never focused on my face and clearly wasn't feeling any pain.

I patted him on the shoulder. "The surgeon will be here shortly, just checking on your IV. Need to make sure, Brody Sachs, correct?"

His head raised slightly and nodded.

"That's what the chart says. Perfect. Lay back and relax, Brody."

He laid his head back on the pillow and closed his eyes.

When Sara started to enter I held up my hand, pointing to Brody letting her know she need not distract him—his pain meds were enough distraction. Backing out of the doorway, she stood guard by it for me.

"You work for APD?"

Brody's eyes opened half-way as he nodded.

"I have a good friend who does also," I said, looking up at Sara.

Brody closed his eyes and turned his head away from me as if he didn't really care.

Ripping open the 60cc syringe, I removed the plastic cover. I drew back the plunger to fill it with air and screwed it in the needleless port on the IV tubing. Having seen nurses pinch off the tubing of my IV's above the injection port, I did the same. I jammed the entire 60cc of air in knowing it would cause an embolus and throw him into cardiac arrest. Since he didn't have any cardiac monitor leads, no one would be alerted and he'd lay there dead until the surgeon arrived. I unscrewed the syringe, started to put the cap back on and stopped…again drew back the plunger, screwed it on, pinched off the tube and slammed in one more bolus of air.

"That's for Aaron Vasquez," I whispered.

I put the syringe in the SHARPS container on the wall, then grabbed his cell phone out of his pants set on the chair. As I walked out, I made sure no one was looking before I pulled off the lab jacket, wadded it up and put it in the dirty laundry basket full of bed linen, stuffing it under the top sheet. Sara and I walked past the McDunn's without a word as I put my latex gloves inside my pants pocket. We went through the two sets of doors back into the waiting room where we donned our caps once again.

We took a seat so I could send a text. I pulled out Brody's phone and went to messages.

"How'd you get past his password?" Sara asked.

"Before I left his room I used his thumb. Then I went into settings and disabled it. He didn't seem to mind." I shrugged and Sara laughed.

They gave me pain drugs. Still be awhile. Need to see surgeon.

"You think he might have been the one to attack Lisa?" she asked.

"With a broken toe requiring a surgeon to come look at it, and him coming in roughly at the same time she arrived... I'd say yes. For the beating she took I sure hope she was the cause of his pain."

"At some point they're going to find out he didn't send a message, then they'll ping his phone," Sara said. "Why don't we put it near where the judge's car is parked?"

"Good idea. I don't think they'll realize he didn't send it until after we have the judge drive out."

"You're setting them up, aren't you?"

"Hoping to. I'd like to take care of one more before we do it though."

I explained what I needed Sara to do before we left the waiting room. Leaving, I put my arm around her and she leaned her head on my shoulder trying to appear to be crying, the perfect distraught couple who got terrible news in the ER.

Inside the parking garage we went to the area near Mac's car. I scrolled through the contacts on Brody's phone until I found Kyle Lansing's information. Bodner seemed like the logical choice to go after first, but he sat in the Tahoe less than two blocks away, so I had to go elsewhere. Ever since I heard the radio DJ's talking about what Kyle did to the unarmed Mexican man, I had a serious dislike for him.

I had no idea where Kyle would be, but I hoped he and the last member of the group might be home since these three were likely the ones who went after Lisa. If I was right, we could even the playing field a little more. If not, we'd make the next phone call and go there.

I wouldn't say I expected a quick response, or one at all for that matter. I put the phone in my pocket as Sara pushed the FOB to unlock Mac's car. I put on a pair of the latex gloves preparing for Brody's phone to ding.

Without prompting, Sara took a pair of the gloves as I opened the text and read: *Enjoy them. I can't believe you let that chick hurt you. You must be getting old, LOL. Heading home. Sarge put me on call.*

Showing Sara the text, she raised her eyebrows, surprised by our luck.

It's about time something went our way!

CHAPTER FIFTY

My phone rang displaying Celia's name. I sent it straight to voice mail knowing we needed to get out of the garage before someone thought we were suspicious.

Once Sara picked up the brick of cocaine, I closed up Mac's car and locked it. We waited for three people walking toward the exit to get out of sight before we took off for the stairs. I popped the trunk on Mary's car before we reached it and Sara seemed relieved once she dropped it in the trunk and pushed the lid closed.

We drove to the front of the hospital. Sara went inside alone to let Mac know we got the brick and explain the plan. We knew there would be some risk to Mac, politically as well as physically. We needed him to buy in before we went any further. I decided to use Sara's phone to make the next call.

I looked on line for the Albuquerque Journal, dialed and asked to speak with Lisa's boss. The secretary put me on hold for close to two minutes. Returning, she asked my name and the reason for my call.

"I'm a friend of Judge McDunn's…something happened to Lisa."

She put me on hold right away, never asking my name again–not that I would have given it to her.

"This is Mike. Who are you?" he demanded to know.

"So you know I'm not BSing you, we had a shootout at

McDunn's last night where four AKs were killed. Lisa came to the area to talk with us and make sure Mac was okay."

"Okay, that's a good start. Now, Lisa. What happened?"

"She got attacked early this morning. She's in critical condition at UNM hospital ER...Mac's there now."

"You think it has to do with the article?"

"What article? I haven't had the time to look at any newspaper."

"We ran the first in a series she worked on. This part had to do with Deputy Chief Chamberlain's promise a few years ago not to put certain officers back on the street, like Kyle Lansing. The article mentions both of them."

"I don't believe so, but I'm not positive. I think we need to meet...I might need your help."

The silence lasted long enough where I started to get uncomfortable.

"Okay. But we will only meet in a public place."

"How's three hours from now at the Starbucks across from the Journal building?"

"I'll be there. I'm wearing a blue and white striped shirt, I have short dark hair, and reading glasses around my neck."

Right then, the passenger door opened and Sara got in the car.

"There's two of us, one's a female. See you then." I hung up.

Sara did the pantomime, show of hands and quick head jerk, asking who had I been talking with.

"Lisa's boss at the Journal."

She raised her eyebrows and stared.

"Thought he might want to know Lisa had been attacked... plus I think we might need his help later. He agreed to meet us in three hours, by his office. He mentioned an article came out this morning regarding Chamberlain and Kyle

Lansing, the first part in a series Lisa had been working on."

"I don't think they even saw the article, otherwise it implicates them as possible suspects."

"I agree. What did Mac say?"

"He said he needed time to talk it over with Sam and Mary. I kind of got the feeling they all know it's risky, especially to Mac's career. The thing is Sam made the comment this whole thing has been nothing but risky from the time the judge began receiving threats. He asked for a couple of hours to think about it."

"Perfect. Hopefully he'll get back to us one way or the other before we go see Lisa's boss. Let's switch, I need to make a phone call while you drive."

Before I made the call, I had her drive us to my car taking a bit longer to prevent being seen. Once there, I made sure nobody had us in their sights, though I couldn't worry about the accidental witness who may be watching. I stuffed two .40 caliber semi-automatic handguns in my waistband, grabbed four extra magazines along with two boxes of ammo, a snub nose .38 and more ammo for it.

As I put everything on the floorboard in front of me, I told Sara to head to Kyle Lansing's home in Bernalillo. The county area there had a mixture of some nice homes and some dumps. I hoped for the dumps, based on my experience with people in those kinds of areas tending not to notice much since they never wanted to be a witness.

I grabbed Sara's phone and dialed Celia's cell, putting it on speaker so I could load magazines. She answered on the second ring.

"Celia, it's AJ. I'm calling from a friend's cell. You might want to save this number."

"AJ, we've been worried sick about you."

We heard a little girl's voice in the background tearfully ask, "He's okay?" She demanded to get on the line and talk with me.

"Brooke, it's me, AJ."

Through more tears, she said, "I thought…someone killed you…like they did my dad."

Her sniffling and gasping breaths between words broke my heart and Sara teared up also.

"Sweetheart, I'm okay, really I am. Honest. Do you believe me?"

"Uh huh," she mumbled between sniffles.

"Brooke, your dad was a really brave man, way more than me. He's like a hero to me, trying his best to do the right thing. I have so much respect for your father and what he did, all I want to do is finish what he started."

"Okay…but you aren't going to die, too, are you?"

"No, sweetheart. I have some really good people helping me. We're going to be fine."

It took me another few minutes before I finally got her to stop crying and tell me a little about the gymnastics competition.

"Thank you," Celia said, when she got back on the phone. "Brooke needed to hear your voice. What you told her about Peter was…."

We could hear her choke up.

"It sounds like she did well at the competition," I changed the subject.

"She did do well…didn't win, but I don't think she cares about it much right now. Brooke needs to be around the other girls, laughing and playing. This trip has been great, especially staying in the hotel with her friends."

"Good! I'm glad. When do you all get home?"

"We're close to leaving so I hope early evening."

"I'm not sure I can make it tonight, but I'll try to get over to say hi the first chance I get."

"What you're doing is dangerous, isn't it?"

"What makes you say that?"

"You sound like Peter did, when he kept trying to minimize the danger, if only for someone else's benefit."

"What I told her about her dad is true, and so is what I said about wanting to finish it."

Silence. Finally, she said, "AJ...please be careful."

"I promise."

I no sooner hung up when I could feel the heated stare. I turned to see Sara's eyes glaring at me.

"You lied your ass off to Brooke. You know very well there's a good chance one or both of us ends up dead."

"Look, I'm no child psychologist. I had a ten-year-old girl crying and I did my best to persuade her to stop. Besides, I know Brooke would be devastated if I get killed the same as her father, but there's no sense in her worrying to the point of being sick over something that hasn't happened." *Yet!*

Sara thought about what I said and added, "About the time I think I got you figured out you go getting all compassionate for her."

"If that's a back-door compliment, thank you."

"You're welcome," she said without looking at me.

CHAPTER FIFTY-ONE

My luck appeared to be middle-of-the-road. Kyle Lansing did not live in a rundown area of Bernalillo. The saving grace was the space between houses in his neighborhood. Most of the places appeared to sit on half-acre lots. He obviously did not care about landscaping given his half-acre only had dirt, and lots of it.

Sara and I put on the hats. I made sure I had the reading glasses on the bridge of my nose as we approached, anything to keep him from recognizing me right away. Parking on the side street so no one would identify Mary's car, we stayed put until a neighbor finished backing out and then drove away.

Nothing seemed to be moving in the area so we made our approach. A dog barking incessantly likely had become white noise to everyone around since it had not rested from the time we arrived.

Mary had some church flyers in her car so we carried them and as we got on the front porch we rang the bell and turned our backs…Sara pointing to the paper like she needed to show me something.

As the door opened I grabbed the screen door, jerking it open while I pointed the semi-auto handgun at him. I could see the shock in his wide eyes, followed by the quick glance to his right.

"You do and you'll die right here." I knew he had a gun close by.

With the tip of the gun I flicked it up twice so he would back up. Fortunately he complied; the last thing I wanted was to have to shoot him right there.

Once inside, I told him to back up to the middle of the living room, drop to his knees and cross one foot over the other. Sara trained her automatic on him while I began searching the house. Like most guys, he had small miscellaneous tools in one of the bottom kitchen drawers along with glue and tape. I pulled out the roll of duct tape and set it on the counter.

"Shoot him if he even twitches." I felt I knew Sara well enough she would have no trouble doing it. I walked through the kitchen door to the backyard.

That is where I found what I hoped would be there… trash cans. Opening the recycle can, I saw a green plastic one-liter soda bottle, grabbed it and took it inside.

Back in the kitchen, I put the .40 caliber handgun back in my waistband and pulled out the .38, putting the muzzle up to the uncapped top of the soda bottle, duct taping them together to hold the bottle in place. Sitting on the counter was a dirty kitchen towel. I wrapped it around the plastic bottle and duct taped the ends to the plastic.

When I walked back into the room, Sara smiled.

"What?" I asked, my hands around the gun behind my back.

"He figured out who I am. Would you believe he actually looked shocked to realize a good cop would turn dirty to stop a sleaze-ball cop like him?"

I laughed, seeing the first hint of her feeling a little positive about what we were doing.

"Stand up and walk over toward your recliner there," I had him stop ten feet short of it.

"Sara, would you mind going out to the car to get that present in the trunk we have for Kyle here."

"I'd love to." she smiled.

After Sara left I grinned. "Kyle, unlike you I won't shoot an unarmed man without at least giving him a chance to defend himself first." I looked at the end table where his Glock rested, then back at him.

Kyle realized what I meant, although I could tell he did not know if he wanted to try it, or not.

"Right about now you're thinking what's he gonna do if I don't go for it. All I have to say to you is compare the odds."

The look on his face told me he had no idea what I meant.

"The odds are one hundred percent I'm going to kill you if you don't go for it. Who knows what the odds are if you do go for it, but sure as hell the odds are better than if you don't."

He obviously had never been in a real shooting where you have to read the person's eyes you're facing. He telegraphed his move by one glance at the table, followed by his glance back at me. When he made his move, I shot him in the gut and the leg before he reached his gun. He fell back over the edge of his recliner.

When Sara came in she saw Kyle on the floor, blood all around him. She also spotted the soda bottle on the end of my gun. Her eyes widened and she alternated her glances between Kyle and the soda bottle. Holding the brick in her hands she stared at me. I was glad to see she had put a set of latex gloves on again.

"Kyle here decided to go for his gun. He didn't make it."

For a second, I thought I'd lost Sara…as if she had

started to rethink the situation and might say she had not bought in to the plan.

Finally, Sara shook her head. "Too bad for Kyle."

Kyle had rolled up on his right side protecting his wounds and I asked Sara to get a large kitchen knife.

Walking to Kyle laying on the floor, I put my foot on his shoulder to make him lie flat on his stomach. I whispered loud enough for him to hear, "You should have never fucked with my friend."

Before he could reply, I put two rounds in the back of his head.

When Sara came around the corner, I asked her to grab his gun and fire it twice in the direction of where I'd been standing, and put the gun under his outstretched right hand after which I put my last round through his right wrist.

"Now what?"

"Cut open the brick, start spreading it around the recliner, around him, and all over him. We want this to look like a *payback* hit."

"You kinda have an evil streak."

"Not really. I've just seen a lot of homicide scenes. According to my nephew, these guys have been ripping off drug dealers and making a profit, killing those who protest. I do believe right is right, and wrong is wrong. Everything about Kyle and SDM is wrong. What we are doing is right, so more innocent people don't die. At least I hope it is."

"Me, too," she said, nodding.

We drove to a shopping center where we threw the gloves in different dumpsters. Further down the road behind a different shopping center we dumped the bottle, duct tape and towel and drove around trying to find a pay phone…not an easy task.

When we pulled up to one, I called the Sheriff's office. Disguising my voice as a Mexican gang-banger, I told how a drug deal went bad at Kyle's address. I did not stay on the line any longer than fifteen seconds.

I wiped the gun down before holding the rough wooden grips in my fingernail tips, waiting for Sara to pull to the curb over a storm drain. I pushed the door open with my free hand and tossed the gun, hearing it drop to its resting place in the drain.

CHAPTER FIFTY-TWO

Going to meet Lisa's editor, we drove to Jefferson Street and parked in the lot at Starbucks. We were about fifteen minutes early, so we picked an inside table in the back corner each ordering a Cappuccino, something I started to enjoy during my time in Italy.

Sara no sooner sat when we saw him crossing the street as I stayed standing so he'd see me when he walked in.

When Mike looked over, I gave him a nod to let him know we were the ones. He looked around as if he needed to make sure there were witnesses in case something went bad and then walked over to us.

"AJ Conti," I looked at him squarely in the eyes, extending my hand.

Mike stopped, looked at my hand, then back at me. I kept my hand extended until he finally shook it, surprising me with a stronger grip than I expected from a newspaper guy.

"I'm a former homicide detective from California, this is Investigator Sara Gray, from APD."

They both nodded, but neither said a word.

"I took the liberty of ordering you a Cappuccino, hope that's okay? Please have a seat."

We all sat down at a table.

"I can see you're on sensory overload here, wondering

if you can trust us. You even arranged for the guy sitting over there at the small table acting like he's reading the newspaper to be your backup."

Instinctively Mike started to look in the direction of his co-worker, but stopped halfway and nodded before turning back with his eyes looking down.

Trying to ease his embarrassment, along with some of his tension, I laid my wallet badge and ID on the table in front of him. Sara did the same, putting hers next to mine.

Mike examined both and seemed a bit more relaxed. He slid them back to us across the table. His eyes shifted between us several times as he sipped his Cappuccino. After he set the cup on the table, he leaned back into his seat.

All right, he's ready to listen.

I ran through a litany of background things that had occurred, relatively certain he already knew about them. Only a few people knew the information I provided, Lisa being one of them. Although it seemed a bit monotonous, it did what I had hoped…relaxed him even more.

I'd discussed with Sara the risk of sharing information of our plan with anyone and decided to keep the risk to a minimum by only discussing with Mike the part about Mac being set up with the brick of cocaine. I locked eyes with Sara, making sure we still wanted to take the step. She nodded.

After I explained the entire process of how we discovered the brick in Mac's car, as well as the two Syndicate cops sitting and watching the parking area, I told Mike I wanted to set up the cops.

Mike's eyes widened and his lips pushed out. Leaning forward, he placed his forearms on the edge of the table, his hands moving to hold his cup.

"I won't have any of my people do anything criminal. That being said…how can I help?"

"Fair enough. Before I go any further, we need to verify we are confidential sources, never to be revealed. Plus, you need to make sure you do not ask any question where the answer might put you in a bad position."

Mike's fingers interlocked in front of his mouth, his thumbs rapidly tapped against his lips. He took one deep breath before he said, "Let's do it. If in some way this helps get those goons who did this to Lisa…I'm ready."

Sara gave me the slightest grin. We finished our brief meeting and Mike left for his office and we continued on our agenda.

WHEN WE GOT IN MARY'S CAR I CALLED MY NEPHEW, Christian. I explained how I needed a brick to mimic a brick of cocaine making sure he understood the white powder could not have even the remotest hint of drugs. Christian knew why I had come to Albuquerque and he did not ask why the fake brick, though I knew he'd share the reason with the people he got to help him.

After I finished the phone call, I read off the address to Trevor Johnson's house, which according to the information Sara had, Trevor rented the house from his uncle, DC Chamberlain.

"Why are we going there?" Sara asked. "He's sitting in the Tahoe by the hospital."

"He's the weak link. Once he finds out two of his buddies are dead he might want to save his own neck. I'm pretty sure Jerry Bodner and Sergeant Pace won't roll over, although you never know."

"You really think Trevor will roll over on his uncle?"

I pondered her question, not sure of anything really.

"Playing the odds, he seems like the one who might have a chance of a life after prison. If we can convince him, he might be able to corroborate Peter's information about who was giving the directions and their illegal activities, but from the inside."

"I presume we are going to his house so you can leave him a note?"

"That's what I'm thinking, my only problem is how do we have him contact us? I don't want to give him either of our cell phone numbers, you know…in case he doesn't want to cooperate."

When Sara looked away, I sensed she was running possibilities through her mind.

"How about Mike?" she asked, looking back at me. "He said he would help and he's dealt with confidential informants throughout his career. If we keep him out of jeopardy where he only tells Trevor where to meet us once he believes Trevor is truly willing to help…."

I ran the concept through my head several times not wanting to put Mike in a bad spot. Convinced, I nodded agreement.

"I'll call Mike, see if he is willing to do it. Head to Trevor's house so we can decide where to place the note."

Sara took off, heading in the general direction of San Mateo Boulevard and I called Mike. He seemed more than willing to do it, immediately reading off the number of his business cell phone.

Twenty minutes later we were on Trevor's street. Like most of the homes in the neighborhood, Trevor's didn't have a garage. We knew he wasn't home, but we sat there for a few minutes to get a feel for the quietness surrounding his house.

Scratching out a note on a napkin, I kept it simple telling Trevor if he wanted a chance not to spend the rest of his life in prison, he needed to call the number I wrote down.

Sara slid on her baseball cap, pulling it low to hide her face. She took the napkin, crossed the street and walked past several houses before she turned into Trevor's driveway lowering her head even more in case he had surveillance cameras. Opening the screen door, she closed it with the napkin tucked tightly between the door and the frame.

Returning to the car, we both took a deep breath knowing the wait had begun.

CHAPTER FIFTY-THREE

Gyrene received a call from dispatch to contact a homicide detective for Bernalillo County Sheriff's Office. Something told him to call right away even though he had no idea what the request was about.

"Detective, Sergeant Pace here. How can I help you?"

"You got a guy named Kyle Lansing who works for you?"

"Yeah, why?"

"We're at his house. Got a call on a drug deal gone bad. Lansing's dead."

Stunned, Gyrene could not find the words to reply.

"Looks like a bunch of cocaine all over the place, including on his body. Preliminarily, looks like he went for his gun and got a couple shots off before they shot him…then executed him."

The detective cleared his throat before he went to the tough part.

"So…Sergeant Pace…did you have any idea Lansing might be dealing drugs?"

"Fuck you," Gyrene growled, knowing anything but an angry response might give away the fact he did know.

All of Gyrene's guys, except for maybe Rook, would sell the drugs they ripped off from dealers. They looked at it like extra income, tax free.

"Relax, Sarge. Had to ask. I've already notified my

administration so you can let yours know though I'm sure the Sheriff will contact your Chief."

"If you don't mind, can you keep me in the loop on what you find?"

The silence lasted for several seconds.

"We'll see," the detective's tone lacked conviction. "Gotta go."

Between the tone and the quick departure Gyrene sensed the detective didn't much believe him about not knowing Kyle was dirty. He figured he wouldn't receive another call, nor would he be allowed beyond the crime scene tape to get a look for himself if he went there.

Gyrene texted Sly and Rook to find out their location, knowing Sly and Kyle were friends he wanted to be the one to tell him. He had already decided to relieve Rook in the Tahoe before he told Sly. He had several reasons to stay with Sly, not the least of which was to keep him from rushing to Kyle's place and creating a scene.

When Gyrene got to their location he gave Rook the keys to his vehicle followed by an order for him to take it to their warehouse.

"You better get some rest, who knows when the judge will leave the hospital so we might be in this for the long haul."

Gyrene waited until Rook drove away before he brought up Kyle.

"I've got some bad news," Gyrene said.

Sly pulled himself up straighter by grabbing the steering wheel.

"Kyle's dead. Apparently he got in a shootout in his house over some cocaine he took off a drug dealer. From what the detectives there would tell me once they shot him, they executed him."

"Mother..." Sly yelled as he struck the steering wheel with the outside of his hand.

Gyrene sat quiet, waiting for the right time. When Sly took a couple of deep breaths to regain control, Gyrene decided to move forward.

"I have no idea who might have done the hit, but I doubt the Sheriff's Office will share much more than they already have."

"I think I know. We hit a guy's house early in the morning after we took care of the lawyer, someone Shooter had arrested for selling coke a few years ago. It was easy, he'd been up most of the night and we caught him off guard." Sly squeezed the steering wheel several times before he looked over at Gyrene.

"He tried telling us he got his drugs from one of the major gangs. He warned us the gang would probably kill him, but they would also want revenge since we ripped them off."

"There's something else...I can tell by the look on your face."

Sly lowered his head, rubbing his hands over his face.

"I handed it to Kyle right in front of the guy...told him it was a gift for joining the unit. We took off our balaclavas after we walked outside...how else would he have known?"

"Kyle's face has been plastered all over the news for the last year. Sounds like the guy recognized him as he got in the Tahoe."

Sly looked at Gyrene and nodded.

"He's going to pay for this if they haven't killed him already. I'll find out who his supplier is before I kill him, then I'll get that fucker, too."

"We need to focus on the judge first. We're going to have

to lay low after him, so you'll have time to deal with those guys afterwards. Besides, you're going to need the time to do some planning so it doesn't look like we retaliated. We don't need the extra heat."

Sly sat quietly for several minutes, taking in everything Gyrene said.

"Fair enough. But as soon as we're done here, I'm going after them...they're going to pay for what they did to Kyle."

Rook drove to the warehouse on autopilot, his mind on Lisa and what damage OM might have done to her. It bothered him knowing he supplied the information about her running habits, especially identifying the best place for her to be attacked. Several seconds later the corners of his mouth broke into a slight grin, knowing she somehow caused OM pain, too.

After he left the warehouse, Rook picked up fast food and drove home. He parked in his driveway, grabbed his bag of food then noticed some kind of paper in his screen door. As he got closer, he recognized it was a napkin and smiled, believing one of the young neighbor boys most likely left it like they had before when they wanted to get their lost ball back from his backyard.

He grabbed the note as he opened the door and once inside headed straight to the kitchen table, letting the note drop landing writing side down. Rook grabbed the burger, pulled off the paper, and took a quick bite before he headed to the fridge for a soda.

Sitting at the table, he popped the top on the soda and took a long drink, followed by a loud burp. Taking another bite, he flipped the napkin over.

Dropping the burger and jerking into the back of his chair as if he needed distance from the note, he jumped up and backed away toward his front door. All the while his eyes stayed fixated on the note.

He checked outside for strangers and had difficulty returning to his kitchen, nausea replaced his hunger.

Standing over the note he read it again, without touching it.

CHAPTER FIFTY-FOUR

It had only been a few hours before I received a call from my nephew, Christian saying he had something for me. We agreed to meet at Bataan Memorial Park Cemetery, roughly fifteen blocks from the UNM Hospital parking structure.

We arrived, with Christian pulling in less than five minutes later.

I walked to his driver's window. "You guys are quick," I said as I looked at what appeared to be a nicely packaged brick of cocaine. It didn't look exactly like the brick we took out of Mac's car, but under the circumstances I couldn't complain about the little differences in packaging details.

"Oh, trust me, they were happy to help," he said with a huge grin.

Christian had always been a person into details so I knew there wouldn't even be a hint of an illegal drug in the package. I handed him Mac's car keys and told him where it had been parked. He seemed eager to help, taking the keys and leaving without any hesitation.

While waiting, we walked around the graves as if we were looking for a particular name, hoping to relax the middle-aged groundskeeper now eyeballing us. Once Sara and I knelt down by one of the headstones, he seemed satisfied. Seconds later he took off in his John Deere Gator for another part of the park.

"Do you think Mac realizes the risk to his career by getting pulled over with the brick in the car?" Sara asked.

"I believe so. I think he wants this thing to end as quickly as possible. Lisa being attacked…and keeping him from helping get those guys would be impossible, regardless of the risk to his career. You and Mac are kind of cut from the same cloth."

Sara looked at me with sad eyes, the realization her career could possibly come to a stop was written all over her face. I laid my hand on her shoulder. When her eyes teared up, she walked away.

Out of the blue I realized I hadn't thought much about needing help shutting down the upper echelon if and when we ever got past the violence from the thugs. I sent a generic text to Kenny Love telling him I might need some guidance, knowing very well he'd jump all over my admitting I needed him…again. Sure enough my phone started ringing a minute later.

"Always needing my help, nothing's changed," Kenny snickered. "Can't you do anything by yourself?"

"Because I'm currently standing in a cemetery I won't disrespect the dead by telling you what I'm really thinking."

I couldn't help but chuckle when I heard him burst out laughing.

"So, what do you need now…?"

"I know, I know, and make it quick, you're busy."

"Exactly."

"I'm going to need some federal help here shortly, if I make it through alive."

"Don't like the sounds of that."

"Yeah, well, they are systematically eliminating anyone in their way—they already tried a drive-by on us. Even if I put a stop to these rogue cops, if we don't bring down the top dogs they'll simply replace them."

"The best I can do is contact an FBI Supervisory Special Agent I know in Phoenix...maybe he can put us in touch with someone in your area. What you really need is the attention of the US Department of Justice."

"Yeah, I agree. I'm hoping any kind of federal assistance makes DOJ take note. Especially since they thought they cleaned up the problems in their last investigation into corruption."

"I'll call the guy I know now, but I'm not sure how fast he can help you."

"I appreciate it. Hey...it goes without saying, I need someone who is a down to earth, realistic type Fed, not one who plays exactly by the book."

"Then why are you saying it?" Kenny asked, laughing before he hung up.

I shook my head and grinned as I watched Sara leaning against the trunk of the car. Somehow, I needed to persuade her to help from the fringes, convinced if she continued to stay with me she'd most certainly lose her career.

Over the top of the car I saw Christian's car pulling into the opposite side of the park then slowing to a crawl as he approached us. He stopped at the back of our car and rolled down the window, tossing the keys to Sara.

"Everything's in place. Oh, did you hear about the AKs?"

We both shrugged, neither of us knowing what he was talking about?

"Several SWAT teams raided AK members' homes early this morning. Two AKs were killed, around a dozen were arrested."

"Really? We hadn't heard anything about it."

"Thought you'd want to know. See ya." He started to drive away, but only went about fifteen feet before he backed up.

"I also heard one of the dirty cops got killed by the supplier of the drug dealer he ripped off…that's the word on the street anyhow," Christian said. He stared at us with a straight-line grin before he nodded and drove off.

"Smart move," Sara said. "Nobody can accuse them of not going after the group who tried to kill a judge…right before they take him down for the coke in his car."

Sara was right, going after the AKs as decisive as they did could prove to be a brilliant move—except for the fact Mac's car no longer had cocaine in it.

"What are your thoughts about Christian's last comment?" she asked.

"The gossip in an office, or the word on the street all have one thing in common…maybe half is true while the other half gets blown further out of proportion with each person passing along the story. Maybe some group is trying to take responsibility for it to up their street cred. I gotta say, I like the fact the word on the street got out so fast afterwards."

Sara nodded and turned to head for the driver's door.

"I'm thinking you could drop me off at my car, then take Mac's keys to him and Mary's to her. I need to stay away from the ER."

"Okay, but I think you need to talk with them, especially the judge."

"There's no privacy inside the hospital so maybe we can do it in the front parking lot by Mary's car?"

Sara agreed so we took off to get my car.

When the four of them walked through the door the looks on their faces told me Lisa would likely live. Mac had already lost one woman he loved so I couldn't have been happier. It took me a long time to get over the murder of my fiancé, Bethany, so I knew what Mac would have to face if Lisa died. Knowing he would not have to go down the same path brought me a sense of relief.

"They found BRSA dead when the surgeon arrived about an hour after you left," Sam said.

Without emotion, I looked him in the eye until he grinned.

"I heard the surgeon say the guy probably had a heart attack and he wasn't at all surprised given the guy's yellow fingers indicating he smoked like a chimney and he looked at least ten years older than his age."

"Lisa one…bad guys zero," I said, then turned my attention to Mac.

He shared the details of Lisa's major injuries saying they had her in intensive care, but the prognosis looked good. Without any prompting, he brought the conversation around to the issue at hand…should he drive away in his car?

"They're not going to stop, are they?" Mac said rhetorically. "I'm a threat to them and they want me gone…dead or alive."

"Look, we don't have to do this," I said. "We can do other things, do some more planning, try to come up with other ways to expose them."

He looked at his sister and I could see that would be her preference, although she did not say anything.

The inherent risks to Mac's career were something I didn't see the need to cover. I felt certain the three of them had thoroughly discussed it before Sara went to get them.

"I'll do it," Mac said.

"You'll probably need to contact a defense attorney to at least have one quasi-available in case you want one right away. Do whatever you need to do to look cooperative but surprised. Mike will have people in place to help us out."

I paused, looking into everyone's eyes before moving on.

"This is going to be a shit-storm for all of you, but if we play our cards right and get a couple breaks, the storm will soon shift."

I gave all three a hug before Sara and I took off.

CHAPTER FIFTY-FIVE

I needed to call Mike, but before I could pull up his name in my contacts, he called me.

"Mike, I was about to let you know Mac will be leaving within the next thirty minutes."

"Not a problem, I'll send my people to the area now so they can be in position. I hope you don't mind, but I felt like we needed more than newspaper people in the area."

"I'm listening," I said, and put my phone on speaker for Sara.

"I thought by catching it on camera, more importantly catching anything they say on audio, we would need solid equipment. So…I contacted a good friend at one of the news stations, a long-time reporter. She's willing to be in the neighborhood so she can get to the car stop location quickly."

Sara's eyes were wide and she rolled her shoulders. I felt the exact same way; our problem was neither one of us had a clue on the best way to use media coverage for something like what we were trying to pull off.

Sometimes you have to accept blind faith in those with more experience.

"Look, Mike, we'll trust your instincts on this and appreciate your help. My only request would be, see if your reporter is willing to be in an unmarked vehicle without advertising."

Sara put up her index finger to cut in. "Tell her, they need to wait a few minutes from the time of the stop to the time the black Tahoe pulls up," she said. "Catching anything the cops in the Tahoe say will be key."

"Got it. I appreciate your faith in me," Mike said. "Now, we have another issue. Your young cop called a few seconds ago…I think he wants to talk. I told him I'd have someone call him within ten minutes. He's waiting right now."

The words were no sooner off Mike's lips when it hit me. Sara needed to do the interview. Worst case, she gets what we need but it does nothing to help her career out personally. Best case, someone like Mike helps to resurrect her career by putting her front and center bringing down the corruption Lisa started reporting on—that is, if things start working out like we planned.

"Sara will call and meet with him."

When I saw the surprised look on her face, I gave her the index finger back, knowing I would have ample time to explain as I drove her back to her parked car at the restaurant.

"Mike, you've been a great help," I continued. "But, I'd like to impose on you for one more thing if you're up to it… like sitting in on the interview?"

Sara dialed the number Mike provided. It rang only once, followed by silence.

"Trevor, this is Investigator Gray. I heard you might want to talk."

More silence. Sara looked at me and shrugged as I prompted her to keep talking before the guy panicked and hung up.

She continued. "Look, I know this is difficult for you. I'm not looking to screw you over. I have a neutral place where we can talk so it's not at the PD."

"Where?"

"An architect's office behind Bank of America Financial Center on Jefferson Street. It's a small office, but they have a conference room we can use. I can even let you in the door off the conference room so you don't have to come through the lobby."

"Just you?"

"No. I want a neutral person there with us. You and I both work for APD so we both have a lot on the line. I won't talk to you without this guy being there."

"Is it that detective from California?"

"I don't know who you're referring to," she lied. "Wait, are you talking about one of the guys involved in the shooting at Judge McDunn's house?"

"Yeah."

"No. Definitely not him. I have no reason to bring him. As far as I know he is a friend of the judge."

"How'd you get my name…my address?"

"Let's say a dead sergeant provided it to me. I think you know which one I'm referring to."

Silence once again. I nodded at Sara letting her know she was doing well.

"You going to arrest me?" he asked.

When Sara looked at me, I shook my head. She looked frustrated as I kept shaking my head and squinting my eyes. She needed to say no.

"No. Why would I?" she asked.

I kept signaling for her to build on her comment and on his confidence.

"I told you, both of us are in an awkward position."

I nodded, still rolling my finger for her to keep talking.

"Look Trevor, the whole thing could fall apart at any time. Or worse yet, the Chief and the Mayor could throw you guys under the bus to make it look as if they were great for stopping some rogue cops. I…I think we can help each other out here."

This time the silence lasted for only ten seconds.

"I'll be there in forty-five minutes. I'll call you when I'm there so you can open the side door. If I think you're fucking with me…I swear I'll start shooting and we'll all die."

"Trevor…I'm not messing with you. I promise."

The three beeps from his ending the call filled the car.

"Excellent job!" I gave her my best smile.

"Thanks," she said.

Sara's entire demeanor changed as she started going off on me about my not wanting her to arrest a dirty cop involved in all sorts of nefarious activities. I didn't say a word, letting her vent to get it all out of her system.

She reminded me of myself when as a young detective my mentor kept me from arresting a man, who lost control for a split second and unintentionally killed his own daughter. I stewed for days over it until the man gradually started trusting me and came into the police department several times to talk. The man told how he knew I had enough to arrest him early on and he appreciated me letting him deal with his daughter's funeral. We arrested him two weeks later. I learned valuable lessons; not everyone is a flight risk. And, people are receptive to a detective who listens and tries to understand their plight instead of swooping in to intimidate.

"You done?" I asked.

Sara's stare gave me the answer.

"This kid is a follower who's in over his head," I said. "He's not going to run. The worst thing he'd do would be kill himself, which he could do in the county jail if someone there didn't kill him first for being a dirty cop."

I paused to let what I said settle in, but only for a moment.

"He could well be the linchpin to us turning this nightmare around. Not to mention saving your career if you play your cards right."

"All right, all right. I hear you."

"Finally," I said with a huge smile, knowing she would smack my arm, which she did.

"So, how do you want me to handle it then?"

"Sara, go in and don't rush it. Slow down the interview… time is on your side. Let it happen, naturally, without pressure. You'll see what I'm talking about. Go in mentally prepared for it to take several hours before he gets to the good stuff."

"Why me? Why not you since you seem to be able to do what it is you want me to do."

"I have a medical examiner to go pressure. Lord knows if we switched, you'd straight up kill the medical examiner for his role in Aaron Vasquez's murder."

It only took a few seconds before her stoic face broke into a little grin.

CHAPTER FIFTY-SIX

Sara called Mike to let him know the meeting with the young cop was set. Mike agreed to go down the street from his office to his friend's architect office to get everything ready.

Before Sara got out of the car I used her phone to call the medical examiner's office so a local number would show up on the caller I.D.

When the secretary answered I tried to sound authoritative and in a hurry when I told her I was Chief Baylor from the police department, almost demanding to speak with Doctor Mullins. Within seconds, she patched me through to his office.

"What do you need now, Dick?"

"I'm not Chief Baylor, but I suggest you don't hang up unless you want to go to prison with him."

The silence told me he was either frozen with fear or wondering if he should at least listen. While I let him ruminate...*I remembered his reactions to Chief Baylor at Aaron Vasquez's home. According to Sara, Mullins looked like he despised the Chief and did not look like a willing participant. We had no idea if the doctor was being blackmailed, but Sara's gut feeling and description of him seemed worthy to give it a shot.*

I restarted the conversation. "If you want a chance to jump off a sinking ship and save your own neck then you'll meet me at the Starbucks across from the Albuquerque Journal in thirty minutes. No cameras, no recording devices, only the two of us talking in a public place so I can prove to you I'm not some hit man sent by Chief Baylor to whack you."

We heard him clear his throat twice, followed by silence.

"Look, DOJs coming again, this time people are going down. It's not going to be recommendations followed by scheduled visits to give Baylor and his cronies' time to prepare. DC Chamberlain wants you taken out by their Syndicate. Based on your silence…I am guessing you'd rather take your chances. Best of luck."

"Wait, wait. I'll be there…Starbucks…thirty minutes."

"Smart. I'll get your attention when you walk in." I clicked off and handed Sara her phone.

"You have nothing to go on besides what I saw when he walked up and the Chief walked towards him at Mr. Vasquez's house. I don't know…?"

"Maybe, maybe not. He's a medical examiner, not a crook. Besides, he sounded panicked when he almost screamed for me to wait. He comes across as a scared doctor whose being played."

Sara took a deep breath laying her head to one side.

"Look, I'm going to do exactly what I told you to do, listen and be patient. Whatever I give him will be BS to scare him, but I guarantee he won't have anything substantive to take back to the Chief. Worst he can do is let the Chief know we're going after him, which he probably already expects. Trust me."

She nodded. "I do like your smart idea picking Starbuck's right down the street in case Trevor decides to go postal on us."

"Don't kid yourself. I needed another Cappuccino is all."

"Yeah right," she said, a huge grin on her face.

Sara got out and stood in the doorway, looking at me without saying another word. The hair on the back of my neck stood up as I sensed we were thinking the same thing, *I wonder if we'll get to see each other again.*

CELIA AND BROOKE PULLED INTO THE DRIVEWAY READY to stretch their legs and grab something to eat. They had only stopped twice on the way back from Denver, once to fill up and once at the rest stop a few miles south of Santa Fe. Celia happily fell in line behind a couple of cars whose drivers wanted to push the speed limit, which helped her to keep her time to six hours.

"Let's leave the bags in the trunk for now," Celia said. "We can grab them after we eat."

Brooke smiled, pleased they were thinking alike.

Once through the front door they went directly into the kitchen and Brooke headed straight to the refrigerator to grab a soda. She took a long drink before closing the door.

"Can't you wait to have that with dinner," Celia asked. "You know you only get one."

Brooke smiled as she set the can on the table and went towards the living room to turn on the television. Brooke froze in her tracks, letting out a violent scream.

Dropping the loaf of bread, Celia raced to the living room. Brooke turned and buried her head, sobbing into her mother's chest. Celia stroked Brooke's hair, telling her it would be all right until she looked up and saw the reason Brooke was so frightened.

Written on the living room wall, spray painted in red… blood red.

Sleeping with the enemy. Tisk, Tisk.

"Oh, my God," Celia whispered as her eyes slowly moved from the wall to view the wave of mass destruction of everything in the room.

She tightened her arms around Brooke as she stepped back into the kitchen where she put her hands on Brooke's cheeks to lift her face.

"Sweetie, listen to me. We need to go to the car. Remember what your Dad always taught us. Don't panic, think about what we are doing. Can you do that?"

Brooke nodded. With tears rolling down her cheeks, she took the first step toward the front door.

Celia wrapped her arm around Brooke's shoulder and began walking, grabbing her car keys off the table. Once outside Celia tried to take inventory of the cars parked in the neighborhood. There were no marked police cars, but she knew they were not beyond following her in unmarked cars.

Trying to remain calm she started the car. "We need to look around and see if any cars follow us. Will you be our lookout?" Celia asked as she backed out of the driveway.

"Aren't we going to call AJ?" Brooke asked through her sniffling and her repetitive short inhales.

Celia reached over and patted Brooke's leg. "Yes, we are. First we need to drive away from here and make sure we are alone. Remember, don't panic."

Brooke nodded, wiping her tears with the backs of her hands. She sat up, trying her best to be tall and started looking around the headrest and checking her side mirror while her mom drove away from their house.

Celia had no idea where to go, but she knew she wanted to stay on heavy traffic roads and populated areas. She had gone a couple of miles without seeing any cars following when she pulled out her cell phone to call AJ.

CHAPTER FIFTY-SEVEN

While waiting for Mullins at Starbucks, I located some pictures of the good Doctor on the Internet.

I spotted him lurching across the parking lot with sudden, almost furtive, movements, his head swiveling so much he had people looking at him. He acted as if he expected a group of mercenaries to swoop out of the shadows and throw him in a van. His fear quashed his ability to reason his involvement had to do with isolated issues in Albuquerque, not a national security problem where mercenaries might actually be involved.

Nonetheless, I stood hoping he would look my way.

"Doctor Mullins, over here," I said once he stepped inside the coffee shop. He picked up his drink order, plodded towards me and pulled the chair across from me away from the table so far he would have had to lean forward to set his drink down. Instead he crossed one leg over the other and held onto his cup with both hands on his lap. I could see his hand shaking.

A familiar odor, though faint, touched my olfactory receptors. I noticed the same smell on my clothing the rest of the day after I attended the autopsy of one of my victims. Mullins probably did not notice the hint of death odor attached to his clothing…his own receptors were no doubt immune to it.

Mullins made eye contact for a brief second before he looked down at his lap. Although I knew I could continue to make him uncomfortable, I needed to work the opposite direction. We had no idea if he could be of help to us or not, but if Sara's instincts were right, I needed to make sure I didn't scare him.

"So, Doctor Mullins, we both know Aaron Vasquez did not commit suicide and you've been asked to cover it up."

His head shot up, his wide eyes locking onto mine. I could almost see the color drain from his face.

"Who...who are you?"

"I'm the guy whose been piecing the puzzle together on all the illegal activity the police chief, the mayor, and their SDM, Syndicate of Death, as they like to call themselves, have been doing. The chief and the mayor plan to move into higher political positions."

"If you know all that, why are you willing to talk to me and help me from going down with them"

A fair question to be sure. I took a few seconds to contemplate.

"Since I've been involved in a number of autopsies," a quick fact I threw in to make him wonder even more about me, "let me put it to you in a way you'll understand. Let's say you're thirty minutes into an autopsy, and the smoking gun so to speak is all the bodily signs point to the deceased being asphyxiated."

I paused for him to recognize the similarity of death to Aaron Vasquez. "You'd be remiss not to look for associated factors, such as clogged arteries that may have led to death sooner than say a healthy young heart."

Mullins nodded, an obvious agreement to the *associated factors* concept. I remained quiet watching him nod again once he made the connection we presumably had the *smoking gun* on the dirty players. Though we didn't have it yet, he did not know that, and his info would be akin to our *associated factors*.

"If I may...."

"Certainly," I said, reaching for my cup.

"How did...how did you connect me to any of this?"

"Your credentials are impeccable, I researched you well before I contacted you, quite impressive. I have no doubt you're an excellent forensic medical examiner, I mean you wouldn't be the Chief ME if you weren't." I took a sip to allow the compliments to sink in first.

"Along with that, it's obvious you're not a crook because everything about your demeanor says to people like us you're a fish out of water in the scumbag world of murder and exploitation."

While he lowered his head to confirm in his own way I was right, I made a quick assessment of what to say next. Something told me to go for it, so I trusted my instincts.

"Doc, a very astute investigator saw you and the Chief together in the front yard at Aaron Vasquez's house when you first arrived. Let's say he or she could tell you were being blackmailed...what the observer overheard confirmed it."

His brows shot up while he leaned back into his chair telling me we were right. It seemed like the appropriate time for a little subterfuge.

"That information prompted us to go digging. It did not take long to figure out not everyone in the police department likes or respects Baylor or Chamberlain. Finding out the reason why you were blackmailed didn't prove to be difficult."

"That son-of-a-bitch. He said he buried it and he personally convinced the little girl's family she would be so traumatized by going through the system everyone would be better off if my son got counseling. He obviously kept some kind of record of it if you found it. What a son-of-a-bitch."

Damn Sara, you nailed it.

As much as I wanted to know more about what exactly happened, especially with Mullins' son, I had to get more on the cover up in Vasquez's death.

"Talk to me about Aaron Vasquez's murder."

It took a few seconds for Mullins to shake free of everything running through his mind about his son.

"What's there to tell? I have no idea who did it, or how they did it. Baylor never said anything to me about those things. He definitely had an idea though, because when he called me early that morning at my house I could tell he knew about him being dead already. He said when a call came in about a dead man, a well-known gay legal professional is how he put it, I needed to be the one to respond, not one of my other MEs."

"What about the scene or the evidence?"

"What a joke. Zero crime scene integrity," Mullins began. "There were more cops and politicians romping through the crime scene than I've ever seen in my entire career. Mr. Vasquez did not leave a note, the car was not running when the fire department arrived even though it had a half-tank of gas, and he had his gym clothes and gym bag with him in the car just like he did every morning to go workout. But…the icing on the cake is his carbon monoxide saturation level."

As Mullins stared off into his own world, I could see the frustration building inside him. He felt anger having to sign off on a case that was anything but a suicide, all in the name of *family blackmail.*

"Doc, what about the saturation level?" I pulled him back on track.

"His was over eighty percent. Most people die somewhere between forty-five and sixty percent. He had to be force-fed, so to speak, a large volume in a short period of time for his saturation level to be that high. A standard hose running to the inside of the car would result in the person dying around the lower levels I described and the car would run out of gas at some point. Neither took place here."

What happened next shook me, almost taking my breath away as I replayed the question several times in my mind before I could answer.

"Do you have a tape recorder?" Mullins asked. "I'm ready to give a statement. I'm done with being a puppet on that asshole's string. And for that matter, I'm done listening to the bitch I'm married to. She was the one who convinced me to call Chief Baylor and ask for his help with our son, who by the way never did get counseling. He's probably molesting children in New Brunswick…he just hasn't gotten caught. I don't care what happens to me at this point, all of this is wrong. I should have had enough guts to stand up and put a stop to it a long time ago."

After I digested what the good doctor said, I had to stop myself from jumping up from the excitement. Instead, I calmly asked him to wait as I went to my car to retrieve the recorder I always carry with me.

CHAPTER FIFTY-EIGHT

My phone dinged about the time I walked back inside Starbucks. I looked at the message from Celia.

Nine-one-one.

I called her immediately.

"AJ," her voice shaking.

"Celia, what's wrong? Are you guys okay?"

"They were in the house…they tore it apart. They painted a nasty message on the wall. We got out of there. AJ, where are you?"

I described the Starbucks near the Journal and Celia said she would find it, assuring me she had not been followed. She agreed to call me once she arrived before they got out of the car to let me know if she still felt she had not been followed.

If we had any doubt, we would have to do something else. The last thing I needed was to bring the cops to see me interviewing Doctor Mullins.

I had tried to give Ralph some time to deal with his emotions, but I needed him, so I dialed his number.

"Ralph, Peter Howard's wife and child are in danger and I need someone to stay with them."

"AJ, I'm sorry I haven't been there to help you more. Of course, where do you want me to go?"

"I understand Ralph...don't worry. I need you to come to where I'm at."

I explained my location and how Celia had begun heading my direction. I didn't want Ralph to see Doctor Mullins, unsure how he would react to the man who covered up the cause of Aaron's death, so I suggested Celia meet up with Ralph in the parking lot. We agreed he could take them to Mac's house figuring the chances were slim anyone would be going there anytime soon, especially if they were trying to nab him in a car stop.

After I hung up, I explained to Doctor Mullins how I would need to take a break or two, without giving him too many details. He said he understood and he would wait. He seemed to have a determination about him, like nothing would stop him from giving me the full statement.

Once I started the recorder, Doctor Mullins laid things out from the beginning. He described how his son had molested a young girl and his anger toward his wife wanting to cover it up instead of getting their son help. I tried to listen as intently as I could, even asking some clarifying questions without leading him, despite my constant checking of the time.

When my phone finally rang I took a deep breath, thankful they had arrived at Starbucks. I stopped the recorder and walked to the door, surveying the area as Celia and Brooke began walking across the lot. Brooke walked beside her mom, holding her around the waist, her eyes looking down. Celia said something and pointed toward me…Brooke took off sprinting toward me.

Stepping onto the sidewalk I had time to kneel as Brooke ran into my arms. I could feel her fear as she buried her head into my chest. When I stood and picked her up, Celia reached the sidewalk. Without hesitation, she too came over into my free arm and hugged me. Her tension was palpable, although she did a better job at hiding it for Brooke's sake.

I convinced them we needed to go inside and as we turned toward the door I could see Doctor Mullins staring at us, a look on his face not unlike that of someone admiring what another person has.

"Are you sure you weren't followed?" I asked as we all sat at a table near the window, a good thirty feet from the doctor.

"Pretty sure, aren't we sweetie," Celia said as she stroked Brooke's hair.

Brooke looked at me and nodded.

"That's what took us so long. I did a lot of doubling back and driving through different residential areas to make sure. Brooke acted as my lookout." Celia winked at me.

"I'm very proud of you for helping your mom like you did." I put my free hand on top of her hand.

"Can we stay with you?" Brooke asked.

"Sort of. See the man over there by himself? I'm taking his statement and need to finish with him. Then I have to make sure my friend the judge, the one you met, is okay. After that I'll come to where you guys go."

I could tell by Celia's face she had questions about what I really meant, but would not ask in front of Brooke.

"I have a retired cop friend of mine meeting us here. He is… or was, Aaron Vasquez's private investigator and he'll go with you guys to Mac's house and stay with you until I get done."

It took a few minutes before I had Brooke convinced I'd meet them there and they would be safe. I gave Celia money to get them something warm to drink and snack on while I continued with Doctor Mullins.

"If I hadn't of overheard you tell someone on the phone they were someone else's wife and daughter I would have sworn they were yours," Mullins said when I sat. "The little girl adores you."

I didn't know what to say. I loved everything about the thought of having a child, and Brooke holding my hand, or hugging me, or telling me about how her gymnastics felt good.

"Ahem…um, no…these guys murdered APD Sergeant Peter Howard, her father, when they realized he had information on them and planned to expose them for what they really are. What you're seeing is me being the first person to come along they could trust, and right now they are being threatened again so they're scared."

Mullins stared into my eyes, slightly turning his head to one side with his own parental look of disbelief of my explanation. Thankfully we moved on without any further questioning, although he seemed to have an even stronger resolve to tell everything after hearing the truth of Peter's murder.

The totality of Mullins wrongdoings, lawfully, not morally, with regards to The Syndicate centered on Aaron's cover-up. Listening to him lay everything out about what he heard and saw at his crime scene, along with comments the chief and mayor made, convinced me he had no desire to hold anything back.

"Doctor Mullins, you're doing the right thing," I said after I turned off the recorder.

"Yeah, well, I'm sorry it took so long for me to have the courage."

"I think we need to keep you safe somehow, at least for a day or two."

"Don't worry about it. I have a hotel in Santa Fe I often go to for a few days to get away. I've always paid cash so my wife would never know. The truth is, she never cared, so it was easy."

I made sure to get his personal cell phone number and the hotel information I'd need to turn over to the Fed's, then gave him mine and Sara's numbers in case anything happened.

For some reason before he left he shared with me his longtime plan of leaving his wife and retiring in some Latin America country like Panama or Belize. I sensed he would be doing so once he got his retirement in order and helped us put the people away he despised.

Shortly after Mullins left, Ralph arrived so I had him meet Celia and Brooke. The conversation only lasted ten minutes, but I could see Brooke relax as she saw for herself how I trusted Ralph to keep them safe.

CHAPTER FIFTY-NINE

Mac stared at Lisa's motionless body, thankful her drug-induced coma kept her pain free. He softly stroked her forehead and kissed her hand before he left the room. Pausing outside the door, he looked back at her once more, hopeful about her recovery.

He pushed the button on the wall opening the door automatically.

Sam and Mary were waiting to walk him to his car. Sam had been able to speak with the primary internist assigned to Lisa's case and he shared information as they walked. Lisa needed to make it through the next twenty-four hours to effectively start climbing out of death's grasp. Still, the various physicians were feeling optimistic about getting her stabilized.

The three had agreed not to search for the black Tahoe AJ told them would be waiting, even though they all had a strong desire to look around.

"Look, Mac, you know how I feel about this so I'm just going to say it…please be careful," Mary warned as the three stood next to Mac's car.

Mac gave her a wink, followed by a half smile before climbing into the driver's seat and putting his crutches behind his seat. The package, looking like a brick of cocaine, drew in all their eyes.

"As soon as you pull out, I'll call the attorney Gordon Rogers recommended," Sam said. "We'll stay here with Lisa."

"Thank you both…for everything," Mac said. Typical of his reactions to things most would consider dangerous or scary, he smiled. "See you on the other side."

Mac sat watching them walk away. Even though the brick did not have any contraband, a real risk to his career loomed over the actions he would undertake. Convinced he had made the right decision, he started the car.

"Let's do this," he said looking at himself smiling in the rearview mirror.

He expected to be stopped relatively quickly after leaving the parking garage. Turning east on Lomas Boulevard, he had barely gone a few tenths of a mile when he saw the motorcycle officer in his rearview mirror.

Mac knew the officer would choose the general area for the car stop, usually based on officer safety, but in his case it could be for any number of reasons. When the officer turned on his emergency lights, Mac started looking for a place to pull over. He hoped to find somewhere that would benefit whomever Mike had watching out for him where they could blend in like a bystander.

Seeing the Catholic Church ahead, he kept driving until he could pull into the lot beside the church with ample areas for Mike's people to position themselves. Mac was pleased with the location and decided if he were questioned by the cop about not pulling over quicker, he could say he thought it would be safer for the cop to get off Lomas Boulevard with so much traffic.

Watching in his side mirror, Mac saw the cop stand by his motorcycle. The cop kept turning to look over his shoulder until a vehicle pulled in behind him. Once it stopped, the cop approached Mac's car on the driver's side. He told Mac his left taillight was out followed by asking for all the standard car and license items. With those in his hand the drama began.

The cop drew his weapon and pointed it at Mac while telling him to put up his hands. Yelling back to whoever had pulled in behind him, the cop saw a brick of cocaine on the floorboard.

Interesting that he already knows it's a brick of cocaine, Mac wondered.

Mac's eyes scanned the area on his left. Beyond the cop, Mac spotted a man standing with his arms crossed and what looked like a large camera lens resting on his shoulder with someone else behind him. With the cop pulling out his gun, people began popping up everywhere around them to watch the action, making Mike's people blend in even better.

Mac heard the cop continue to yell at him…not to move his hands while he shifted his eyes to his right. Behind a group of four or five people standing near the church, Mac would have sworn he caught sight of a parabolic listening device. Looking back at the cop, Mac hoped he did not give them away, whoever they might be?

Following the officer's instructions, Mac opened the door. Off to his left a person came into plain view who Mac recognized.

"Officer Bodner, fancy seeing you here," Mac's hands still up in the air.

"Get out of the car," Sly ordered. "Shoot him if he does anything suspicious!" He looked over at the motorcycle cop.

Mac did not move, staring at Bodner the entire time.

"Get out of the fucking car," Bodner yelled.

Mac shifted his eyes to the motorcycle cop with his gun trained on him.

"Officer, there is no way for me to get out of this car without reaching behind me to grab my crutches, right where you think a brick of cocaine exists." Mac waited for a sign the motorcycle cop understood Mac's dilemma.

"Officer Bodner here is hoping I reach for the crutches. That way, you can shoot me, saying it was a furtive movement. So, I'm staying right here until someone hands me my crutches. That is, officer, unless you want to force a handicapped judge to get out of his car on his hands and knees after you refused to let him have his crutches."

Sly saw the motorcycle cop looking as if he was beginning to side with the judge. Sly's face reddened and he yanked open the back door, grabbed Mac's crutches, slammed the door and threw them against the open front door.

The motorcycle cop nodded.

Mac grabbed his crutches and went through his methodical method of turning in his seat to get prepared. Mac slowly explained to the motorcycle cop how he needed to straighten his leg and lock the brace into place, causing a clicking noise. He told the cop it sounded similar to the cocking of a weapon, but he had to lock the brace in place or he could not stand.

Seeing he had the cop's buy-in, he explained how once he stood he needed to swing his shorter leg to make that leg brace lock in place, causing a similar sound. When the cop began to lower his weapon seeing Mac posed no threat… Mac continued with the leg brace process.

The judge thanked the motorcycle cop, who nodded one last time as he put away his weapon. Mac sensed the cop just happened to be in the area when Bodner requested a car stop and he was not part of the charades.

"So, Officer Bodner, how did you know about this supposed brick of cocaine in my car anyhow? Did you put it there?"

"There ain't no supposing about it, you're toast."

"Hmmm, must be some kind of new technology I'm not aware of to be able to accurately determine the presence of cocaine without testing it first. Unless, of course, you planted it."

"I'm outta here," the motorcycle officer called out to Bodner. "I'm sorry, Your Honor." He took off toward his motorcycle, ignoring Bodner's demands for him to come back.

"Looks like every cop has not bought into your dirty schemes."

"Shut the fuck up, you're going to prison for a long time. You won't last a month with all the bad asses there that you sentenced."

"Well, Officer Bodner…one of us is going there, that's for sure."

Gyrene moved to the back of Mac's car when Sly went up by the motorcycle cop. He listened closely to everything the judge said. Seconds before the motorcycle cop decided to jump ship and leave, Gyrene had a sickening feeling.

He tried to look around without drawing attention, but it was too late—he spotted the camera staring right back at him, and the parabolic mic a few feet away from it.

The phone call from the Bernalillo County Sheriff's detective popped into his head. Kyle had supposedly died over cocaine he ripped off from a drug dealer. The picture of what really happened came into perfect view in his mind.

Having figured out what was actually occurring Gyrene let the motorcycle cop leave without pulling rank and giving him a direct order to stay, deciding instead not to ruin the innocent cop's career. He knew what he had to do, but he decided he needed to make sure Sly didn't kill the judge first. The brotherhood in his mind had dissolved, making his decision easy…he wasn't about to mention to Sly what he saw in the crowd.

CHAPTER SIXTY

Sara and Mike had been in the conference room for over an hour waiting for Trevor. During their careers, both had experienced the letdown of wanting to speak with someone important to their investigation, who ultimately changed their mind and failed to show. They had the feeling their meeting today might be another of those experiences.

"He's not going to show," Mike shook his head.

"Probably, but let's give it another thirty minutes at least," Sara said.

"What's going through your mind…why more time?"

"I don't know, something about the tone of his voice when I spoke to him. I'm sure he's battling internally…should he or shouldn't he? I sensed he knew by the note he's going down and only he can control his destiny of how much prison time he gets. Unless he chose door number three…to kill himself."

Mike nodded, contemplating her rationalization as he walked to the large glass window looking into the lobby area of the architect office. Everyone had left except the secretary now organizing her desk before leaving.

"You think maybe he's waiting until everyone leaves so no one else is here except for us?" he looked over at Sara.

"I wonder? It's almost five thirty. Who all are still here?"

He looked back into the lobby as the secretary turned off her computer.

"The secretary is the last, and it looks as if she's getting ready to leave. She knows not to alarm the place so we should be good."

"We'll give it a good thirty minutes once she drives off. You walked here, and I parked down the street. The parking lot should be empty."

Twenty minutes later, they heard a knock on the back door.

Mike went to answer it while Sara positioned herself along the same wall, her hand on her gun as a precaution. When Mike opened the door, both men stared at each other. It was an awkward moment till Mike signaled with his hand for Trevor to enter.

When Sara saw Trevor's hands were free of any weapons she walked toward him, extending her hand.

"Sara…Sara Gray," she said, leaving her hand outstretched.

"Trevor," he slowly lifted his hand to shake hers.

Sara gestured for him to sit...her note pad and pen positioned in front of the chair at the head of the table.

Trevor looked back at Mike, who did not move after closing the door.

She nodded her head sideways to get Mike to sit down, knowing Trevor would not relax with Mike standing behind him. Mike quickly took a seat.

"He's Mike, he's not a cop or a fed as promised on the phone. He's a supervisor at a business near here."

"At the Journal," Trevor said to Mike before turning back to Sara.

Sara could see Trevor's discomfort from her not being up front with him about Mike. She felt doing so again might cause him to leave.

"Yes, you're right," she nodded and wanted to say more, but knew there was no good explanation for not telling the man where Mike worked right now. Instead she sat down, hoping Trevor would join her and Mike at the table.

Trevor pulled out the chair, reached for the Glock on his right hip and set it on the table…muzzle pointing in Mike's direction. Finally, he sat down.

Sara turned to Mike, who had done enough interviews of tough guys in his career to know not to show fear. He calmly sat back in his chair, hoping the racing of his heart was not showing in the veins in his neck.

Cognizant of not wanting to make another mistake, Sara picked up her pen and looked into Trevor's eyes. She knew he held all the cards. "You're free to get up and walk out at any time. All I want to do is talk."

"Why should I say anything to you instead of killing you?"

Sara put down her pen, leaned back into her chair, and sat quietly.

After a few seconds she spoke softly. "Trevor, you may be young, but you're intelligent," she tried to stroke his ego. "Something tells us…of anyone in your band of brothers, you are the only one who has compassion. Let's be honest, you're the youngest in the group, you have the least experience, and if it weren't for your uncle, DC Chamberlain, you would have gotten all the crappy jobs in your unit. Plus, you didn't have enough time on the job to get a special assignment, much less one working for the Chief and the Mayor."

Trevor's eyes widened as he stared at her then lowered his head, looking at his hands on top of the table.

Sara wanted to say more, but AJ's words kept telling her to be patient and listen. She sat quiet while her and Mike waited.

"I didn't want her to get hurt," he gradually lifted his eyes to look over at Mike. "I'm sorry."

When Trevor lowered his head again, Sara nodded at Mike.

Mike leaned forward while choosing his words. He knew the importance of Trevor's statements.

"I appreciate you saying that, Trevor. I can tell you're sincere. Lisa is not out of the woods yet, she could still die."

Mike paused, wanting the possibility of Lisa dying to weigh on Trevor. Sara nodded again, prodding Mike to keep going.

"Lisa told me a while back she thought the youngest one in The Syndicate wasn't like the others. I can see in you a person who is not cold blooded, and I'd like to see what you could do with your life if you worked with good people."

Trevor raised his head, his eyes alternating between them.

"I was glad when OM, sorry, *Brody*, came back to the car with a broken toe after he attacked her."

"Yeah, well, trust me, Brody won't be hurting any women ever again," Sara said, hoping Trevor took her comment to mean they already had him in custody. "And neither will Kyle, for that matter. So, you can see, between the information Lisa discovered, the information Sergeant Peter Howard left us, and the information I've uncovered, this whole thing is about to implode. This is your chance to save yourself from a life in prison."

"I really liked when they praised me, especially for things like tactics or preparation. You know, using my brain. I didn't know…I didn't know how to tell them I did not want to be part of all the killing, especially when they tortured people. They'd kill me if I tried to leave the unit."

"Now you don't have to worry about it, the unit is coming

to an end," Sara said. "The only question is what are you going to do now? Stay loyal to people you have no respect for, or try to fix some of the wrongs?"

"I sat in the car for a long time thinking about this. I'm ready to tell you everything…on the record, if you can get the DA to cut me a deal."

Sara sank back even further in her chair, shocked by the reality she had no way of contacting the DA without notifying her chain of command, none of whom she trusted. The thought of having Trevor so close to telling everything and it falling apart made her stomach churn.

"Hey Kiley, how are you?" Mike spoke into his cell phone. He smiled at the shock crossing Sara's face now realizing he had the DA on the line.

CHAPTER SIXTY-ONE

The text message from Kenny told me to answer the call I would receive within the next few minutes. My cell began to ring in less than a minute.

"AJ Conti," I answered.

"AJ, FBI Special Agent Oscar Palenzuela. Your buddy must be well connected. He spoke with a Supervisory Special Agent in the Phoenix branch where I worked a number of years. I'm here to help, so let's get started."

"I hope you know what you're getting yourself into."

"I've been in Albuquerque for a few years. We've suspected there were rogue cops here for a while now, but our hands were tied after DOJ did their thing a few years ago and were supposedly monitoring things."

"So, how can you get involved now?" I asked.

"Like I said, your buddy must be well connected."

Ain't that the truth, I smiled knowing Kenny had more contacts in his cell phone than anyone I knew and they were legit. Plus, he had the pictures to prove it.

I was surprised when he said, "We've already discussed within our office the possibility of a DOJ agent responsible for monitoring might be on the take getting kickbacks to look the other way. With your buddy's phone call, we've received approval to assist you. So long as we can go after the DOJ agent when we're done assisting you."

"Absolutely. Thanks."

We agreed not to discuss specifics over the phone. I had Oscar meet me within the hour at a parking lot near where I knew Sara and Mike were talking with Trevor. When he arrived, I gave him a quick rundown of what had happened so far. My focus stayed more on the brick placed in Mac's car, my conversation with the ME, and Sara interrogating Trevor.

"How high up do you think it goes?" Oscar asked.

"According to Peter Howard, the APD Sergeant they killed, all the way to the top. Plus, the ME was blackmailed by the Chief. We think the Mayor may also be involved based on the councilwoman being attacked and threatened."

"Have you cut any unofficial deals with anyone?"

"No. I think the ME would probably like witness protection. He made it pretty clear he will help take down the Chief, but he does not plan to stick around if he's not needed. Investigator Sara Gray has Trevor Johnson in an interview right over there," I pointed to the building.

"She sent me a text before you arrived. Seems Trevor is willing to talk if he can cut a deal. They've already contacted DA Hildebrand, who seems more than willing to help considering her upcoming reelection."

Oscar took out his phone and started making calls. It wasn't long before I sensed he did not want DA Hildebrand involved. He sought approval from an Assistant U.S. Attorney to go in and try to get a statement from Trevor while the federal prosecutor worked on the deal they might offer him dependent upon the depth of his testimony, their ability to prove its accuracy, and his willingness to testify.

When we knocked on the door at the architect's office, Sara let us inside. Trevor's face showed surprise while he acted like he expected me to show up at some point. He even gave me a friendly nod as if we knew each other.

"They kept saying you were nothing but a washed-up detective," Trevor said looking over at me. "I tried to tell them…they better take you serious, but they never listened to me. Guess they have no choice now."

"I appreciate your vote of confidence." I noticed a grin come to his face.

"This is FBI Special Agent Palenzuela. I've been with him the last thirty minutes and I know he's doing everything he can to work with you on a deal."

SA Palenzuela reached out and shook Trevor's hand. The age-old gesture of long-ago warriors made Trevor sit up taller.

Smart move, Oscar.

"Trevor, Investigator Gray will take possession of your weapon now since you no longer feel the need to kill everyone in the room." I smiled at my own joke, hoping to relax him further.

Trevor nodded, pushing the gun down the table to Sara. Without us asking, he stood and put his hands on his head knowing we would want to make sure he did not have any other weapons. Oscar patted him down and took the extra magazine he had and handed it to Sara. Trevor sat after Oscar patted his shoulder to let him know he was done.

Glancing at Oscar, I nodded at Trevor. When Oscar returned a quick nod I believed he read my mind. I wanted to say more to Trevor since he seemed to have a semblance of respect for me.

"I hope you know I'm not here to screw with you," I slowly shook my head. "I think your uncle, Fred Chamberlain, most likely pushed you into this Syndicate thing you guys have going, but I've never believed you specifically wanted to be part of their crimes."

"Man, how'd you know?" Trevor's shoulders relaxed and his face looked relieved. "I just wanted to be a straight up cop…working the streets, you know? Not doing the kinda things those guys did to people."

"Investigator Gray and I discussed exactly what you just said. But, in order for Special Agent Palenzuela to really help you we're going to need *something* from you…something the group did we can verify. It would be a show of good faith, making it easy for the Investigator to take to the Assistant U. S. Attorney proving your information's credible."

Trevor nodded and his eyes looked up searching his memory; his mind worked through the things he had seen. After a long pause, he dropped his head. I knew from experience he was gonna tell us something important, something he was embarrassed to admit.

Oscar slid forward ready to start a conversation. I threw up my hand to flag him from talking and he sat back in his chair.

"That gay attorney, the dead one…one of his last clients, Viktor, they killed him at our warehouse," Trevor said. He stayed away from being forced to cut off Viktor's finger.

"They cut up his body, then made me take the buckets of him out to the west mesa where that serial killer dumped bodies ten years ago. There's already new construction really close to that dump site, so I had to find one a little south of there. I had several buckets in my car and I dumped each one in a separate spot, but close to each other. I can draw you a map. It should be easy to find."

AFTER ANOTHER SPECIAL AGENT ARRIVED TO TAKE Trevor downtown to their headquarters, we all left. Mike

split off to go check on his people to see what they had fi
Mac's car stop. Sara and I jetted out to the dump locat
Trevor drew on the map.

Surveying the area, we could see how coyotes ha taken some of the body parts. Still, we were able to finc four spots within ten feet of each other covering human remains. We would only be able to prove it was Viktor Laine through DNA or teeth comparisons, but the clothing Trevor described Viktor wearing looked to be a match from the remnants we found in the dump area.

"What are you shaking your head for?" I asked.

"They go to the extent of cutting him up after killing him. Then, they make Trevor bring the cutup parts out here so the coyotes can take away the evidence. But, they're stupid enough to tell him to bury Viktor's parts where the serial killer buried all his kills…which were all female by the way. Then, they have Trevor bury the clothes with the body parts when they could have disposed of those in so many other places we would never make the connection?" Sara threw up her hands.

"You would think cops, of all people, would have a better sense of not leaving a death trail," I said. "Good thing for us wearing a badge doesn't automatically increase one's intelligence quotient." We both laughed, something we needed to let off some steam

I always loved working with the FBI. Their highly trained personnel loved getting involved in serious cases like ours. Most importantly, they had resources—lots and lots of resources. In less than thirty minutes after I called Oscar, a team of forensic crime-scene personnel showed up to take over the recovery of what we believed would turn out to be Viktor's remains.

CHAPTER SIXTY-TWO

Officer Bodner questioned Mac for over an hour in one of the interview rooms at headquarters. Mac could not tell for sure, but he believed nothing was being recorded based on the language and threats being used.

"You're a dirty fucking judge and you know it. You're lying your ass off saying you don't know anything about a brick of cocaine in your car."

"Officer, this is getting old," Mac shot back. "I've asked for my attorney to be present, you've denied me that privilege; I've asked to be booked if you're going to book me, another privilege denied; and I suspect you are *not* recording this conversation since you are continuing to violate my rights."

Bodner moved close to Mac, trying to intimidate him by standing over him for several *long* seconds.

"You got lucky at your house. This'll work out better," Bodner whispered. "When you get to prison, you ain't gonna have enough luck to keep from getting shanked by one or more of those pissed-off assholes you sent there."

"I'll take my chances. Unlike you, Officer Bodner, I treat people with respect. It's worked out for me so far. You outta try it."

Bodner's jaw tightened, he looked mad. Without thinking, he threw a punch landing on the left side of Mac's face.

The armrest of the chair Mac sat in prevented him from going to the ground. Blood filled his mouth and he spat on the floor once before he pulled himself upright with the opposite arm rest.

Gyrene bolted through the door and wrapped his arms around Bodner, who now looked as if he wanted to throw another punch.

Mac recognized Gyrene as the second officer who accompanied Bodner when they followed Mac to headquarters.

"Intelligence is not one of your strong points, Officer Bodner," Mac said, wiping blood from the corner of his lips with the back of his hand, staring into Bodner's eyes.

Bodner struggled to get free, consumed by anger. Another officer in a regular uniform, not the black fatigues Bodner and his sergeant wore, came in to help drag Bodner out of the room.

Shortly after they left a young officer came in, telling Mac he needed to book him in the county jail for possession of a controlled substance with intent to distribute. He left the room for several seconds, returning with a paper towel so Mac could wipe the blood from his face.

"I'm sorry, Your Honor," the officer said. "We're not all like him."

"I know," Mac said, a half smile on his lips. "And thank you," he said, holding up the paper towel.

Twenty-five minutes later Mac stood at the counter in front of one of the deputies, separated by thick metal caging running from the counter to the ceiling, to answer questions and officially be booked into jail.

"My attorney is right outside. We have the money for bail."

"I'm sorry," the sheriff's deputy on the other side of the

cage said. "We have orders from above you have to finish being booked, then change into an orange jumpsuit."

"Who gave the order?"

"My lieutenant," the deputy said. "Officer Bodner said you made comments about killing yourself, so we have to put you on suicide watch…and you have to be seen by our psychologist."

"He's lying, I never said anything like that."

"Not the first time we've heard that about Bodner," the deputy said just loud enough for Mac to hear.

Mac chuckled. A flood of memories from his time as a public defender filled his mind, memories of how dirty cops can mess with people for no particular reason…other than *they can*.

"I'm sorry, Judge McDunn. I have to follow orders." The officer looked around to size up those near him, and then leaned into the cage. In a low tone he said, "Nobody here trusts Bodner. He likes fucking with people like you. Trust me, you're the farthest thing from a person who needs suicide watch."

Unsure he could hold back from saying things too loud, Mac nodded.

The deputies placed Mac in a small cement cell with only one metal chair and no crutches, where he sat waiting for three hours unable to move, unless he wanted to crawl along the filthy cement floor.

The female psychologist went off on deputies for taking away his crutches, yelling at them to use common sense instead of following every order.

After a deputy brought Mac his crutches and another chair for the psychologist, she apologized several times. She asked Mac a total of three questions before she stood and declared him fit to be released.

Thirty-five minutes later four deputies' escorted Mac down the hallway, out the back door, and to his attorney's waiting car, trying their best to keep the throng of reporters from preventing Mac from leaving.

"Judge McDunn, were you transporting a brick of cocaine as alleged?" The question came from a female voice beyond the bright lights.

Mac turned, putting on his stoic courtroom face as he looked into the middle of the brightness.

"No. I believe the majority of the men and women in law enforcement are good people, trying their best to do a difficult job keeping our community safe. Unfortunately, some let power and prestige get in the way of doing what they were originally hired to do."

Mac turned and got in the passenger seat, his attorney driving away the instant the door closed.

GYRENE SAW A YOUNGER VERSION OF DC CHAMBERLAIN in Sly, especially when he got so focused on screwing with one person he did stupid things, like punching the judge in the face. He despised Chamberlain, and he had to hold back from going off on Sly.

"Not very smart punching the judge in the face."

"He's lucky you guys held me back or I would have hit him again. Besides, there's no recording of it. If he tries to say anything happened…we'll say he slipped and fell."

Gyrene nodded for Sly's benefit, but in the back of his mind he knew his days of backing up Sly in his lies had come to an end.

Feeling Sly had gotten so caught up in his anger and

resentment towards Judge McDunn, Gyrene could almost predict how Sly would handle the evidence taken from McDunn's car.

"You going to do a quick test for a presumptive positive result on the cocaine before you book it into evidence?" Gyrene asked.

"Hell no. It's been a long day and we already know it'll be positive. I'll let the guys in the lab do all the testing."

"Sounds good to me," Gyrene said, intentionally reinforcing Sly's belief they knew it would prove to be cocaine.

What a dumbass, Gyrene shook his head.

"You're right about it being a long day," Gyrene said. "How about you dictate your report real quick while I book the brick into evidence so we can get outta here?"

"Damn, a sergeant willing to carry some of the load," Sly laughed at his own attempt at humor. "That'd be great, thanks."

If he only knew, Gyrene smiled.

In the evidence area Gyrene took the brick out of the unsealed paper bag Sly had used. With a permanent marker he wrote on the top of the brick that it had remained sealed and no presumptive positive test had been done. He then signed, dated, and put the time on it. Using his cell phone he took several pictures of the brick and the evidence bag with all of the information on it. After he sealed the bag with the brick in it, he took several more photos.

Gyrene returned to the report writing room where Sly sat dictating his report. He sat at one of the dozens of computers where he began looking for social media accounts for AJ Conti. Finding what he was looking for, he looked over the top of the computer and listened to Sly dictating to make sure he still had time to send a message.

CHAPTER SIXTY-THREE

Mac sent a text to let me know he'd been released and his attorney would be taking him home.

My return reply said Ralph, Celia and Brooke would be at his house. Sara and I decided to meet him there to get an update.

By the time we arrived Mac's attorney had left. When we walked in, Mac, Ralph and Celia were sitting in the living room. The two fellas had beers in their hands.

Sara headed for the kitchen and I went to check on Brooke before I sat with Mac to get caught up.

Quietly, I opened the bedroom door trying my best not to wake her. Hearing her heavy breathing, I made my way over by the bed and saw she had curled up into a little ball. I pulled the sheet up over her and rubbed her forehead, watching her for several more seconds. The soft touch on my shoulder surprised me. Celia stood next to me, looking down at her little girl like only a mother could.

"It took me a while to get her to sleep," Celia whispered. "I had to lay next to her. She kept talking about you, wanting reassurance you would be okay."

I could not deny the warm feeling knowing she worried about me, maybe every bit as much as I worried about her. Bending over, I stroked her hair one more time before nodding toward the door for us to leave and let her sleep.

“Do you think you’ll be here in the morning when she wakes up?” Celia asked after we closed the door.

“I’m not sure. The FBI is involved now so I’m hoping they take the ball and run with it, but I’d hate to make a promise I can’t keep.”

I could see the disappointment in Celia’s pained expression, but at the same time I could see she understood my desire not to give her false hope.

Sara had already started catching the guys up on what we knew from the ME and Trevor Johnson. I was pleased she skipped over the hospital and our foray into Bernalillo County earlier in the day.

“Did the kid tell you who killed Aaron?” Ralph squinted, his jaw muscles flexing like someone who needed to know in order to take care of them himself.

“He gave Mike, Lisa’s boss at the Journal, and me the impression there were two of them,” Sara answered.

She glanced at me as if she hoped I’d be okay with her identifying them. I shrugged to show I was not really sure if we should or not.

“We think it would have been Kyle Lansing and Jerry Bodner,” she said.

“We heard through the grapevine Kyle Lansing got killed earlier today by some drug dealers he ripped off,” I added.

“The *grapevine*?” Ralph asked.

“My nephew,” I said.

“Yeah, he’s supplied us with varying pieces of information, all of it accurate up to now, so we have no reason not to believe him,” Sara added.

“Nice to finally have a little luck on our side given Sam overheard a doctor say Brody Sachs died in the emergency room today from a heart attack,” I said.

I could feel Mac's eyes staring at me long before I looked over at him. I had tried to lie to him on two different occasions when we were kids; his stare had been enough to get me to quit—until I became a cop and needed to use it to roll a suspect in an interview.

Without turning my head, I did a quick glance at everyone else, quietly sighing when I realized none of them saw the look on Mac's face. Scrunching my face, I looked at Mac because I couldn't lie directly to him. Mac knew from his defense attorney days not to ask a question he didn't want to hear the answer...he turned his head towards Sara.

"I gotta go," Ralph stood, crushing his empty can before taking it to the kitchen trash.

"There's been nothing strange since we arrived. Now that it sounds like you guys are getting it under control, I don't think the girls need a bodyguard anymore," Ralph said on his way back to the living room.

Celia stood to give Ralph a hug.

"You take care of that little girl. She's special," he said.

Ralph looked like there was something else he wanted to say but held it back. When he closed the door behind him, I felt the lights of Albuquerque would soon be in his rearview mirror, never to return unless we needed him to go to court.

Mac shared everything with the rest of us about his car stop, arrest, booking, and conversation with Bodner.

"I don't think Bodner saw it but there were definitely people taking pictures in the parking lot where I pulled over," Mac said. "I'm not sure if Mike's people brought a crowd with them or not, but there were quite a few people before I actually got arrested."

"Mike arranged for some news people to be there, so we're hoping they got something good on camera and statements from their parabolic mic to help bolster our case," I said.

The ding from my phone surprised me since it wasn't a regular text. Nonetheless, the message got my attention.

We should meet!

Without realizing it...I stared long enough at the text to make the others feel uncomfortable.

"What is it?" Sara asked.

"It's a Facebook message. I seldom get one."

I handed her my phone so she could read it...and was surprised when she read it aloud. It dinged again and Sara said the message told me to text the number on the screen.

"Any idea who it's from?" Mac asked.

"No. It's either a setup or it's someone who has more information for us."

Celia stood and went into the bedroom without a word.

I whispered, "Celia's worried how Brooke will take it if something happens to me."

Mac squinted at me for a couple of seconds followed by a glance over at Sara. She rolled her eyes back at Mac and he grinned.

"If that's what you want to believe...?" Mac smiled.

I knew what he meant since Sara had already been giving me her thoughts on Celia's admiration for me beyond just someone she could trust. I needed to focus on the message so I ignored his comment.

> *Who are you?* I texted, verbalizing each text for their benefit.
>
> *Sgt. w/SDM.*

Why me?
I'm tired of this. Thought I could help you.
When? Where?
One hour. Our warehouse, I'm sure Rook told you where it is.
One hour, got it.

Their concern for my safety was palpable, long before I confirmed it with the look in their eyes.

"After everything that's happened, don't you think he's setting you up to take you out?" Mac asked.

I didn't say anything right away, trying to choose my words carefully.

"There's no denying the risk. But, we can't surround it with a SWAT team without the probability of not getting information he may be offering." I looked at each of them, making sure they at least acknowledged I had to go.

"Right now, we're close to having the SDM under control," I said. "But, without more, do we have enough to bring down the shot callers? The ME and Trevor are good, but only if they testify. I say the more we have the better…it's worth the chance."

My phone dinged with the familiar text sound. I looked at it and then passed the phone to them.

"He knows the brick was fake, yet he booked it into evidence still perfectly sealed…at least I hope that's what he is trying to tell us," I said. "If he knows anything about negotiations, it's a good faith gesture to let us know he wants to help."

Sara finally broke the long silence saying, "You're going to do it regardless of what we say."

"I've known you most of my life and I knew you would

do it the instant you tried to justify it," Mac said. "She's only known you a few days and she can read you like an open book. You're losing your touch."

Between Sara chuckling and Mac's huge grin…I couldn't help but smile.

CHAPTER SIXTY-FOUR

I called Oscar to tell him someone wanted to meet with me and share information. It took some time to convince him to agree to my terms before I shared whom I'd be talking with…Sergeant Pace. I intentionally held back the time and location to allow Oscar time to come to grips with the good that could come from the meeting. What I needed to avoid was him wanting to take back his agreement so an FBI SWAT team would go in to get Pace. Once I gave him the information he barely had ten minutes to meet Sara and me at the warehouse, definitely not enough time to change his mind.

Oscar parked a warehouse away near our car and Sara got his attention with her flashlight. After he made it over by us, I headed for the door as Sara grabbed a heavy piece of steel from the trash bin to keep the door propped open should they have to come save my ass. I took a deep breath and entered with my Glock in my hand.

Sergeant Rob Pace stood Spartan-like a good forty feet away close to the whiteboard they used for assignments. His being in full dress blue uniform caught my attention. The fact it was his Marine uniform surprised me. He looked heroic in his military uniform with his white-gloved hands by his side, obviously proud of that portion of his life.

Not seeing a handgun I lowered mine to the low-ready position as I made my way to within twenty-five feet of him. I had already scanned the room for possible cover or concealment if things went south. There were none. I figured I might as well get close enough to increase my odds of a kill shot…if needed.

"Why the Marine uniform?"

"Because it's time I do the right thing…the honorable thing…something that automatically disqualified wearing my police uniform. I've done nothing honorable in that uniform since promoting to Sergeant."

The look on his face held a mixture of dual expressions at the same time. I had seen those same expressions many times in my interviews of suspects, but his face held both a shine in his eyes as he stood proudly wearing a uniform that clearly meant the world to him, while at the same time doleful for what I presumed were his actions as a member of The Syndicate.

"Coffee?" he asked as he turned and walked toward a table with a full pot of coffee sitting on its warmer.

"No thanks."

"I hope you don't mind if I have some." He filled a small cup half-way.

I didn't say anything as he turned toward me, the cup in his left hand and a thirty-ounce red coffee container in his right. He walked over to the end of a table twenty feet from me and set down the container.

I looked at it, then at him, hoping for an explanation.

"None of the other guys made coffee like this," he said, extending his cup toward me before taking a sip. "They liked that fancy piece of crap over there with the little coffee pods."

Pace set his cup down so he could take the lid off the container and extended his arm and poured the entire contents on the table. He pinched the clear plastic bag now sitting on top of the coffee grounds and tossed it to the corner of the table closest to me.

"That should be everything you need."

"What are these?" I asked, although I had a pretty good idea.

"Two digital voice recorders. They have a USB drive built in…you push a button and the male portion pops out. Plug them into your computer and you have everything you need. One is Chamberlain only. The other one is any time I had a meeting where the Chief or the Mayor were involved. I could have used just one, it has something like a thousand hours of recording time. I wanted to be safe. Plus, if one were ever lost or destroyed…I at least had the other."

"Impressive!"

"I never trusted DC Chamberlain from the first time I met him when he told me how they wanted this special team they could count on to help them out. From that first meeting, I never met with him, the Chief or the Mayor when I didn't have a recording device rolling."

"Why?"

"Did you trust your administration?"

He had a point. I had to shake my head in support of him.

"The unit started out doing good work, straight forward stuff like any special ops unit across America would do. After we were all several months into it…they started wanting more. I realized their aspirations were so lofty I knew they wouldn't hesitate to throw any of us under the bus if they needed, that is if they didn't have us killed. So, my instinct to cover my ass was right."

"Did I understand your text correctly about the supposed brick of cocaine being in evidence…unopened and untested?"

"Yes, it's exactly like Bodner took it out of Judge McDunn's car, we never tested it."

"Why did you do that?"

"Bodner's nickname in the unit is Sly, because he is when it comes to deciding how to put together an op and executing it, or how to do things like extort money off the relatives of the people who won awards from the city, either before or after we killed them. There was no way to slide that money back into the city's general fund without drawing serious attention. So, since it was all his idea the admin let us keep the money to split up between us. You'll see when you do financial checks on all these guys."

Pace reached over to grab his cup and took another sip.

"I never really liked Bodner, he reminded me too much of Chamberlain. I figured you'd need the brick to clear McDunn's name. You won't need it for Bodner though."

"Why not?"

"I told him to meet me here thirty minutes after you and figured it would give us enough time to conduct our business before he gets here." Pace took the last drink of his coffee before setting the empty cup on the table.

"You ever see the movie, *A Few Good Men*?" Pace asked.

"Yeah, a couple times."

"I liked Lt. Col. Markinson. He had honor." Pace took on the voice of the actor…"*I don't want a deal and I don't want immunity. I'm proud neither of what I have done or of what I am doing.*"

Pace glanced down at the handgun in his holster and then at me. Although the quote from the film was not when Markinson took his own life, the message was clear.

Something told me Pace had accumulated the evidence we would need, but he had no intention of ever testifying in court. I sensed if I said anything else Pace would pull his weapon on me and a gun battle would ensue. One way or the other, Pace planned on leaving this warehouse in a body bag.

Who am I to get in the way of honor, especially if it means none of us has to get shot? The thought rolled through my mind with my Glock still at the low-ready position.

I looked into his eyes and down at his weapon. When I looked back into his eyes…I nodded.

Pace clicked his heels as he stood at attention and saluted me, mouthing the words Thank You.

I watched the man unholster his Beretta M9A1, place the muzzle under his chin and pull the trigger.

CHAPTER SIXTY-FIVE

I slid my Glock in my waistband in the small of my back at the same time Sara and Oscar came racing through the door. They stopped, seeing Pace on the cement floor.

"AJ, what the hell happened?" Oscar asked. "How the hell am I going to explain this?"

Without answering, I walked over to the table and retrieved the plastic bag. Picking it up, I handed it to Oscar.

"Simple. You say the man wanted to die with honor instead of suicide by cop. He had a gun under his chin... we're only supposed to shoot to kill, not intentionally wound someone. So his *'death, while tragic, probably saved lives.'*" I knew they wouldn't understand the movie reference, but it seemed appropriate given the circumstances.

"Let the contents in that bag explain the rest. If it's what I think it is you might even get an *Atta-boy* out of it."

Oscar looked at the bag, then at Sara as if she could provide an explanation to my actions.

Smartly, Sara shrugged.

"We've got more important things to discuss. Pace called Bodner, he's supposed to show up here any minute."

"Holy crap," Sara looked around the warehouse. "This place is fricking bare, no place to hide."

We heard squeaking of breaks followed by the engine as the vehicle parked near the roll-up door. I directed Sara to my right by pointing and pumping my index finger several times. Then I did the same with Oscar to my left. The angles would keep us from shooting one another. I grabbed my Glock and took a couple of steps back toward the table with the coffee on it. Pulling out a chair, I sat facing the door with the Glock covered by my left arm as I leaned forward and put my forearms on my legs.

Lowering my head, I hoped Bodner wouldn't recognize I was not Pace until he was well into the warehouse. The last thing I wanted was for him to tuck tail and run leaving us chasing a killer outdoors putting lives in danger.

I counted the footsteps until I heard the sixth, a number in my head rationalizing I might have got my wish about him getting inside far enough for us to stop him if he tried to flee.

"What's up?" Bodner's voice was heard…followed by, "What the *Fuck*?"

I knew he spotted Pace's body. Raising my head, I pointed my Glock. By the time I extended my arm, he had out his weapon with the muzzle rising toward me.

My eyes caught the bulletproof vest as I watched in slow motion his muzzle climbing in my direction. I pointed low, firing two rounds before I heard shots ringing out from what seemed like all directions due to the echo inside the warehouse.

I aimed for Bodner's head, but the incoming bullet striking my right shoulder caused my hand to flinch and my round to miss. Worse, my Glock fell to the cement.

Diving to the floor to retrieve it with my left hand, my body rolled once to my right. I pointed my weapon at Bodner who had dropped to his knees. All the shooting stopped as his arm sat still in an L position, his handgun hanging by his side.

The hesitation seemed like an eternity, but in reality lasted less than a few seconds. I saw him squeeze his eyes, a dark stare right at me as he started to raise his gun. Having already aimed at where I wanted to hit…I put my last round through his head before he could pull his trigger.

I saw Oscar first. He ran towards Bodner and put his foot on the man's hand still holding the weapon. When Oscar nodded back at me, I relaxed my arm, putting my elbow on the cement.

Sara emerged, taking my Glock from my grasp. "Let's get you up in the chair."

"Sara…get me an ambulance…now," I said rolling on my back.

The funny thing about years of learning to trust your instincts, of knowing your body and its limitations, you have to fight through the fear of realizing your instincts are accurate especially when it comes to your own demise.

Sara's eyes widened and her mouth opened, but no words came out.

The bullet got an artery, my mind tried to tell me. *I'm getting weak quick.*

Grabbing her cell phone Sara stood, walking toward Oscar. I could hear her talking in the background, but listening would take away from what I needed to do.

Trendelenburg, I thought, *raise your legs up…*the vision of me as a young paramedic passed through my mind as I put pressure on the wound. *Stay calm and position yourself properly.*

I lifted my leg to reach for the chair, leaving my back flat on the ground. I knew my opportunities for success were limited to two chances at best. The toe of my shoe caught the front edge of the chair and I closed my eyes, counted to three and pulled. Through beneficence the chair moved closer allowing me to put both heels up on the front of the chair and say a thank you prayer.

Instantly I felt a positive change in strength and clarity from the blood in my legs rushing to my vital organs, but I knew the strength would pass soon and I'd return to slowly losing those without immediate help. I closed my eyes to focus on slowing my heart rate.

At that moment Brooke's face and huge smile came into my vision as if she were right in front of me. Oddly, the voice in my head was Bethany's, talking from heaven and telling me not to let the beautiful little girl down.

Thank you, Sweetheart, I thought, a tingling in my skin when Bethany's face appeared, her cute little grin with dimples shining in each cheek.

"Oh my God, he's unconscious?" Sara said.

"Not yet, but I'm getting close," I said, trying to open my eyes. Both of them were kneeling beside me. Sara's hand was on my good shoulder. "Sara, put pressure on my wound."

"They're close, I can hear the sirens," Oscar said. "Hang in there, I'm going to go flag them down."

I weakly nodded and he was gone. Looking into Sara's eyes my cheeks did not want to move as I tried to smile. "Sara, I can't thank you enough for all your help. Promise me…do not roll over and quit. You're a great investigator."

Tears glistened in her eyes as she touched my cheek.

I closed mine, being overtaken by a dark and drifting feeling, similar to times in the operating room. Hearing things going on around me, but not being able to identify them as darkness crept up and took me.

CHAPTER SIXTY-SIX

Oscar's boss, the Special Agent in Charge, arrived at the warehouse thirty minutes after AJ had been rushed by ambulance to the hospital.

"Sara, this is SAC Griley, he's in charge of my area in our office here," Oscar said.

Griley suggested they step away for privacy.

"Oscar, give me your best assessment," Griley said.

He looked at Sara, paused, and said, "Well, sir, I believe we need to act quickly. We need to get with the Assistant U.S. Attorney to listen to the recordings given to us by the dead sergeant. Before the shooting and before he took his own life, he told us the recordings will implicate people at the top."

Oscar hesitated because it is always easier talking about dirty cops from another agency than it is someone in your same basic position, like another federal agent.

"He also said there's another person on the take…a DOJ Agent who is in charge of monitoring the supposed turnaround of the PD after DOJ's last investigation."

Before Griley could say anything, several sets of headlights from the black Lincoln Town Car and APD patrol cars blinded him. Looking through the lights, the three could see a taller man in a suit with two police officers in uniform flanking him now walking towards them.

"I'm Deputy Chief Fred Chamberlain. We are taking over this scene. Investigator Gray, you'll go with these officers," he said, his right arm swinging to his side as if ushering her.

SAC Griley extended his arm in front of Sara to keep her from stepping forward while he took two steps toward Chamberlain.

"Mr. Chamberlain," he began, intentionally not showing respect for his rank in order to assert control, "Gray's not going anywhere. This is an FBI investigation and an FBI crime scene. Investigator Gray happened to be working for us during this operation and will remain under my direction until such time as I release her."

"That's bullshit," Chamberlain growled. "I've been told two of my officers are dead in there," pointing at the warehouse, "and she had something to do with it. She works for me and by God she's going with us."

"Interesting?" Griley stared into his eyes without another word.

"What's so damn interesting?" Chamberlain hissed.

"Agent Palenzuela, don't you find it interesting how Mr. Chamberlain here suspects two of his personnel are dead even though nothing has been released yet? You don't think he has some people in this complex who are on his payroll do you? I mean, how else would he know information like that?" Griley said, his eyes still glaring at Chamberlain.

Several FBI agents including their SWAT team on the scene made their way over to Griley after hearing Chamberlain raising his voice at their boss.

"Mr. Chamberlain, would you mind explaining to us how you had such information about our crime scene? Or, would you rather get in your car and leave before I have my personnel take you into custody as a material witness?"

The officers flanking Chamberlain had already taken steps back realizing they had no authority, not to mention being outnumbered. It took Chamberlain several seconds before he came to the same conclusion.

"This isn't over," Chamberlain said, looking over his shoulder as he headed for his car.

"Oh, no, it isn't. We'll be coming to talk to you about this very soon!" Griley held up the plastic bag with the LCD recorders.

Chamberlain stopped to look and nearly jumped inside the car when he saw the bag.

While the cars were driving away, Griley turned to Oscar and Sara.

"I sure hope what you think is on these...really is. Otherwise I stirred a hornets nest I'm not sure I can protect us from. You two come with me, we need to meet with the attorney."

MAC HAD BEEN SITTING IN THE PEACEFUL DARKNESS OF his living room thinking about Lisa and how important she was to him when his phone rang.

"AJ's been shot, they're taking him to UNM emergency," Sara blurted out. "I can't leave here, please get over there."

"I will...."

"Call me." Beep, beep, beep.

Mac had never been one to profess any belief in one religion over another, but with two people he deeply cared for in the hospital fighting for their lives he put his head in his hands and asked for His help.

"Was that AJ? Is it over?"

Startled, Mac turned to find Celia looking at him.

Mac's hesitation caused her to run down the hallway to the bathroom. He started to roll his wheelchair behind her, but stopped when he heard her crying.

CHAPTER SIXTY-SEVEN

Mac called his siblings to let them know AJ had been shot. Sam agreed to pick him up since Mac's car had been impounded.

Mary did the same thing she did after learning about Lisa's attack, she put out a prayer request through her church to get a prayer chain going.

Mac changed shirts while waiting for Sam. When he rolled into the living room, Celia sat on the couch with her knees drawn up, hugging a pillow.

"My sister is willing to watch Brooke if you would like to go to the hospital with my brother and me."

Celia almost spoke up, but stopped when her lip began quivering. Wiping her eyes with her hands, she took a deep breath. "I want to…I really do." Sniffling, she wiped her eyes again. "I'm not sure I could handle being there?"

She buried her face in her hands as Mac rolled up to the side of the couch and put his hand on her shoulder. There were no words to comfort her. No one could guarantee AJ would live.

"Brooke will be crushed…I couldn't have her alone with a stranger if…please call me as soon as you know something."

"Do you know anything yet?" Sam asked while he drove.

"Nothing," Mac said. "Worse yet, I don't know who to call because I don't know who to trust."

"What about Sara…I thought they were together?"

"They were. I know they called the FBI guy they've been working with and the three were supposed to meet. She sounded scared, as if she couldn't talk or maybe she was in a rush."

Sam wanted to ask if anyone else had been shot, but knew it would be futile.

They parked in employee parking at UNM Hospital. Sam had seen enough trauma in his years as a physical therapist he could maintain calmness. He knew there was no need to rush…it wouldn't make any difference in the outcome for AJ.

The quietness in the hallways stood out as Sam reached for his plastic ID on the lanyard around his neck, passing it by the scanner on the wall. When they rounded the corner near the emergency room, Sam showed his ID to the security guard before they headed to the nurse's station.

Sam asked to speak to the ER nursing supervisor hoping the fact he knew her for a long time would get him answers.

When she arrived, Sam explained there existed no blood connection, but they considered AJ a brother. After he found out the bullet hit AJ's axillary artery and he'd been rushed to surgery, Sam asked if she would let the operating staff know AJ had family in the waiting room.

By the time AJ came out of surgery a new day had dawned. Sam stood when the surgeon walked into the waiting room.

"Hi Sam," the surgeon greeted him. "I hear you and AJ Conti are brothers somehow." His head leaned to the side as if he needed an explanation before he went into sharing patient information.

Mac, who had finished locking in his braces stood up and said, "Kind of a long story, Doc, but suffice it to say our parents treated AJ as one of our family and he has been for over thirty years now."

Sam said, "Doc, you and I have known each other for a long time. I wouldn't jeopardize your career unless I really believed he's our brother. When AJ wakes up, ask him who we are? I'm certain he'll say family."

"I see...well, the surgery went well overall. AJ lost a great deal of blood because the bullet hit an artery in his shoulder. It was touch and go for a while, but I think everything is going to be all right. I want to keep him sedated for today as a precaution."

When the doctor turned to leave they smiled and sat down, ready to start making phone calls.

CELIA HAD NOT SLEPT AND SAT ON THE COUCH WITH A blanket over her legs sipping coffee, her mind going over everything that happened in the last several months. When her phone rang, it startled her. Seeing Mac's name, her hands started to shake, nearly spilling her coffee before she could set down her cup. On the fourth ring she answered.

It was a short reassuring call from Sam. Hanging up, Celia's tears of joy were partly for AJ being alive, but more for not having to tell Brooke he died.

The door to the bedroom creaked and Brooke walked through wiping the sleep from her eyes.

"Mom, why are you crying…and smiling?"

Celia patted her lap, reaching out to help Brooke climb up and snuggle into her mother's arms.

"Where's AJ, is he sleeping?"

"Kind of," Celia said. "He got hurt but he's okay…really, he's okay. He's asleep at the hospital, but when he wakes up, I promise we can go see him. Would you like that?"

Brooke had pulled away to look into her mother's eyes, but hearing he would be okay, she nodded and settled back in her mother's lap.

CHAPTER SIXTY-EIGHT

Mac had an attorney friend, who had accurately predicted who would be elected to high political positions along with appointments by the Governor for the last five years…well before they took place. The news of Mac's arrest was the lead story in every conceivable press and news agency within the state and region so it did not take long before Mac's friend called.

"Zeke, please tell me you're only calling to check on my well-being?" The silence answered his question.

"I wanted to let you know what I'm hearing…so you had some time to prepare," Zeke said.

Mac took a deep breath. "I'm ready."

"Your Honor, I'm so sorry…but the disciplinary board of the New Mexico Judicial Standards Commission is coming after you."

"Zeke, it was a set up. The brick they confiscated is not cocaine, its nothing."

"They have no plans of waiting for you or your defense team to prove any of that. What I'm hearing is they want you replaced in the Sandoval case. I don't know who Sandoval has pissed off, but they want him to go down for the murders of Gary and Barbara O'Brien. You were in the way, so with the shooting at your house and supposed drugs in your car…they have an opening and they're taking it. I'm sorry."

Mac knew there was nothing to say except to thank Zeke for his friendship and giving him the heads up.

He called his defense lawyer, who seemed as stunned as Mac. The disciplinary board had no obligation to listen to Mac's defense team before rendering a ruling, much less waiting for months for everything to blow over and Mac to be cleared of any wrongdoing.

At the end of their discussion, Mac went to Lisa's hospital room and sat beside her, holding her listless hand as she continued to sleep. The shock of his legal career coming to an abrupt halt made him nauseous. The longer he sat, the clearer it became. He needed to retire so he could save his pension before they took it as part of the disciplinary process.

He lightly stroked Lisa's forehead, kissed her hand and left. At the first opportunity, he called his defense attorney to ask him to make contact with the Commission to get the ball rolling.

The corruption in this state goes well beyond APD, he thought.

THERE WAS A SENSE OF IMMEDIACY IN THE FBI CONFERence room, a fear that without rapid intervention there were others in APD who could easily be recruited to replace SDM, no different than when SDM replaced ROP. It took several hours for the Assistant U.S. Attorney, Oscar and Sara to go through the taped conversations from Sergeant Pace. With the information from the medical examiner, Trevor Johnson and the tapes, the attorney put together a schematic of the various crimes, who committed them, and what directions were given by administrators, namely DC Chamberlain, Chief Baylor, and Mayor Sampson.

When they were done, the attorney felt comfortable getting arrest warrants for Chamberlain and Baylor. The Mayor had more distance and less direct contact with Pace, so to lock him in she needed someone else to roll. She suspected her best option would be Chamberlain, expecting defense attorneys for the Chief and Mayor to claim Chamberlain went rogue on his own. Her hope was to possibly cut him a deal to get him to roll on the other two once he realized they were pointing the finger at him.

Separately, she prepared to do an arrest warrant for DOJ Special Agent Shawn Nester for receiving payouts to look the other way and produce false reports on the success of the APD after the previous DOJ investigation demanded changes. While she waited for the conclusive financial evidence from the audit of his finances to finalize seeking the warrant, she placed a call high enough up the DOJ chain to ensure the fallout would run downhill and Nester would be put on leave in the interim. As a realist she expected more than one head would roll in the DOJ system before the fallout of their coverup got fully exposed to the press, although all she truly cared about was Nester.

CHAPTER SIXTY-NINE

When I awoke, the grogginess did not last long. Given the time line by the nurse of when I arrived at the ER, got out of surgery, length of time I'd been sedated…I figured it had been well over two days since I last ate. Before long, I began pestering my nurse for food. When I asked for something from a fast food restaurant, I got back the standard look of *yeah right*.

Sam came by first and caught me up on what he knew. He told me Mac would be signing his retirement papers later in the morning. I was pleased to hear he put a positive spin on retiring, saying he would have more time together with Lisa.

Knowing Sam had to leave, I didn't ask about Lisa's condition figuring she must be improving if Mac could see their future together.

Sam stopped in the doorway, half turning to look back at me. "Oh, your surgeon doesn't believe in people spending any more time in a hospital than absolutely necessary. If I were you, I'd check to find out when he'll release you."

"My kind of doc. Thanks Sam."

Other than some pain in my shoulder I felt pretty good after I finished eating. I hoped for a real shower, but the nurse's tilted head without answering my question told me

I would be enjoying a sponge bath. After being shot, and fading in and out in the warehouse, nothing could derail my happiness…not even a sponge bath.

When visiting hours began I heard her footsteps running down the hall long before I saw her pretty face. Wearing a huge grin, Brooke raced to the left side of my bed and climbed up to give me a hug.

Seeing my nurse and Celia standing inside the door, each with their own big smiles, I smiled up at Brooke. "What are you doing here at this hour little girl?" I asked. "Aren't you supposed to be in school?"

Brooke's head sprang from my chest. "Mom said I could go in a little late after I came to say hi."

My nurse left and Celia came to my bedside her smile never fading.

"Hi AJ."

"Celia, it's great to see you," I reached across and she took my hand in both of hers, holding on for several seconds.

"Thank you. Both of you. You guys visiting makes my day."

Celia winked and let go of my hand.

"I'm going to take Brooke to school and then I'll come back to get you."

"What are you talking about?"

"The nurse whispered in my ear she's certain with how well you're doing your doctor will release you. So, I'll come get you."

"Bye AJ, see ya later!" Brooke gave me a kiss on the cheek. "I'll see you when I get outta school, or maybe after gymnastics." She hopped off the bed and walked away with her mom. They waved and headed out the door, leaving me feeling way better than what I expected.

It wasn't thirty minutes when the doctor arrived to

let me know my blood work all looked good and I could be released.

"I expect to see you in a week in my office." He started to leave and stopped in the doorway, turning around to face me. "I think you should know, you were knocking on Death's Door, a few times. Strange as this may sound, Surgeons talk about how they get this weird feeling in the operating room sometimes, knowing a patient isn't meant to die…just yet. We do enough surgeries and sooner or later we come across patients we sense something besides the surgery saved their life. You were one of mine." He turned to leave and over his shoulder he reminded me, "See you in a week."

Strangely I knew exactly what he meant. When I was a paramedic right out of high school, I came across a couple of people who never should have lived, yet somehow they walked out of the hospital. The weird part for me had to do with an overwhelming sensation that somehow Bethany held my hand from the warehouse until long after my surgery and in Intensive Care.

I knew a lot of people would think I might be crazy if I told them about that feeling, but something told me my doctor would understand.

Thank you, Bethany, for being with me and holding my hand. I love you.

Once Celia drove away from the hospital, I went through the arduous process of one hand texting with my non-dominant left hand. I wanted Mac to know I'd been released, but more importantly my thoughts were with him while he went through the process of signing his retirement papers.

Next, I sent a short text to Sara to see how she was doing. She texted back saying she was fine…still working with Oscar and the federal prosecutor. The grapevine relayed to her how no one at APD knew what to do about her exactly, so she had not received a word from them. She added a smiley Emoji, telling me how she was glad I was okay. She looked forward to seeing me soon.

CHAPTER SEVENTY

Celia quietly drove without interrupting me, probably sensing the importance for me to touch base with the people who shared my ordeal. Her soft demeanor did not last when I said she could drop me off at Mac's.

"You're coming to my house, end of discussion. I'm not about to leave you all alone right after you got released from the hospital."

I let it drop, until a minute later when I asked, "Can you at least make me a fresh pot of coffee? I'm going through withdrawal."

She turned, giving me her stoic look for two long seconds and laughed.

Pulling into her neighborhood, I instinctively began to look at every car.

"I haven't seen anything suspicious last night or this morning," she said. "Not even a regular cop car driving through."

"Good. I'm hoping Oscar, Sara and the federal prosecutor can lop off the head of this nightmare. It's likely the remaining few dirty cops won't have the courage to start up another rogue group, leaving the good ones to take back the streets and control of the agency."

Parking, we took one more look around the streets before going inside. At the kitchen table I sat where I did the first time we met. The aroma of fresh brewed coffee filled the room. If I had a vice, it would be fresh coffee.

Celia left the room, saying she'd be back in a minute. I sat patiently waiting while scanning the various opened mail on the table. Sticking out of the top of one of the envelopes, I saw large red lettering on a paper. Leaning forward, I read D E L in red.

Listening for Celia, I heard her doing something in the back of the house. I reached over and removed the paper further to see the remainder of those letters in red, I N Q U E N T. From what I could figure out, Celia was behind in her house payments by several months.

I took out my phone and snapped pictures of the necessary information before I stuffed the paperwork inside the envelope. The trouble with having one useful hand to make the paper and envelope look untouched ended up not happening. I slid them under other envelopes and hoped it would work.

The thought of them having to give up their home caused me pain. I didn't know Peter personally, but I felt the people in Albuquerque had no idea what sacrifice he made for them to have a police force they could trust. I called back to Celia to let her know I was briefly stepping outside to make a call.

With close to five hundred thousand dollars left in my bank and one point two million in my portfolio, thanks to Bethany's life insurance and Kenny Love getting me into investing right out of the academy, I made two phone calls, one to my broker and one to the person at the bank I always met with regarding important matters. I made sure to put the two of them together hoping they could somehow pull off my request…to pay off the one hundred and fifty-seven thousand dollar debt for Celia's house.

I learned long ago never to underestimate what rules can be circumvented in the interest of doing a good deed for someone.

When I went back inside Celia was already pouring the coffee and we sat at the table sipping and enjoying the peace and quiet. Soon Celia began telling me all about Brooke's time in Denver with her gymnastics team.

"You know, I had been dreading Denver before you showed up," Celia said. "I knew we were going to have to give up gymnastics and Brooke was heartbroken while trying to stay strong for me. That was supposed to be her last competition. Instead, thanks to you, she had so much fun up there."

"I'm glad, to hear she was smiling, and having fun…it makes my day. She's been through a lot…so have you. I told you before, you and Peter have a special little girl."

Celia went to the sink where she started putting dishes away and I continued to sit and drink my coffee…feeling a tension building around us.

"I love Peter with all my heart," Celia said, her back still to me. "And yet, when I heard you were shot and I might lose another who I care for deeply, I nearly lost it. Still, I know I must stay strong for Brooke…she's the only thing keeping me together."

I presumed she wiped away tears when I saw the backs of her hands go up near her eyes.

"AJ…I really do care for you, probably more than you know…and Brooke adores you." She hesitated. "I sense you care for me, for us, too. But, I'm not ready to move forward."

"Celia, I know exactly how you feel. I felt the very same way after Bethany was taken from me. You're right…I do care for you. I have from the moment I met you. And

Brooke, she lights up my life, what else can I say. But I'm not expecting anything—I totally understand. I'm happy to spend time with you as a good friend, who cares about you. But I have to say, I much prefer to talk to your face than the back of your head."

Smiling, I waited for her to turn around when she realized I wanted to lighten up the moment. She did turn and leaned on the counter like she needed it to hold her up.

I held my breath until she finally broke into a sweet smile sending a warm rush through me. Walking over, we hugged. Her closeness gave me a feeling as if we'd made it over a huge hurdle. I was glad we'd remain linked, regardless of the depth of our bond.

We spent the rest of the day trying to put her house back in order from the illegal search and destruction that tore the place apart. We agreed the most important thing for Brooke's sake was to get the wall painted displaying the ugly red message. I would be the distraction so Celia did not have to face what happened alone.

When Brooke got home, we took her to gymnastics and then out to eat. I could see the tiredness in both of their eyes when they dropped me off at Mac's house. Like good hosts, they watched from the car to make sure I got to the door before smiling and waving goodbye.

I stood at Mac's door, recalling once again the sensation I had in the warehouse. Bethany telling me I needed to live for Brooke. Seeing the light in Brooke's eyes today, I knew she celebrated my not being taken away like her father. The doctor's words confirmed I was not supposed to die.

I closed my eyes, silently thanking God for my life and Bethany for her support and guidance.

CHAPTER SEVENTY-ONE

The fallout from a wrongful arrest could be profoundly damaging for the United States Attorney's office. Arresting a Chief of Police anywhere turns into a political hot potato, even more so when the Chief is allegedly orchestrating hits to further his political future. The prosecutor and investigators believed they had pieced together the elements of the crimes needed to charge Chief Baylor and DC Chamberlain. Along with the paperwork to get arrest warrants, the decision from the top was to let an independent panel of attorneys within the office, including some supervisors, go through what had been put together before seeking the actual warrants.

It had been three days since my release from the hospital and Oscar and Sara agreed to meet me at a downtown sandwich shop not far from the Federal Building. For reasons other than all cops like to have their backs to the wall in a restaurant for safety, I arrived thirty minutes early.

I hadn't felt comfortable for the last two days when I left the house. I wanted to keep an eye on the front door, along with seeing through the front windows as to who might be hanging around outside.

Pushing the four-seat table at an angle, it now allowed for them to also be able to see the same things. When they arrived, I stood to give Sara a hug. She looked happier than I had ever seen her, which didn't take much given the circumstances under which we originally met. Oscar stuck his right hand out, awkwardly rescinding it when I flashed my fingers in the sling. He moved to his left hand somewhat robotic as he processed what would be the right procedure.

I chuckled and said, "Good to see you, Oscar," and we sat at the table.

Oscar's facial muscles relaxed having gotten past the awkward entry.

The first fifteen minutes, we ate while I caught them up on my shoulder, along with how well Lisa was recovering. She had recently been moved from ICU to a bed on the medical floor.

"So, are we ever going to get those arrest warrants?" I asked.

Sara leaned back and looked over at Oscar. I suspected she felt like a fish out of water being a local cop now dealing with only federal agencies and personnel. The basic concepts of going after offenders is the same, but how things are done are often different.

Oscar cleared his throat and sat back, crossing his leg and turning away from me. Not a lot of difference between good guys and bad guys when it comes to body language *showing* they are hiding something or they are embarrassed by the answer they *do not want to give.* I referred to it as the *adult fetal position.*

"I can't say AJ. I wish I knew more, but it's gone beyond the normal levels…we're being told the delay is to make sure we have everything we need to file charges. We think it comes down to nobody at the top wants their career fried if we move too fast and it falls apart."

"Kinda makes sense if you look at it from their perspective." I could see by the four wide eyes staring at me they thought I was nuts.

"Seriously, you'd probably do the same," I said. "My concern is the likelihood Chamberlain amasses another group and starts taking out witnesses like us."

"It's been mentioned by the prosecutor to her direct boss," Sara said. "We were there when she said it."

"I hope you two are being careful. See the guy across the street sitting on the far right of the bus bench?" I waited for them to zero in on the character. "I've been feeling uncomfortable the past day or so, as if I'm being followed. That guy has sat through two buses coming and going."

Oscar did a double take between me and the guy on the bench, followed by him leaning forward with his arms on the edge of the table. "A guy taking advantage of an open seat and reading a newspaper downtown is pretty normal here, AJ."

"I agree, if he had on a suit. Survey the area, tell me I'm wrong about eighty percent or more of the men in the visible area aren't in a suit." I hesitated knowing he would look. "The men down here not in suits are here because they have to be, not because it's where they hang out and read the newspaper. That guy has a cop's haircut, cop sunglasses, a baseball hat sitting atop his head squarely instead of leaning to one side or backwards. Plus, he's got on new jeans to go along with the I'm-a-construction-worker boots."

Oscar shot a quick look at Sara, who nodded.

"Tell me this guy wasn't pulled out of a patrol car, no undercover or stakeout experience, and told to watch one of us."

Silence.

When I suggested we do something to prove or disprove my concerns, Oscar exited through the back door. When he got in position on the same side of the street as the man on the bench, Sara and I walked out of the restaurant. We stood there and watched as Oscar started to approach the man, calling out he wanted to talk to the man from some distance.

Like we expected he stared at Oscar, and looked over at us, then back at Oscar. He dropped the paper and took off in a fast walk as if he was in a walking marathon.

I turned to Sara. "Be careful, please. You and I are probably who Chamberlain has it out for the most. Mac signing retirement papers makes him less important. The only reason for them to go after Oscar is to kidnap and torture him to get the location of Trevor and the ME, which Oscar probably doesn't know, but they would never believe it."

"I must've got caught up in thinking we had what we needed so I haven't been paying attention. I promise I'll start. I think you probably convinced Oscar to do the same." Sara smiled. "Gotta go, AJ. I'll let you know if we hear anything on the warrants."

CHAPTER SEVENTY-TWO

I turned to leave when Sara walked off, but something told me to look around for the guy who ran from the bench when Oscar got close. I watched him run north and turn west at the intersection where he went out of sight. Knowing Oscar and Sara would walk in the same direction back to the Federal Building, I wanted to be sure he was not waiting for them.

Sara walked north as Oscar did the same on the opposite side of the street. When the light changed to green, she crossed first to catch up to him. While she waited, she saw Oscar making his way west, looking over his shoulder several times as if he was trying to wait for her.

I trailed quite a distance behind Sara, crossing the road heading west almost at the same time she did, but on the opposite side of the street. I could see Oscar way ahead of her still heading west while trying his best to walk slower so she could catch up. So far, nothing caught my attention until the same man stepped out of the lobby of a building on my side of the street. He had his phone in his hand while looking in Oscar's direction.

I could see Sara chuckling as she watched Oscar almost run into a parking enforcement officer now overseeing the tow truck operator hooking up to a small black car. Oscar turned back to Sara wearing an embarrassed smile.

That was when we both saw the flash from the explosion with shrapnel flying in all directions. Sara ran toward the blast site screaming Oscar's name. Closing the distance between them, reality set in when she looked at the body parts down on the pavement.

Along with everyone around me, I hit the sidewalk. Searing pain shot to my right shoulder. The smell of smoke and burning flesh filled the air, along with a constant ringing in my ears.

Pushing myself up to my knees, I scanned the smoke and debris filled air in front of me, but he was gone.

Sara, where's Sara?

Looking across the street, I saw Sara holding her ears taking small deliberate steps toward what used to be a car. I ran over and stepped in front of Sara to keep her from walking up to the carnage.

Two citizens stepped around us, presumably to provide aid, and I saw the effects of gunfire before I heard it as both men flopped to the ground. I grabbed Sara's shoulders and pulled her down behind what was left of the nearest car. A quick glance told me both men had been shot and one was obviously dead.

More shots continued to hit the car glass and the wall of the building across from us. I pulled out my Glock and made eye contact with Sara. The faraway look in her eyes now gone, replaced by her narrow eyes.

I pointed to myself and with the tip of my Glock tried to make a semicircle. Sara nodded and I moved in a low crouch. From the trunk area of the car I counted to three and took off toward the opposite side of the street. I could hear Sara from her position firing rounds to cover me. When I reached a parked car on the opposite side of the street I dropped to one knee behind the engine block and did a quick look around it.

Our man from the bench stood in the middle of the road alternately firing rounds towards Sara and then me. The instant he fired his second volley of rounds I stood and took aim. Looking down the sights I could see his body slowly turn in my direction for another volley when I pulled the trigger, several times. I first shot at his torso and then at his hips in case he wore a vest.

The man's leg caved as he fell to his right. I took off running toward him, and saw Sara doing the same. The man tried to crawl. Keeping his eyes on us now twenty-feet away, he put his weapon to his temple and pulled the trigger.

The stench from burning rubber and screeching tires of a black Crown Vic minus plates grabbed our attention. Sara and I both fired at it causing glass to shatter before it made a quick turn out of sight.

Looking at each other, we assessed the other for bullet wounds. The only blood showing was my right shoulder where my stitches ripped open. I figured it couldn't be too bad with the amount of adrenaline flowing through me.

"Oscar…we have to go look for Oscar," Sara reminded me.

"No!" I barked, making sure she understood I wasn't about to let her go. "We gotta get to the Federal Building, to that prosecutor you've been dealing with."

Sara looked over her shoulder at the blast sight, then back at me. She nodded and we took off. Our weapons stayed low and ready in case we came across more assailants.

Entering the building with our guns still drawn meant we were met by a dozen people, who immediately drew down on us. Fortunately, Sara's quick comments about working with Oscar and identifying the prosecutor she had talked with bought us some time. Several agents holstered their weapons and ran outside when Sara said Oscar might have been killed by a car bomb a couple of blocks away.

Two young agents took our weapons and escorted us to the fifth floor and when the door opened the prosecutor stood waiting for us.

"Jen Hayes," she said, looking right at me.

Before I could respond, she turned and started power walking, her high heels not a detractor. She motioned to us to follow. We ended up in a conference room with two young agents posted by the door when Jen left.

"What's taking so long," Sara asked after fifteen minutes.

"There's a huge mess a few blocks from here they have to contain, plus Jen is probably trying to get her ducks in a row before she tells whoever hasn't authorized those arrest warrants their lack of expediency killed a federal agent."

I looked at the agents and saw their puzzled faces looking back at me. Hearing me say someone dragging their feet caused the death of one of their own didn't sit well and they started whispering among themselves. In the meantime, they no longer watched us as if we were terrorists.

When I pulled out my cell phone one of the agents came over.

"All I want to do is text someone to say I'm alive," I looked into his eyes. "I'll even show it to you before I send it."

A long pause ensued as he contemplated what to do.

"Look, you know the right thing to do is at least let me tell someone we're not dead…please?"

He nodded so I handed the phone to Sara.

"Please tell Celia no matter what she hears on the news, we are alive and ask her to please let Mac know. And, for her to be careful."

Sara's fingers flew through the message almost as fast as I said it. She turned it toward the agent who nodded and walked away without reading it. She hit send.

CHAPTER SEVENTY-THREE

We sat in the conference room for four hours, along with our two guards who were kind enough to bring us coffee. The door burst open and five people walked into the conference room. Jen and Special Agent in Charge Griley were the only two faces I recognized.

Jen proceeded to introduce the remaining three who all outranked her. They were in the room only long enough to thank us for killing the man who killed a federal agent and several other innocent people.

Jen relaxed when they were gone and released the two young agents.

"I wanted you both to see these."

Opening a file, she pulled out two pieces of paper and laid them on the table in front of us.

Sara and I stared down at the arrest warrants for Chief Baylor and DC Chamberlain. I felt a tingling of success while at the same time a sense of sadness for all the people who they injured or killed out of greed.

"We have agents ready to go take them into custody," Griley said.

"Can you do me a favor?"

"Absolutely!" he said without hesitation.

"Can you send a car over to UNM Hospital to get Judge McDunn? And if it's possible, we would like to be there to witness the two being put in the back of your cars for transport to jail."

Griley smiled, pulling out his phone as he headed for the door.

"What happens now?" Sara asked.

"Unfortunately we'll need you two to come back here after the arrest," Jen said. "A great deal has happened and we need to record everything you both have witnessed and your accounts of what took place. It will go a long way in backing up what we already have from the medical examiner and Trevor Johnson, plus the recordings from the sergeant."

"Any word on the guy down the street?" I asked.

"Yes. We have identified him…he was an officer for APD. We are also guarding another APD officer who is currently receiving treatment at a hospital for gunshot wounds and believe he was the driver of the getaway car you both shot at. Thanks to some honest workers at the city corporation yard where all city cars are worked on, we also have the car he tried to hide in one of their work bays."

The door opened and Griley leaned his head inside. "Let's do this."

MAC GOT OUT OF THE FBI CAR AND MADE HIS WAY OVER to us. The three of us did not speak. Instead, we focused on the only positive to come from a mountain of pain and suffering.

Seeing Baylor and Chamberlain in handcuffs being led to a waiting FBI car gave me a sizzling sense of gratification.

Chamberlain had a smirk on his face seeing Mac. "Too bad about your girlfriend and the judicial commission forcing you to retire."

"Most of us work hard to protect the citizens we work for and defend the justice system," Mac said. "Good luck finding protection where you're going. There's not enough solitary confinement or prison guards to protect you from what's waiting there."

Before he could respond the FBI agent grabbed a handful of Chamberlain's hair and forced him into the car.

"Chief Baylor," I called.

He stopped and turned toward me.

"You've betrayed the oath you took to protect and serve… you've betrayed the badge. Worse yet, you've betrayed the good men and women who willingly put their lives on the line to serve this great city. May God have mercy on your soul."

Chief Baylor's head dropped as his shoulders slumped.

CHAPTER SEVENTY-FOUR

Since Sara had worked with Oscar for two days, her interview in an office of a senior FBI agent only lasted a little over an hour.

Mine took almost three hours, conducted in an interview room complete with a one-way mirror and video camera. All of the questions by the agent were straightforward and designed to help prove Mac had been in serious danger.

When the agent was done with the interview, SAC Griley walked in, releasing the agent who interviewed me. Griley waited for the door to close before he took a seat across from me.

"The room behind the glass is cleared out and nothing is being recorded. We're off the record now, AJ."

I had no idea where Griley might go with the conversation, but I did my best to relax and not do anything to make him think I was afraid to talk to him.

"The dead bodies before we got involved were alarming. Obviously with what they did to Oscar and those innocent people, Baylor, Chamberlain and their followers don't care about anyone but themselves," Griley said.

Sensing this might be heading in a positive direction, I leaned forward and gently laid my arm in the sling on the table.

"AJ, between you and me…I want to thank you for all you did to put a stop to SDM, and I mean *all* you did. Nobody will ever acknowledge it in public, but sometimes a war like they waged on McDunn and you requires special tactics."

I couldn't tell the extent of his knowledge, but I was pretty certain he had some idea of my nefarious activities.

"Thanks Agent Griley."

When he extended his hand, I took it with my left hand, feeling he truly appreciated our efforts.

"Oh, I thought you might want to know, Jen Hayes has been busy this whole time. I guess the mayor went on record saying The Syndicate and the actions by Baylor and Chamberlain were disgusting and he was not involved in any way. Chief Baylor immediately wanted a deal once he heard what the mayor said. He's been talking ever since."

"What about Chamberlain?"

"He's playing games, talking but saying nothing. I think he's trying to prevent going to jail until lockdown for the night so he can slip in unnoticed."

"Yeah right," I laughed along with Griley.

In the two weeks that followed Lisa's series on the corruption inside Albuquerque Police Department helped reach record numbers of sales for the Journal. She had already been assured her position would be waiting for her no matter how long her recovery took.

"It looks like Lisa will be released from the hospital by the end of this week," Mac said with a huge smile.

"So, when's the big day?" I asked.

"What are you talking about?"

"When's the wedding? Please don't tell me after all of this, you don't realize life is too short not to latch on to a great person like Lisa, especially since she can put up with you." I laughed and dodged the pen he threw at me.

Mac grinned. "We have decided she should move in here when she gets out. That's a big step for us so have a little patience."

My phone rang. It was Celia and when I answered, I heard her crying.

"Celia, are you okay? What's wrong?"

"I'm great, AJ," she said, sniffling.

"I don't get it, then why are you crying?"

"I think you know why. I just opened my mortgage statement."

I smiled, knowing her tears were those of joy.

"AJ…thank you. I don't know what else to say."

"You've said enough, really."

"How can…how can you afford this, on a cop's retirement?"

"Celia, don't worry about it. I have a little more than a monthly check, trust me. The only thing I ask is for you to go to school for interior design like you always wanted."

"I will, I promise. Can I ask one more thing?"

"Sure, go ahead."

"The city changed their position and now determine Peter was killed in the line of duty, which allows me to receive Peter's benefits. Did you have anything to do with that?"

"I don't know what you're talking about?" I lied.

"AJ…I know it had to be you…thank you so much," she said before the tears started again and she hung up.

"Speaking of relationships," Mac smiled, telling me nothing had gotten past him.

"She's not ready to move forward and I totally understand. Celia and Brooke deserve a chance to have a good life after what the PD did to them. They killed Peter, tarnished his good name and put those two through hell."

"You're a good man, AJ."

I have a good friend who continues to show me the way.

THE END